THE WHITE ZULU

Being a Memoir of Isandlwana and Rorke's Drift, including Hints on Piano Theft, Theatrical Costumery and Acts of Arson, in the Service of Queen Victoria, God Bless Her.

BY HOWARD WHITEHOUSE

ZMOK
BOOKS

Cover Art from "The Defense of Rouke's Drift"
by Alphonse de Neuville, 1880

The White Zulu by Howard Whitehouse

This edition published in 2018

Published by Winged Hussar Publishing

Zmok Books

1525 Hulse Road, Unit 1

Point Pleasant, NJ 08742

ISBN 978-1-9454303-5-0

LCN 2018901936

Bibliographical References and Index

1. Zulu War. 2. Fiction. 3. War

*This story is dedicated to the memory of three men called George —
my father and both of my grandfathers. My maternal grandfather,
George Aldridge, lived his whole life in Hove, and knew the area
well. None of them went to Zululand, but when I was six my
father took me to see 'Zulu', and thus sent me on this journey.*

CHAPTER ONE

Hove 1928

The man ran desperately, feet skidding on the hard ground as he lunged for safety. Terror was etched deep into his black face, and he cried out an incomprehensible shriek – perhaps to his ancestors or his Gods – as the sabre lashed fiercely a few inches from his head. He heard his assailant shouting, the voice that of a British senior officer with his blood up. "Take that you heathen swine! Run! You bring no credit to the Zulu nation!"

The officer's speech meant nothing to the refugee. He understood the actual words well enough, but he had no idea what the mad old duffer was barking on about. Tears of pure fright washed pale streaks down his dark cheeks; he prayed to reach the back gate into the alley before the sword swung again. The fleeing man lunged for the gate, hauling it back on creaking hinges. He darted between buildings and out into the street. The lights of the Freemasons' Tavern[1] shone like a beacon of safety. He ran, pausing at the next corner to make sure there was no pursuit. The officer was standing at the gate, brandishing an ancient cavalry sabre. A youngster in hotel page's uniform stood next to him, as if holding the old soldier back. The running man, in return, waved a brush-like object at his attacker, as if incanting an ancient curse.

"I'm bloody well never sweeping the chimneys 'ere again!".

* * *

The summer of 1928 was a season of bounty for the seaside merchants and hotel proprietors of England. The sun beamed down beatifically, each hour of its shining presence catalogued as proof that fine weather and the British summer were not the total strangers they sometimes seemed. Parties of London trippers rode by train or charabanc[2] to the resorts of the south coast. Pale female bodies

1. The Freemason's Tavern still stands on Western Road in Hove.
2. A single-decker bus, used for excursions rather than scheduled public transport.

sported daring bathing costumes watched keenly by young men in outrageously baggy flannels. Fast roadsters raced down from 'Town' to Brighton, bearing what Mr. Noel Coward had baptised the 'Bright Young Things', for weekends at the Grand. It only took an hour, if you really flew. There were tea dances at Sherry's, shows at the Hippodrome and the Theatre Royal and entertainments on both of the piers. It was a fine time to be young.

Except if, like George, you had to work.

George Chapman worked, all the time it seemed. He was the youngest, and most menial, employee at the Empire Lodge Hotel, Lansdowne Place, Hove. It was 'Four minutes from the sea', but only if you ran really fast. The owners, a father and son named Quint, had argued about that detail. As a selling point it was of doubtful effect. The Bright Young Things did not come to the Empire Lodge. They found it 'staid', or 'stuffy'. They found the sedate – but always elegant – Regency streets of Hove tame in comparison with its companion town to the east. Brighton, always racier, drew the crowds, from shop-girls to the daughters of dukes. It had an aquarium and an ornate mock-Oriental structure built by the Prince Regent as 'the Royal Pavilion'. Hove was altogether a quieter place. George, who had lived there all his life, pronounced Hove to be 'dead as a doornail.' It was a phrase he'd got from a detective novel. The official guidebook did not view the town in that light at all; 'dignified' was the preferred term. Hove, according to George, was full of old codgers, retired civil servants and army officers, playing bridge and bowls. All very dull indeed. The dullest of them seemed to find that the Empire Lodge was exactly what they wanted in a hotel, moved in – with George carrying their luggage up three flights of stairs – and stayed forever. They might, indeed, be the dullest people in England. Except for the Colonel.

* * *

George was supposed to be polishing the kitchen knives when he overheard the two Misters Quint as they discussed today's incident, one of many in which the oldest resident had brought shame and potential litigation down upon the Empire Lodge Hotel. That, at least, that was the view of Young Mr. Quint.

"Look, dad. We can't have that maniac staying here anymore. This morning he took his bloomin' sword to Jenks the chimney sweep. Jenks'll never come back, and likely nobody else in town'll do it either. And this is not the first time that stupid old geezer has made us the laughing stock of the neighbourhood." George paused in the hallway to listen as the senior Quint answered.

"I'll not have you talking that way, Edward. Your mother and I did not bring you up to use vulgar language. Colonel Bagshot is a hero. He served in the Afghan War! He avenged General Gordon! He was first on the beach at Gallipoli!" Old Mr. Quint was adamant.

"Oh, stuff and nonsense, dad! He's a senile old lunatic who sees flippin' Ashantee warriors on the top deck of Brighton buses and gets brought home by a constable once a month."

As far as George could hear, Old Mr. Quint had made no reply to that. At least, he never caught it because he heard Cook coming and had to duck back to where he was supposed to be cleaning the knives as per her orders. Still, it was clear that the Colonel had gone and done it this time.

CHAPTER TWO

Hove 1928

George tapped at Colonel Bagshot's door. He could hear the old man muttering on the other side. The boy balanced the tea-tray and turned the knob. The Colonel was, for some reason, engaged in an animated monologue. His sole audience was a large tabby cat. The cat showed little interest and may indeed have heard the story before.

"Henry Hook lunged with his bayonet at the warrior leading the ravening hordes of Zulus. The bloodlust was on him, cursing the foe in ancient West Country[3] oaths and using his farmhand's muscles to drive the steel blade into the Zulu's chest. 'Got yer, ye heathen savage!' he cried, jamming a cartridge into the hot breech of his Martini-Henry[4]. As a second Zulu stormed forward through the shattered remnants of the door, I swung my own rifle, like this ---"

To illustrate the point, he swung a golf club furiously about his head, loudly upsetting a hanging fern in a clatter of broken pottery. The cat yawned.

"Of course, I never got credit for saving the garrison at Rorke's Drift. Well, they'd have had to take back all those Victoria Crosses."

The Colonel was speaking to George now. He recognized a sympathetic listener. The boy put down the tea things. It was four-thirty on a Monday afternoon, and evidently time for another recollection of wars gone by. The incident with the sweep – or, as the Colonel remembered it, with the marauding Zulu warrior – had sent the old fellows' mind wandering in that direction. George did not bring up the issue of Mr. Jenks, or what had convinced the Colonel that a perfectly ordinary tradesman engaged in a perfectly ordinary trade was, in fact, a savage African killer of men anxious to rip out the guts of English holidaymakers.

---

3. Henry Hook, despite his portrayal as a Londoner by the actor James Booth in Zulu, actually came from Gloucestershire in the West Country.

4. The Martini Henry was a single-shot breech-loading rifle, adopted by the British army in 1871. It was a black powder weapon known for its powerful recoil, with an extreme range of around 1800 yards (although shooting at this distance was generally discouraged!). Replaced in the 1890s by the magazine-fed Lee Metford, the Martini Henry remained in use by 'native' forces as late as WWI.

Charles Edward Hezekiah Bagshot, officer and gentleman, master of disguises, raconteur and probable liar, was sitting in a moth-devoured armchair. His skull shone where the hair had long ago retreated, before the tight skin sagged into a mass of wrinkles from the forehead downwards. His white moustache was clipped and disciplined; his eyebrows, beetling enthusiastically, were emphatically not. In this, his final and greatest disguise, he appeared as a small, elderly man in pressed, threadbare tweeds, regimental tie, and the kind of leather brogues that begin to turn upwards like Persian slippers after forty years of strenuous wear; George polished them daily and knew them well. The Colonel maintained proper military posture in a way that was wonderful to behold though, like all old horsemen, his knees would rather turn out than in. He looked like any other retired officer – and George saw dozens of them on the seafront each day. But the boy knew that Colonel Bagshot – "Binky" to his peers – was unique. He was one of the great unsung heroes of the British Empire. He said so himself.

The Colonel's military service was varied, an elaborate history in which he moved about from unit to unit, campaign to campaign by a Byzantine sequence of transfers. He had been commissioned into the 10th Hussars[5] – that was always *The Regiment* – but his exact status in the Punjab Frontier Force, the Sultan of Morocco's personal guards and certain cannibal tribes of the deeper Congo was difficult to assess. He spoke vaguely of what he termed *exchanges* and *secondments*;[6] there were temporary appointments and brevets awarded for gallant conduct – often taken from him later by Enemies in High places, as he hinted darkly. Why, if he'd just stayed with the Regiment and played polo, he'd be receiving the pension of a full General! His chum 'Bungo' had been a young officer in the regiment and had gone on to the post of Governor-General in Ottawa. Bungo (now as Viscount Byng of Vimy) hadn't seen half the service that old Binky Bagshot[7] could claim.

In the year George had been working at the Empire Lodge he had heard more than a few of Colonel Bagshot's stories – manly tales of derring-do at the untamed frontiers of Victoria's empire. The Colonel had served, it seemed, in every campaign fought by the British army from the outbreak of mutiny at

---

5. The 10th Hussars had been formed as a dragoon regiment in 1715, but converted into – first – light dragoons (1783) and then into the fashionable Hungarian-styled hussars during the Napoleonic Wars. Distinguishing itself in Spain and Portugal, and at Waterloo, the 10th became a high-status unit, whose officers required a private income far in excess of their army pay in order to follow a life based on fine horses, expensive sports and an extravagant social life. Very occasionally it took a break from these exhausting activities to campaign at the far frontiers of the British empire.
6. An *exchange* is exactly what it suggests – the swapping of one officer for another. A *secondment* is a temporary transfer. A brevet is a local or short-term promotion that might or might not be made officially permanent.
7. Julian Byng was a near-contemporary of Colonel Bagshot in the regiment. His distinguished service culminated in commanding the Canadian forces on the Western Front in WWI, and subsequently the post of Governor-General of Canada.

Meerut in '57[8] onwards ("Traitorous hounds!" he had railed at the memory of the revolting sepoys, though arithmetic suggested he could have been hardly more than a toddler at the time). In 1918, after decades of service, Colonel Bagshot's active career finally ended. Serving against the Turks in the Holy Land he had (as he explained) been unfairly removed from his command following an unfortunate – but entirely understandable – confusion between the words 'Austrian' and 'Australian' in his orders. Being oblivious to the presence of certain units belonging to the House of Habsburg[9] amongst the enemy forces (he admitted that he might have nodded off during one or two briefings; they were very boring and always held right after lunch) the Colonel had, quite naturally, assumed that a particularly rumbustious ANZAC brigade had finally stepped over the line into open rebellion.

But taking the kind of quick, decisive measures required to deal with mutiny – the kind of thing involving megaphones, a machine gun battery and several armoured cars – caused a diplomatic row that no protests of innocence could quell. The Colonel's use of the phrase "Antipodean sheep-shaggers", bellowed through the megaphone at several thousand Australian soldiers, had not served to improve the situation. After a series of what were termed 'unnecessarily excitable' telegrams between Bagshot's command post, Army HQ in Jerusalem and the War Office in London, the Colonel found himself unexpectedly retired from active service. "Bloody cheek!" he called it.

---

8. The origins of the Indian Mutiny are complex, and are beyond the scope of a brief explanation. The important thing to note is that, while the exact date of Colonel Bagshot's birth remains unclear (due variously to a fire, a sunken ship, and rats eating his birth certificate) it is unlikely that a four or five year old ever led a cavalry charge shouting "Hurrah! Hurrah!" as he was occasionally wont to claim.

9. A very limited number of troops from the Austro-Hungarian empire served on the Palestine front alongside their Turkish allies. The suggestion that they were sent purely to cause this sort of confusion among the more deranged British officers seems unlikely to be true.

CHAPTER THREE
Hove 1928

The Colonel's rooms were, to George, an astonishing escape from the everyday world of bus rides along the seafront, watching the town football team[10] wallowing to muddy defeat, and always – always – mornings spent scrabbling to avoid the scathing displeasure of the cook, (known only as 'Cook') and Old Mr. Quint. Old Mr. Quint was not only proprietor of the Empire Lodge Hotel but a churchwarden and guardian of public morality – in particular, George's. The young man's actions, whether it was appearing for duty with cap askew, or wasting his money going to see Harold Lloyd at the pictures, were somehow symbols of the decay of modern society. Since the armistice, civilization had collapsed; you could read about it each morning in the Daily Mail. Standards were, however, maintained to the last at Mr. Quint's establishment, and even the 'Boots' – the lowly position which was George's – as expected to repel the barbarian hordes.

Actually, Colonel Bagshot viewed the universe in terms not very different from Old Quint. In his rooms there was safety from the troubled and troubling outdoor world of Rudolf Valentino (lately deceased), bobbed hair and the Labour Party. In his rooms Victoria reigned yet. In his rooms it was hardly Lansdowne Place; indeed, it was hardly England at all, but a hothouse composition of the tropics. It was always a strict seventy-nine degrees, the steam radiators sweating away. The potted palms and ferns ran riot, as if a suburban conservatory had studied hard in an effort to become the jungles of Burma. There were African masks and pieces of Indian brasswork, bizarre knives and polished clubs. There were photographs, shields, banners, and old bamboo wicker furniture that had seen a dozen cantonment bungalows before Pickles got to it.

Pickles was a handsome and well-rounded ginger tabby who alternated tremendous idleness with brief but ferocious assaults on the household fixtures. The hotel rules forbade pets, of course, but the Colonel contended that Pickles was an exception. Dammit, the Colonel himself was an exception.

---

10. Brighton and Hove Albion, founded in 1901 were, in the 1920s, a fixture of the Third Division South – the lowest in the English Football league.

George sat down. His employers could hardly mind his being detained for a few minutes by the hotel's oldest and most distinguished resident, even if he did attack the tradesmen with a cavalry sabre. Besides, the Colonel had only today settled his account with the management, an event of some rarity and a cause for minor celebration in the back office. As George saw it the Colonel had plenty of money, counting his army pension, a small private endowment and an alleged annual grant from the Maharaja of Kashmir for some past kindness, ("Old bastard'd be selling matches outside Murray's Hotel in Bombay if it wasn't for me!"). He never really spent any of it. His extravagances ran no further than a regular, and large, supply of single malt Scotch, books (quite a lot of them, military history and biography), a singular and virulent tobacco mixture by Vafiades of Cairo and frequent reinforcements for his considerable army of lead soldiers by British and continental makers. Parcels arrived from Germany, heavy things for their size; the disastrous financial state of the Weimar Republic meant that Georg Heyde and Co[11], of Dresden, were more than happy to serve the Colonel's recruiting needs in return for his Sterling drafts. But Colonel Bagshot knew that appearances matter. A gentleman ought not to pay tradesmen whenever they ask for their money. It was just not done. George's employers, for all Young Mr. Quint's elephantine pomp and circumstance, were only tradesmen. So, if Heyde and Company joyfully received a cheque on the Bagshot account, it was likely that the Empire Lodge Hotel would have to wait. Today the wait had ended, and the Colonel was a hero in Old Quint's eyes. He could delay the servant lad if he wanted.

The Colonel peered at George, and flicked tobacco ash from his beflannelled knee. "Yes, the Zulu Affair. January 1879. You'll recall that during the first season of the Afghan War, I had gone down with a touch of the cholera. Unless it kills you, cholera isn't near as bad as you'd think – it don't compare to a bite from a Black Mamba or a nip from a spiteful camel. Or, it should be said, with sharing a railway carriage with an enthusiastic Jehovah's Witness. Just a lot of throwing up and considerable activity at, um, the other end. Also hiccoughing and a high-pitched voice. However, my constitution was still somewhat weakened and what with my wound from Ali Masjid[12], I was feeling distinctly poorly. I mentioned this to the surgeon by way of polite conversation, and before I could say 'Pass the port' the damned fool wrote me a ticket for six months leave in England. I didn't want to go; it was six weeks by steamer, and once I was home I might not make it out again for the opening of festivities in the spring. Afghanistan can be charming in April. Besides, my aunt would probably pack me off to some

---

11. Germany was the home of the tin soldier, and the Heyde company specialized in historical figurines, nominally 54mm in height. Colonel Bagshot was able to take advantage of the parlous state of the German economy to buy these cheaply. The main domestic manufacturer of model soldiers was William Britains and Co, founded in 1893, who remain in business today.
12. The action at Ali Masjid (Nov 21, 1878) saw the defeat of an Afghan army by Sir Samuel Browne and the Peshawar Field Force. Two squadrons of the 10th Hussars were present at the battle.

ghastly Alpine rest cure, drinking vile spa water and being rigidly polite to elderly Teutonic matrons. So, I protested to my commanding officer, Lord Ralph Kerr. He told me that the 10th Royal Hussars didn't need the services of an officer who couldn't stand up without clutching his washstand.

Anyway, I was sitting in a canvas chair on the deck of this frightful steamship – the first thing out of Bombay for dear old England, via the Cape rather than Suez, as it happened – trying to keep my dinner down. I was reading a copy of Clarendon[13] on the Civil War – the real Civil War, not the American disturbances – when a scruffy merchantman hauls up off the larboard beam (which is the left side) and hails us. In those days whenever ships met they'd swap news, gossip, what-have-you; in this case, though the bearer was hardly acceptable company, the news was excellent. There was war in South Africa!

Now, modern attitudes being what they are, you might not appreciate what a fine thing it was for a young officer to hear that he might have the chance to be killed or horribly disfigured in some desolate and benighted part of the globe. You see, war meant not only the chance to get into a decent scrap – which, having been bullied through public school, most of us loved – but also the opportunity to get ahead. Once upon a time soldiers used to toast 'a bloody war and a sickly season', since that was a way to shunt side some of the fellows ahead of you on the promotion ladder. As you can imagine, modern medicine had made things worse for us young 'uns, since you couldn't expect the fever to carry off a few gouty majors the way it had in Wellington's time. Couldn't buy yourself a promotion anymore, either, since the government abolished the purchase of commissions[14] – though frankly, I was glad since my private resources were a touch shaky when I started out. Damned expensive regiment, and fashionable, 'the Shiny Tenth'; I wouldn't have got in if it hadn't been for Great Uncle Henry's having been the Colonel's squadron commander forty years before. Many a good man got jumped over by fools and sots with a few guineas jingling in their pockets. The 10th was deadly expensive, at least six hundred pounds a year when the regiment was in England, ideally twice that; cheaper in India, of course. Still, when the Prince of Wales is your Colonel-in-Chief, you'd not expect pork pies and jellied eels and three-shilling brandy, would you? Now, I believe that the officer class should be composed of gentlemen – the men like to be led by a fellow who talks nicely, and the conditions at most English boarding schools fit one so nicely for

---

13. The Earl of Clarendon's *The History of the Rebellion and Civil Wars in England* was written in the years before the Earl's death in 1674, but not published until the early years of the Eighteenth Century. It remains a classic account of the Civil Wars.

14. Traditionally the practice was for prospective officers to buy their way into a regiment, then purchase promotions as vacancies came open. This meant that regimental rank was largely determined by wealth rather than seniority or, indeed, competence. From 1871 a reformed system based on seniority was put in place, but officers' pay was relatively low so a private income – often a very significant income – was needed to augment it, especially in 'fashionable' regiments like the 10th Hussars.

a winter campaign up the Khyber – but cash and gentility don't have a lot to do with one another. Murderous brutes, good on a horse, and nice table manners. Nothing wrong with a bit of snobbery with violence."

The colonel liked that one.

"War with the Zulus, no less. Fine strapping, manly fellows, as I'd heard. So, residual cholera and a two-inch gash from a *tulwar*[15] notwithstanding, I was feeling quite chipper when the old barge pulled into Durban roads. Durban's a shocking harbour today, after thousands of pounds worth of improvement. In '79 it was much worse. Ships had to risk a sandbar across the harbour, of uncertain and pernicious depth. The prudent skipper would lay out in the roadstead and let his cargo and passengers be unloaded by a sort of dog-basket on a gibbet into little bobbing tugboats – 'lighters' they call them – and splash their way unsteadily through the heavy surf. That's what the captain of our vessel chose to do; if anyone wanted off at Durban, they could ruddy well take their chances because he wasn't going to. There were two or three of us soldiers aboard – a sickly captain of gunners and a couple of subalterns of foot, I think – all keen as mustard to be at 'em. We were dropped like a catch of herring into the lighter and engulfed in spray and coal smoke until we clambered out onto the Government wharf. I can see us now, a merry band of young men, holders of the Queen's commission, standing soaked to the skin on a patch of damp sand with all our belongings bedraggling up the beach. We were cheering: cheering with all our lungs and tongues and bold British hearts. It was a stirring moment. The gunner went down with pneumonia and died two days later. Still, can't have everything. It was marvelous to see such spirit!"

In the deep downstairs a bell rang.

---

15. A sword in the Indian style, known for a much sharper edge than European service blades.

CHAPTER FOUR

Hove 1928

The Colonel had laid out an array of lead soldiers on the table. They were British soldiers of the late Queen's time, red coats and white helmets, marching in columns. Some of them weren't exactly in the right pose to be marching in columns and seemed to be protesting their deployment by aiming their rifles at the necks of the man in front. George looked at them with care and deference.

"D' ye know what regiment?" demanded the Colonel.

Each of the figures had a patch of grass green paint at the collar and on each cuff, neatly touched in, with narrow white piping between the red and green. Sometimes the Colonel paid extra for 'special' paint jobs for units he particularly liked, rather than the factory finish produced by shifts of young women at Mr. William Britain's establishment in North London; this was partly for the extra detail, and partly, George believed, because the Colonel really didn't think it appropriate that 'gels' be allowed to paint model soldiers. No, there should be a home for disabled veterans where these things were done ----

What regiment? "24th foot, sir, now the South Wales Borderers."

"Quite right," beamed the Colonel. "I have a story to tell."

* * *

On landing at the Point, we demanded the latest news of the war. The war, it seemed, was advancing well. Lord Chelmsford, the senior commander, had decided to take on the Zulus in the middle of the rainy season so as to give us an advantage of some sort. Perhaps he thought that, since the Zulus had no waterproofs or galoshes, they would have to stay at home while we advanced in sensible boots and proper headgear. As it was, it simply meant that our gallant forces had to struggle through a land completely devoid of decent roads, employing a vast gaggle of rented transport, in a constant state of soaking exasperation. I watched an irate Dutchman whip a handful of black men into a vain attempt at manhandling a wagon. South African ox-wagons are the size of a minor cathedral, so wheedling it out of a stretch of sucking swamp – artistically placed at the point where two streets came together – was no easy matter. I couldn't see that curses and blows were going to fix things either, since the blacks were more concerned to stay out of reach of the flailing overseer than move the bloody cart. "He shall smite them with the edge of his sword; he shall not spare them, neither have pity, nor have mercy," as it says in Jeremiah, though I'd have thought the flat of the sword would have done just as well. There were two spans of trek-oxen, thirty-two hefty beasts, and advancing not one single inch.

There were soldiers working, drilling, carrying things, falling over one another. There were civilians loafing, gawking, getting in the way, their children apparently eager to hurl themselves under the first gun team to pass their way. There was the livestock, animals of many descriptions doing their collective best to clog the pavements, looking as stupid as infantrymen and leaving their calling cards underfoot – the animals I mean, not the infantrymen; not in the British army at any rate.

The main stores depot was a full two miles from the Government Wharf, so everything that landed had an unusually good chance of being lost, spoiled or stolen before anyone in authority had the chance to register it, let alone decide where it ought to go.

It was sheer bloody chaos, of course. I felt right at home. If it had been any better, there would have been something wrong. Good organisation's not a British thing, you know. We don't feel right if things go too smoothly – we're not ruddy Germans! And I've seen much worse. I was privileged to see the shambles the Italians made of merely getting off the boats at Massowa in '95[16] on their way to their ghastly Abyssinian catastrophe; of course, they didn't have the centuries of amphibious balls-ups that we could boast, so it's only natural. They were sheer innocents at the art of messing things up from the outset.

I seized hold of a lanky young fellow in the double white striped trousers of the Commissariat and addressed him in the way one talks to dogs, foreigners and the congenitally imbecilic.

"Who is in charge here?"

---

16. The disastrous campaign that culminated in the utter defeat of an Italian army at the hands of Menelik of Abyssinia at Adowa in 1896 is a remarkable combination of bad luck, political interference and sheer incompetence at a generalship level – the Italian troops fought well against overwhelming odds. Binky seems to have appreciated every minute of it.

"Eh?"

"Who commands here?"

"Well, you might talk to De Ricci. He's assistant to the head of the Ordnance Stores. Or there's a staff chappie from his Lordship's HQ – I think he's around. And old Wright, the DCG's[17] up at his office, I expect. What do you want? Who are you with? Oh, hang on a moment ----"

The commissary turned and jabbered at a little man in a huge Boer hat. There was much waving of arms, and both turned around, neither satisfied with the result of the exchange.

"Horribly short of fellows, I'm afraid. Need some good men in the Stores and Transport departments. De Ricci's quite exhausted. What is it that you want anyway?"

What I wanted was a job. What I didn't want, if I could avoid it, was his job. Appointments at base camps have a disturbing tendency to become permanent if you are any good at them. Standards are low, so you might be considered dangerously competent if you manage to load up a mule cart with a batch of camp kettles in under a fortnight. Death for your career, of course. They hardly ever give medals to those who gallantly issue greatcoats. Many a bold cavalry officer who dreamed of charging with the Light Brigade, all death and glory, ended his service checking horses' teeth at a remount depot.

Not I. I was off into the crowd as a damp corporal respectfully requested a moment of my harried comrade's time. My erstwhile comrades from the India steamer could play wagon-wallah if they liked, but I was off to fight the Zulus.

---

17. Deputy Commissary General – the officer who bore actual responsibility for stores. His duties overlapped with those of the quartermaster's department, allowing room for additional confusion and arguing.

CHAPTER FIVE

Hove 1928

The Empire Lodge was not the most fashionable hostelry in Hove, or even on Lansdowne Place. The hotel's style Lodge was rambling Victorian on top of faded imitation Regency. The rooms were too big or too small – the Colonel had three small ones in a suite – and the furnishings heavy and florid for modern taste. The food was stodgy and the service slow. In the past the elder Mr. Quint and his late lady wife had disagreed over many things, Mrs. Quint claiming that if her husband wasn't willing to make concessions to the tastes of a post-war generation of gentlefolk, he ought to drop his prices to accommodate the more proletarian trippers who stayed with the guest house landladies for *two quid a week*. Mrs. Quint put on a cockney accent when she'd said that; she'd never normally refer to a pound note as a 'quid'. Mr. Quint had said that the Empire Lodge had a traditional tone, and if fashionable London wished to waste its money on flashy hotels and foreign cookery, he'd settle for a few select guests who appreciated what he termed 'English quality'. Mrs. Quint had replied with some curt comments involving rising damp and ancient plumbing, but her spouse had stood firm on what he called his 'No riff-raff ' policy.

Since Mrs. Quint stepped in front of a speeding Austin Seven while visiting her sister in Sackville Road, the tone of *English quality* had prevailed, so that the Lodge relied on elderly residents, together with a few sternly traditionalist or naively unsuspecting summer visitors. What this meant was that the Colonel was not only a staple financial contributor to the upkeep of the place – which showed how ropey things had become – but an emblem of all that Mr. Quint felt the Empire Lodge stood for. When the Colonel ran up the heating bill, it was alright. When Pickles attacked the maid, it was acceptable. When the Colonel looked down his nose at Mr. Quint, it was, well, *old fashioned*. Mr. Quint, a thorough snob, thrilled to have a military gentleman look down on him.

The staff, indeed, sniggered to one another that if the old Colonel was to kick Old Mr. Quint down two flights of steps it would probably make his whole day.

Most retired army officers nowadays were just like ordinary people. They'd got their commissions in the Great War, read Agatha Christie novels and sold Life Assurance or Morris Oxfords. No tone at all.

So, if the Colonel wished to detain the boy telling his endless tales, well, it was alright.

* * *

One decent meal at the Natal Club – cutlets a touch gamy, claret surprisingly good – and a bath later, I was off to the station for a train to Zululand. Well, not to Zululand, perhaps, but towards the provincial capital, Pietermaritzburg. The sooner I was out of Durban the better if I wanted to see active service. The town had been picked clean of horseflesh, so buying a couple of ponies was out of the question; I'd do that closer to the Zulu country, in the higher interior where I wouldn't be paying twice the value for a nag previously infected with some ghastly tropic equine disease. The coastlands are terrible for that.

Trains are a wonderful convenience. A native porter took care of my luggage – being a saddle, half a dozen tin chop-boxes, a small Gladstone bag and a portmanteau from Silvers in Cornhill St – and helped me into the single passenger carriage, quite properly reserved for officers. There weren't any, save for me. Other ranks were relegated to open wagons. There weren't any of them today either, because they were all off at the blasted front, ready to hammer the Zulus.

It was pouring down. I didn't care. I was taking the evening train – the only train – to Pinetown. I was content.

Ignorance is, as you know, a condition of bliss. I discovered that Pinetown, the end of the line, was only twelve miles from Durban. The black line connecting the port and the capital, shown prominently on the map I had bought at the station, was apparently some kind of engineer's pipedream. I hoped to see elephant, rhinoceri, hartebeeste and wilderbeeste and all kinds of exotic African beeste. I did see a few forlorn cattle. I was satisfied to alight at Pinetown anyway. The track underwent a series of desperate undulations which demanded a policy of alternating brutal coercion and tender nursing from the driver and fireman to get the locomotive into action. At one point the stoker was walking alongside, placing stones under the wheels to prevent the whole thing sliding into oblivion. Damned inadequate. I could tell you I've felt safer slung across a yak at 16,000 feet on the way to Lhasa in '04, but that would be an exaggeration. As you know, I never exaggerate. Still, it was no day trip to Hastings.

24

At Pinetown I put up at Murray's, which I was assured was a hotel – not much like its namesake in Bombay, I might say. It was a sort of corrugated iron shed, with the better rooms facing out onto a long verandah, the less luxurious facing out directly onto a patch of bog. The service at breakfast was of a most irregular sort, with the landlady and her vicious brood of offspring holding court at one end of a massive table – the only table – in the barnlike main room. Black servants flittered about in a disorderly manner, as if they had heard a waiter described but never actually seen one. I was one of a number of guests, as Mrs. Murray chose to call us; well, 'hostages' sounds bad, especially if you're charging for the privilege.

"Captain," she said. There's not a lieutenant in the army doesn't brighten up at being addressed as 'captain'.

"Yes, Ma'am."

"Do you think that Cetshwayo will give way at the last minute? I mean, with our boys over the frontier, will he see the error of his ways?"

I was about to begin the sentence, "I bally well hope not----", when I realised the import of what she had said. 'Over the frontier'. I hadn't heard that in Durban. I inquired whence she had this piece of information.

"From that nice staff orficer who went down to the coast first thing today. It's all over P.M.Burg. There's been a fight and all sorts of Kaffirs[18] killed, theirs and ours. Our brave white boys are alright though, two orficers slightly wounded. That nice Lieutenant Harford as used to live in the colony, he tooked a bunch of 'em prisoner. 'Ang the lot as an example, I say."

"Er, quite," says I, a touch off balance. "When did this happen, my good woman?"

"Last week I think, Sat'day or Sunday. Do you think the Zulus will invade British territory?"

"I would certainly hope so." She gasped. Probably didn't see it quite the way I did. I couldn't see that this news was good.

They'd started without me. I'd have to hurry like billy-o to be there for the main festivities.

Mrs. Murray's eldest was trying to cadge a cigar from a fellow at the far end of the table. It's a disgrace what poor breeding can do to an eight-year old. The waiter clattered over with a tray of beef, roasted into abject surrender. Mrs.

18. The word *Kaffir* (derived from an Arabic word meaning 'infidel') was in general use as a term for black Africans. It does not seem to have been especially derogatory at this period, although later came to be seen as an insult.

Murray hurled some imprecation at him in what might have been an attempt at a native dialect. I ate and went to ready my kit for the morning.

That evening I had a chance to look over a little book I'd picked up in Durban. It was by some colonial called Fynn or Fynney and had the General's approval[19]. He was a very dull writer, but a couple of bits caught my attention:

The Zulu army, which may be estimated at from 40,000 to 50,000 men, is composed of the entire nation capable of bearing arms. The method employed in recruiting is as follows: - At short intervals, varying from two to five years, all the young men who have during that time attained the age of fourteen or fifteen years are formed into a regiment, which --- is placed at a military kraal --(better than luring the unemployed with flashy uniforms and free beer, like in England!) -- *As the regiment grows old, it generally has one or more regiments embodied with it, so that the younger men may have the benefit of their elder's experience, and, when the latter die out, may keep their place and keep up the name and prestige of their military kraal----'*

I read on. Clearly this was a real army, recruited by a distinctive method rather like the year's new boys at a public school. They had companies – called *amavivo*, apparently – and regiments, with proper ranks. Each regiment had uniforms of a kind, with the senior regiments having white shields and being allowed to marry; the youngsters had coloured shields and remained bachelors, which was not unlike our own army. I can't imagine a British colonel, in fact, who'd allow his whole regiment to marry; you'd have hundreds of women and screaming babies on every troopship. The married men wore some kind of head-ring apparently. There was a great deal of rivalry between regiments, and fights broke out if they were stationed together. That's nothing new; there's a certain regiment of lancers who'll come out swinging if you should refer to an embarrassing episode from the Sikh war by yelling "Threes about!" in a public house.

Fynney decried their knowledge of drill, referring to *'the few simple movements which they perform with any method, such as forming a circle of companies or regiments, breaking into companies or regiments from the circle, forming a line of march in order of companies, or in close order of regiments not being deserving of the name. The officers, have, however, their regulated duties and responsibilities, according to their rank, and the men lend a ready obedience to their orders.'*

There are units in our army you'd not say that much for – some of the slacker infantry regiments. There was mention of a lot of mumbo-jumbo about magical portents and witch-doctoring, but again as I say, army traditions are odd. The 14th Hussars make a great deal of drinking the Loyal Toast out of Napoleon's brother's pisspot[20].

---

19. The Border agent Bernard (F.B.) Fynney's *The Zulu Army and Zulu headmen; Published by Direction of the Lieutenant-General Commanding*, Pietermaritzburg, 1878.
20. In the aftermath of the Battle of Vitoria (1813) the French baggage train was captured. The 14th Light

The Zulus were apparently were quick, and had little in the way of encumbrances – you know, mess silver, banquet tables, that sort of thing. *'As might be expected a savage army like that of Zululand neither has nor requires much commissariat or transport. The former consists of three or four days provisions, in the shape of maize or millet, and a herd of cattle --- accompanies each regiment. The latter consists of a number of lads (udibi boys) who followed each regiment carrying the sleeping mats, blankets and provisions, and assisting to drive the cattle'.*

Crossing a river was something they did well: *'if the breadth of the stream which is out of their depth does not exceed from ten to fifteen yards, they plunge in, in a dense mass, holding on to one another, those behind forcing them on forward, and thus succeed in crossing with the loss of a few of their number.'*

This was all certainly an eye opener. They sounded like clever fellows. I tried to read a copy of Lord Chelmsford's instructions for the campaign, which spoke a lot about getting the wagons into something called laagers at night, and digging trenches, but frankly it made me fall asleep. I woke when the train stopped in a hissing jolt.

Dragoons share of the loot included the chamberpot of Joseph Bonaparte, King of Spain and brother to the *Corsican Adventurer*.

CHAPTER SIX

Hove 1928

It was during the morning hours that George was most often able to slip away from his duties to listen to the Colonel. Over the past several months George had taken on certain jobs in connection with the Colonel, because nobody else would do them. Molly the house maid was forbidden to do more than the most peremptory cleaning in the Colonel's rooms for fear of breaking some bizarre artifact that might appear on the washstand or throwing away some object her limited judgment told her to be broken, spoiled or deleterious to the public health. She denied that she'd touched any West African fetishes and wouldn't know one if it said 'boo' to her, which the Colonel took as evidence against her. Anyway, she was terrified of Pickles, who had once chased her along the landing and up onto the next floor out of sheer feline joie de vie. So, George cleaned the Colonel's rooms, to a standard both of them considered satisfactory, and listened to the Bagshot history.

* * *

I waited for the Pietermaritzburg omnibus. This was a primitive affair much like your Buffalo Bill's Wild West Show stagecoach and belonged to a man named Welch. The station was crowded with passengers waiting to board – seven or eight of them, all Natal men, farmers, small traders and a doctor. The luggage was perched on top, strapped into submission but fighting back gamely.

Already inside the coach was an elderly lady who conspired, by use of voluminous skirts of archaic fashion, to take up most of the carriage. She had a wicker hamper of patent medicines, and I instantly realized that any threat to her dominion would be answered with an unanswerable offer of some vile lozenge or syrup. You couldn't turn her down without appearing a bounder – she'd say you looked so dreadfully out of sorts – and then she'd got you. She could have the seat.

I decided to ride on the roof with the bags and the native servants. We set off smartish, and I was impressed by the stamina of the horse team. Most of the transport in Natal is ox or mule drawn.

We clambered up Field's Hill and Bowker's Hill – it might have been Botha's, the servants of the English and Dutch passengers disagreed – but a bloody great stretch of incline anyway, churned with wagon tracks slurping through great lakes of jam-like mud. The blacks seemed to like having a British officer on top of the coach with them and pointed out all the landmarks. The country was cut up with swathes of wagon tracks going hither and yon for fifty yards on either side of the path chosen by Mr. Welch's postillion. The road from Durban to PMB was a road in name only; it was more a General Direction. We changed horses at an Inn called the Half-Way House, where the old lady left us, and I took a seat inside.

The passengers were talking. I got interested when the war was mentioned, which was soon. Everyone had heard of the affair of last week and seemed to have known of it long before I did. There had been an attack on the kraals of a Zulu chief, one Sihayo, whose recent conduct had been abnormally barbarous; indeed, it was the shocking misconduct of two of his sons – who had crossed the border in pursuit of unfaithful wives, nabbed them back across the river and murdered them quite without mercy – that had brought the Zulu question into focus. Our men had given them a licking, but no real advance had yet been made into Zulu territory. Apparently, the routes of access into Zululand made the track we were on seem like Tottenham Court Road. Which was good news for me.

"Off to the war, young man?" quizzed the doctor. I agreed that I was. "Don't you be fooled by the Zulus. Too many folk think they will run off into the bush as soon as they see a red coat. They won't play hide and seek like the East Cape Kaffir tribes – the Gaikas and Galekas – did last year, either, which is an infuriating game to play but not what you'd call dangerous. The Zulus believe in a good, stand-up fight and don't mind losing a few warriors in the process."

I opined that we should be recruiting them rather than fighting them. We fought the Gurkhas back in the 'teens and the Sikhs in the 'forties and signed 'em to our colours in crowds the minute the war was up.

"You joke, young fellow, but believe. They'll cut you up in a moment if you let them. Nobody has really seen the Zulus in battle these last years, though you can still meet old Boers who fought them forty-odd years ago. I've never seen it myself but when I was a young physician in the northern part of the colony I treated some Zulus who had been wounded in a big fight between Cetshwayo –

as is king now – and his brother back about '56 or 7, I think. The battle had been weeks before, and all the chaps are walking fifty or a hundred miles with horrible spear wounds, smashed bones, septicaemia and all. Must've been in terrible pain, terrible. Never heard a murmur of complaint."

Definitely, we could use a battalion or two of these laddies. With the medical services offered by the British army, a certain sense of stoic resignation is extremely helpful.

The conversation became general and animated.

"Chelmsford 'll finish them off in a week".

"No, the redcoat's will botch it and our local lads will have to bail them out of it. I have a cousin in the Natal Mounted Police and he told his dad, which is my uncle ---"

"Mounted coppers, my eye! Jumped-up day labourers! Navvies on nags and cheap uniforms that smell like something died. Now, the volunteers, they're the boys. Gentlemen, like."

"Ah, the Natal Hussars. The Durban Mounted Rifles. The pride of the colony ----"

It was clear that opinion was that these local lads could smash up Cetshwayo on their own, with the Queen's regulars there to make up the numbers and dig the odd latrine. I'm not fond of colonial units you know. All they want to do is steal other people's cows, recommend one another for the Victoria Cross and demand Martial Law so they can press the blacks into forced labour on their farms while they put their feet up. I didn't say so though; tact is one of my virtues. A few minutes later I was proved right, as they all agreed how marvelous it would be when the Zulus were beat and had to get jobs for white men, and how wages would come down. If I hadn't been spoiling for a fight, I'd have cleared off home just to show 'em what I thought. If I wanted to risk an army to get cheap workers for scallywag merchants and manufacturers, I'd recommend that Disraeli order an attack on Manchester; it'd be a damn sight more convenient, and the railway goes there already.

After a bit the talk turned to horseflesh, and prices and diseases, and of course they were all pleased that the army's necessity had sent prices up; they were quite comfortable, oh yes. The doctor turned to me. "But you, sir, will be in need of a good pair of horses?"

"Yes, but your discussion gives me scant hope of affording good horses. I don't have a lot of cash at the moment, and I don't suppose the local dealers would take a cheque from a passing cavalryman."

"Oh, don't mind us. I believe that you can find a bargain – well, at least a fair price – at one of the inns between here and PMB. The Free State and Transvaal men will be bringing their animals for sale. They'll be looking for a wild profit, but they are all wild back country folk – blessed near savages themselves – so they'll be content with half of what the townies would ask."

Robbers judging the work of other robbers, thinks I.

"Try the inn at Camperdown. We'll be stopped there a good while, and if you find something to your liking, you can get off there and continue directly for the war".

They all agreed, thinking, no doubt, about the extra inches of posterior room my absence would afford. One lying bugger opined that the driver would surely give me half my fare back if I got out at Camperdown.

Still, they were right, after a fashion.

CHAPTER SEVEN

Hove 1928

Colonel Bagshot's daily habits were eminently predictable. He would rise early and take a brisk hour's march on a set schedule; Monday took him through Hove, past St Anne's Well Gardens and the County Cricket Ground, while Tuesday featured a long walk – a *gasht*, as he called it – along the seafront towards the Marina in Brighton. The rest of the week was planned on similar lines. He'd return for breakfast and newspaper, then retire to his rooms for some hours to read, parade his miniature armies, or work sporadically on his never-yet-completed memoirs. After lunch the Colonel might go hacking on the downs, for which purpose he kept a rather elderly horse at a stables out past Hangleton. In the past he'd ridden to hounds with a local hunt, but after one too many sips from a flask of Talisker – oh, he loved his drop of whisky – he was given to slip beyond the line between reminiscence and delusion. One winter's morning he became convinced he'd spotted a band of Mahsud tribesmen – cunning bastards, clever even for Pathans, he swore – in white robes and turbans, lurking in the gorse for the pack to pass by. Then, no doubt, they'd open up on the red-coated gentry with a rough volley of jezail fire and the sudden rush of Khyber knives. The Colonel had tried to deploy a firing line, but the squires, physicians and estate agents of Sussex seemed hopelessly unaware of the correct drill. The Master had been very apologetic but was firm on the point of the Colonel's not coming back, ever.

"Blackguard even returned my full year's fees!" harrumphed Colonel Bagshot. George just smiled and agreed that it was all very unfair, even if he couldn't understand why being given all your money back was somehow worse than not at all. The gentry were odd people.

The old hussar wasn't all that welcome at the Polo Club at Midhurst, either. He was far too old to play, but tried anyway, and still seemed able to commit all kinds of illegal manoeuvres involving such things as foul-hooking and riding down the unwary opponent. George had no idea what foul-hooking was, but clearly it wasn't allowed.

33

"This modern game is too prissy by half," declared Colonel Bagshot, and went on to explain that real polo was the wild Hindu Kush variant played in the valleys of Gilgit and Chitral. "Chop a man's head off, use it as the ball!" The club secretary almost fainted at this suggestion. "Tradition in the hills!" insisted the Colonel. Be that as it may, nobody in Sussex was about to play with a severed head as a ball. "A goat's bladder" offered the Colonel. The committee did not take up this suggestion.

There was no pig-sticking to be had anywhere in Sussex that year, and if there had been, nobody would have told the Colonel about it. The prospect of an elderly man with a horse, a spear and a pint of single-malt seemed like a clear invitation to a civil suit for anyone who wished to organize such an event. The horsey set knew all about Binky Bagshot.

* * *

The Boer was a Free State[21] man, come down over the Drakensberg to sell horses and make what he evidently hoped, and I feared, would be the kind of financial windfall that the prophets might rail against. Natal had been stripped bare of livestock of every kind by Lord Chelmsford's preparations for war. You could have sold a pantomime horse for fifty guineas outside the Belgrave Hotel in Durban. The horses I had seen so far had barely been fit for a Frenchman's breakfast, and I was still on foot.

Cavalrymen have some set ideas about horses that seem a touch odd to most civilians. One ought to avoid bright chestnuts and light bays; they are spirited, to be sure, but delicate and unreliable. Dark chestnuts and bays are much hardier and usually good-natured. Glossy black horses are excellent; rusty blacks are pig headed enough to command a regiment. Iron greys are tough and healthy, light greys are the opposite; only an idiot rides a white horse in war, anyway – you might as well paint a bulls-eye on your helmet. The best horses for real work are blue or strawberry roans. They are easy to train, good natured, stamina of a Gurkha. Of course, they don't look smart, so many an otherwise intelligent Johnnie has passed over a trustworthy roan in favour of some glossy, expensive steed who will let him down for a handful of carrots.

Another cavalry tradition holds that you can read a horse's character from the white stockings above its hooves. A horse with one white leg is a bad 'un. Two is decent; you could sell it to a friend without fear. Four socks means you can rely on it for a while, at least. But three stockings are what you want – a horse that will take you on a canter through Hades on a half-scoop of oats and a tin cup of muddy water.

---

21. The Orange Free State was an independent Boer Republic at this time.

I picked out a little Basuto mare; strawberry roan three stockings, about thirteen and a half hands. I'm not a big chap, so I bought her for daily work up in the rocks and crags; the Boer threw in a pack saddle with her to carry my kit when I wasn't mounted; she cost me thirty quid, so I couldn't run to a pack pony in addition.

I wanted a charger as well. A cavalry officer has to have a proper charger, something with a good stride and a bit of breeding. "And the remnant were slain with the sword of him that sat upon the horse" as it says in Revelation, though it also says that him what had the sword kept it in his mouth. Probably had no proper scabbards in those days. I can't imagine where I thought I was going to be charging – there wasn't a regular cavalry regiment in two thousand miles, and the local volunteer units weren't about to thunder knee-to-knee into the teeth of a Zulu *impi*, sabres in hand. They didn't have any, for one thing.

I could charge gloriously on my own, of course, and they'd probably paint a picture of me doing it and hang it in the regimental mess – "Old Binky, who impaled 'imself on two thousand assegais".

The dealer called for his 'boy!', and a slender young black in a hand-me-down woollen suit led out two horses of sixteen hands or so; the iron grey gelding looked powerful, but had a trick knee, I thought, and questionable teeth. The chestnut looked fair, two stockings, forty-five guineas. I inquired carefully.

"Tell me about this one."

"Ah, mine frind, docile as a lemb. Easy to teach. A good 'orse, yiss. A joy at a canter, a pleasure at a gallop."

He'd not mentioned the trot. Free State horses, I'd been told, couldn't trot.

"And the trot?"

He gave me a leathery facial twist that I believe may have been intended as a smile. Half his moustache disappeared inside his mouth. Quite vile.

"Mister, this 'orse'll be heppy to let you trot all day."

An hour later I was riding north on the chestnut, the pony tethered behind with all my luggage strapped to her back. I was the best part of eighty pounds lighter in the wallet, which was then eight months' pay for a subaltern[22], but I felt like a Hussar again. I even strapped on my sword to impress the locals. Tally ho!

---

22. A subaltern (or 'sub') was the period name for a junior officer – a first or second lieutenant.

It's a rule of mine to name horses after battles, especially the many victories of the Tenth, the Shiners, my own beloved home. I had named the little pony Benevente, after a glorious action of The Regiment in Spain, during the retreat to Corunna. It was 1808, a few days after Christmas. Great Uncle Henry told me all about it when I was a young sprog. He'd been a junior sub in the 10th Light Dragoons – not yet officially listed as hussars but dressed as such with big brown fur caps with red bags – and it was his first campaign. Our lads were hiding behind some houses with just a few piquets – mounted sentries – out watching the edge of a river for Frenchies. Paget was commanding the brigade – Paget as became Lord Uxbridge, as became the Marquess of Anglesey, chap who lost a leg at Waterloo. Fine officer, excellent eye for the lay of the land. He saw that if the French came on and our piquets fell back all disorderly, the enemy would eat it all up and make a mad dash forward instead of reforming after crossing the river. Six hundred Frogs – bloody Chasseurs of the Guard, Bonaparte's crackerjack light horsemen – trot across the ford, and spur on up the bank all excitable-like. Then we had 'em. Charge! View halloo! Threw 'em all back into the water, cold as a witches' tit, served the bastards right! Uncle Henry said there were prisoners by the dozen. One man of his squadron took a sabre to the French general and made him captive. Oh, we crowed about that one.

Anyway, the pony was Benevente, the charger I called Waterloo. I don't have to tell you about that battle.

I was moving at an easy trot, enjoying the air, when I heard a pounding of hooves along the track behind me. Turning in the saddle I saw the Boer's native groom approaching at a gallop, his hat flapping behind him on a string and his pony laden with an unkempt bundle of old clothes. "Wait, baas!" he called out. "I come with you!"

I don't take runaways under my wing every day, but I'd seen the way the horse dealer had treated the young black; Boer servitude isn't far from slavery, and I'm against that, as a rule. Besides, I needed a groom and he seemed a likely fellow. He assured me that the pony was his, and that he hadn't stolen anything on his way out of the old Free Stater's service.

"What's your name, lad?"

"Me Joseph. Missionary name. Live with missionaries since little boy. Christian boy. 'Prentice boy to Mr. Erasmus longtime. Look after horses. Good with horses. Cure many sicknesses. Good boy. Mr. Erasmus cruel man. Much beatings."

"But what if he tries to catch you?"

"Ah, there is no frog that does not peep out of its pool."

"Ah, no doubt, young fella, no doubt". You fathom that one.

It wasn't much of a conversation, as you'll gather. Still, he seemed like a nice enough young chap, attentive to the horses. He was, apparently, one of those displaced persons whose kinfolk had been subject to the random turbulence of Zulu politics; his parents had left Zululand in something of a hurry when he was a small child, and he had fallen into the meanest class of servants in the world of the white settlers. It was obvious he was damned lucky to have met me.

The road to Pietermaritzburg, such as it was, wound up hill and down dale through beautiful country, like the Sussex Downs. I sang a bit of Gilbert and Sullivan – they were just getting popular then – and some martial hymns; the young Kaffir whistled along in the general region of the tune.

"Onward Christian Soldiers, Marching as to war,

With the Cross of Jesus, Going on before!"

Pietermaritzburg had little to offer. It was a dull provincial town, no decent restaurants and one bookshop, belonging to a chap named London, whose son was in the Natal Carbineers. He showed me photographs, as proud parents will. But I was here for the soldiering, and there wasn't a lot to be found. Chelmsford's whole entourage was up at the border, camped just beyond the Buffalo River at a place called Rorke's Drift. The camp at Ft Napier was well-nigh deserted. Nobody seemed exactly sure how far away this was in miles – the bookseller told me it was beyond places called Greytown and Helpmekaar, as if that was of any value to me – and might be somewhere between a day and a week by horseback. I asked around the handful of loafers drinking coffee, such as it was. One old man told me to sell my horses and hire an ox-wagon.

"Why should I do that?"

"Oh, you shouldn't, most certainly. But I would be able to tell you how long it would take by ox-wagon."

Bloody Colonials.

CHAPTER EIGHT

Hove 1928

Cook wanted to know where George was. Colonel Bagshot was always holding him up when there was work to do. The sausages delivered today were off – you could just smell it – and she wanted the boy to take them back to the butchers in Church Road. Since Mrs. Quint had been *Taken From Us*, Cook had accepted the responsibilities of housekeeping for the hotel; Mr. Quint was happy to let her – bless his heart he had no idea, really, about the running of the house – and his son Eddie was spoiled and full of his own opinions. Old Bottomley, the silly old man who was senior porter needed to be told what to do all the bloody time. Otherwise he'd just sit and smoke or go off to the pub or the betting shop. So, it was up to her to keep things going. And she needed the boy to run errands. That flippin' Colonel had a lot to answer for, if you asked her. And he was very rude about her cooking. Very rude. It was uncalled for. She wished he'd go back to India, or Africa, or to any one of the many residential hotels within a stone's throw of where she was standing. Be a bloody nuisance to someone else.

Of course, he wouldn't.

* * *

It was seventy miles, as it turned out, from Pietermaritzburg to the front, which I did in two days of squelching perspicaciously up country with my young Zulu laddie behind me grinning from ear to ear. I like a cheerful servant; I once had a miserable Scotch orderly who dolloped out guilt, blame and complaint with the after-dinner brandy. He went down with enteric fever; that and a kick from a battery mule – animal probably couldn't stomach his whinging any more than I – and all he could do was whine about how sick he felt. I can't stand a moaner. He was getting better, too, but being a mean-spirited old sod, he couldn't accept that things might turn out alright, so he fell off the hospital ship off Fernando Po, and was ate by sharks. I wrote to his mother and felt damnably guilty about telling her about his heroic death in action, in the service of Queen and Country;

the rotten bastard spread shame and despondency even after he kicked the bucket. But I digress.

I met a column of Royal Engineers going to the war. They weren't doing very well – all kinds of difficulties with mule wagons getting up hills and having to leave half of them in a puddle while the mules were double-spanned to heave the first batch of wagons up the greasy slopes. The captain, Jones, seemed the sort who revels in his own miseries, but I hadn't spoken with a live soldier in days. I didn't count the aged and rejected noodles left at Ft Napier.

"Rough work," Jones grumbled. "We were supposed to be with Chelmsford already, but they gave us the remnants of the mules – all sick and sorry – and half the riding horses aren't shod. The Kaffir drivers aren't the pick o' the litter. My sappers aren't much use. They don't know how to pack a wagon; half of 'em can't pitch a tent without it falling over the first gust o' wind. They'll eat anything they see on a tree, too, think it must be some delicious tropical fruit. Silly sods would eat pine cones if they found any."

Jones warmed to his list of complaints. "Rain in deluges, every day. We've been on the road more than a week, all three-pair o' boots soaked through. We've got ox-wagons too, can't keep up with the mules when the going is decent, and have to be outspanned to graze eight hours a day. Wish I could eat eight hours a day, eh?"

I certainly agreed to that. "Any news of the war?"

"Only what we heard from our people at 'Maritzburg. One white and three natives killed on our side, perhaps fifty Zulus on t'other. We're never going to get there in time. I had to wait and chafe while we fixed a broken swingle bar[23] outside Pietermaritzburg, when we'd only just got started. Then I came on to find one of the ox-wagons stuck nine or ten miles behind the leaders, and nobody had taken a blind bit of notice. That was the day before yesterday, – no, three days ago – and we didn't move again till yesterday. It's damned slow work, anyway. And they made us send a subaltern on ahead with a cart and some sappers, so we are short an officer. Fancy staying with us to help out?"

No bloody fear. Another offer of a job I didn't want.

"Can't blame you. Still, young Commeline is coming along well. He's my junior man, been caked in mud for days and seems to like it. I'm glad to have kept him and sent Chard on ahead. When you get to the main column, do say hello to John Chard from the 5th Field Company, R.E. He's a dull sort, but he'll enthrall you with tales of ponts and revetments and profiles. He really likes profiles. Ask him about them."

---

23. A swingle bar is part of the hitching gear for an ox wagon. It is a wooden bar used to separate the chains behind and between draft animals.

I hadn't the slightest idea what he was on about. Ponts? Revetments? Engineers live in their own little world, you know. Quite mad, but somehow tedious at the same time.

There was a thud and a screeching clatter. A wagon was four wheels in the air, like a dead dog. Everyone felt constrained to shout and wave their arms about.

"Second one today," said Captain Jones. I chose this moment to move along.

Greytown had a pleasant inn, marvelous food for the African frontier; I'm frankly surprised Chelmsford hadn't forcibly conscripted the cook for Headquarters, but she was a powerful woman and could've held her own against a platoon. Helpmakaar was dull and characterless; until quite recently it had consisted of two houses and a few outbuildings. Sopping wet, of course, as was everything and everywhere in Natal. The place is set on a hill called the Biggarsberg and was named "Help One Another" in back country Dutch because the old Voortrekkers set aside their usual squabbling to cut the passage up the steep slope. It was one of the few places where an army stores depot added materially to the beauty of the setting.

I was within an ace of my goal, Army Headquarters, and no doubt a heroic welcome for a gallant officer with actual experience of fighting cunning native types. They'd have me in charge of something useful by the morrow – perhaps a troop of game but undisciplined local gentry to be licked into shape according to Queen's Regulations. They'd be colonials, of course, but fellows of the superior classes, and not bloody Australians[24] at any rate. I rode onwards.

The little Basuto pony crested the rise as the path turned around a rocky hill, and I saw the swell of the Buffalo River cutting across my path, like an ambitious gutter. Beyond, in the mist and drizzle, was the land of the Zulus. Below, at the river's edge I could see knots of men, busy as ants. They were pushing and tugging at what seemed to be an empty date box on a piece of string. Closer still was a collection of thatched sheds and dry-stone walling. The whole scene struck me as absurdly cozy. Joseph, who had apparently been here before, pointed and spoke of the cluster of barns as a Swedish mission, bought by well-intentioned newcomers as a centre of Christian evangelism at the edge of heathendom. Being such people, they had paid over the odds for it from the estate of the builder, a trader (which means a hard-bitten old cheat with a taste for cheap spirits) by the name of Jim Rorke. The trader was dead, but the settlement and the river crossing were generally known by his name: Rorke's Drift.

I got on my charger for the grand entrance – I didn't want to show up on a spotted pony the size of a Dalmatian – and followed the track past the buildings (merely

---

24. In fairness, it must be said that the Colonel is editorializing based on his experience in the Great War at this point. As a young officer in 1879, he had no reasons to dislike Australians.

disreputable-looking sheds when seen close up), now under new management by the 24th regiment of foot.

A sentry had seemed uncertain whether to challenge or salute me. It's amazing how three pints of mud and an oilskin cape undermines the appearance of rank.

"I say!" I said.

"Sir!"

"Show me to your officer."

The sentry led me to Lt. Gonville Bromhead, who told Private Cole to return to his post. Bromhead appeared over-age for his rank, all mutton-chops and fatigue. He offered me a drink. "Dreadful stuff, Natal gin. They call it 'square-face', I believe. The good stuff's all packed up. We'll be moving on in a day or two. They've been working on the road".

I accepted the offer. 'I'd love a drink!".

"Pardon me?" he replied and pointed his ear in my direction, as if to pick up the sound better. I accepted his offer again. Deaf as a tree. I associate that with artillerymen, generally, not foot soldiers. We each drank a glass – none too clean

H– of some fairly disgusting clear liquid, and I took advantage of Bromhead's offer of a bath and shave. The hospital cook, a broad man with a Gloucestershire burr to his voice brought a pale of hot water, and filled my bath; one of those rubberised canvas affairs, folds up small, absolutely the thing if one is to maintain standards.

Then it was off to report to the general himself.

CHAPTER NINE

Hove 1928

Edward Quint had a day off work at the bank. He stretched leisurely in his chair in the resident's lounge after breakfast. Eddie – his father refused to call him that – was reading the morning paper. He was looking over the prices for a new motor car. He'd never owned a car, but perhaps it was time to get one. Thomas Harrington Ltd. had a second-hand Talbot for sale that sounded reasonable. He might go and have a look at it. Stonehams in St. John's Rd sold Vauxhalls, expensive but swish; you could have a Bedford saloon for £520. If you had £520. Working at the bank didn't offer the prospects he'd once expected. He might get an assistant manager's job at one of the Brighton branches, but everyone would apply for that.

The hotel wasn't making money the way it should. His dad was too old fashioned. Mum had been the one with the business sense. Cook was a tyrant, and all her cooking came out of that Mrs. Beeton[25] book from eighteen-something. She boiled the met and veg into complete submission.

But with a bit of advertising – sharp advertising – you could get the punters in. That Colonel Bagshot had three rooms – three, honest to God – for the price of one at any other hotel. If the Eddie could get rid of him, the hotel could get two quid a week, a bit more, even, for each of those rooms for London visitors. The Empire Lodge could get a jazz band – not real Americans, but local blokes – and put on dances. But not with a clientele like Colonel Bagshot. Getting him to pay up was like getting blood out of a turnip. He was months behind on his account, and it was ridiculous how Dad celebrated whenever old Bagshot gave him a tenner towards it. And nobody had said a word about the incident with old Jenks the sweep – well, the sweep did, over the telephone – but dad had never brought it up to the Colonel. It was as if everything the batty old man did was just fine.

---

25. Isabella Beeton's *Book of Household Management*, published in 1861, was a monumental (1112 pages) tome which became the 'bible' of Victorian cookery and housekeeping.

A new Morris Minor was only £125. Not very posh, but alright, really. An Austin Seven was cheaper, but dad wouldn't go for an Austin Seven. Not after mum's accident. You wouldn't think anyone could get killed by such a small car.

* * *

I knew they would fob me off with some underling. I should have expected the worst, but somehow, I never do. The general was off examining the new road. His Military Secretary, one Major Crealock, were he available, would see what he could do for me, except that he was frightfully busy and so I'd have to speak with his assistant, FitzClarence.

You can tell these types. They have Chippendale bureaux in their tents.

The man opposite me was lounging in a leather armchair, his feet propped decorously on a desk that looked like it had been borrowed from Blenheim Palace. He was young, pink-cheeked, and affected in the most nauseating way. He was Lieutenant Algernon Fitzclarence of the 60th Wifles — Rifles — once a disreputable but effective unit of German and American frontier louts, but nowadays an expensive club for the less useful members of the minor aristocracy. Made you weep for England.

I told him who I was and what I wanted. He looked at me as if I was an insect.

"Ye-ess, I see. You were hoping for an appointment with the Field Force. You are an *Indian* are you not? Fwom the wecent altercation in Afghanistan? No snake charmers here, my man. No elephants. Still, the Major served quite extensively in *the East*, you know."

He said *the East* as if it was a disease Crealock had recovered from. It was a prejudice of the Home Army, ancient in origin, that a canter in Hyde Park was more valuable an exercise in the military art than ten years on the wild fringes of India keeping the Zakka Khel clans honest.

I loathed him on instinct. His exact position on the staff was unclear, but he spoke deferentially of His Lordship and His Lordship's Military Secretary; he probably drank their bathwater. He was a complete worm. They say a worm can turn; this one was clearly intent on turning me down.

"You're a little bit late, you know. The line wegiments are fully stocked with officers, and I believe that even the Kaffir contingents have officers, after a fashion. And you're a cavalwee Johnny. Not weally on my list, you see?"

I wanted to kick his backside. Hard. I'd been in his tent probably five minutes, and I'd had about all of him I could stand. Still, acts of Common Assault are best limited to the Queen's officially designated enemies if one hopes to prosper in Her Majesty's service. Even kicking a tradesman is frowned upon nowadays.

"Your hussar talents might be useful, however. We do have a lot of mules to look after."

"I know nothing of mules," I told him. I did, but it doesn't help to advertise. Not to fellows like him.

"Horses, mules, whatever. All equine y' know". He yawned. He yawned at me.

The list of reasons I should not punch his fat head through the canvas wall was fast growing shorter, when an older man appeared in the doorway. His voice had the same carping quality of vindictive authority, though mercifully without the same contrivance around the 'R's.

"Algy. Give this officer something appropriate to his rank and see him on his way. We have matters of importance to discuss."

Hello, thinks I. You can recognize the porker from hearing the piglet's squeal. This must be his divine excellence Major Crealock.

"Bagshot, I have just the job for you."

CHAPTER TEN

Hove 1928

George seldom got the chance to hear the Colonel's stories in a single sitting. It was lucky that the old chap was so good at remembering where he was in the telling, because he so seldom remembered anything else. There had been at least one occasion he'd been brought back to the hotel by a constable, raving about Fuzzy-wuzzies on the Palace Pier. One day he'd been convinced that the Royal Pavilion, set a short bus-ride away in the supremely English town of Brighton was actually the Maharajah of Jaipur's palace and demanding a word with His Majesty about selling a polo pony. There had been a lot of talk about that.

George recognised that he and the Colonel were kindred spirits. Their only relatives were old women who bossed them about. The Colonel had an aunt living somewhere in Oxfordshire, ancient and completely batty, but no other family. He'd inherit a house and property, unless she'd changed the will again. As far as Colonel Bagshot was concerned, the Cat's Home could have the place. She'd probably outlive him anyway.

George had a grandmother who lived a few streets away from the hotel, whom he visited every Wednesday, and some aunts and cousins. His father had gone out for a packet of Woodbines in 1914 and never come back. He might have been killed on the Western Front, or he might not. George had been two years old when he left. His mother had died of the influenza the year after the war. It had been Gran's house, school 'til he was fourteen, a job as a butcher's boy (which he had hated) then here at the hotel. Old Mr. Quint had chosen him for the page's position more from a sense of civic duty to a local orphan than any real interest in the lad. But he had a room below stairs, regular meals, Wednesday afternoons and some Saturdays off. Molly was nice, very pretty, and old Bottomley gave him cigarettes, though they made him sick. Young Mr. Quint, Eddie, was too – what was the word for it? – *arrogant* by half. Yes, arrogant. Acted like a big shot, as they said in the American detective books. But he was away at the bank, or out with his pals most of the time. You had to watch out for Cook, though. Cook had a nasty streak. Not so much a streak as a broad band of malice. He'd read that phrase in a thriller and relished it.

Still, he'd put up with everything. It was a job, and a lot of people didn't have one.

* * *

My new job was no plum. It was, in fact, a raspberry. I had the honour of becoming second transport officer to No. 2 Column, presently at Middle Drift. No. 2 Column was the smallest force in Chelmford's army, made up of the least prestigious troops under the command of the least reliable officer, posted where it could least come to any harm. It might, in fact, not go anywhere at all, which fairly well undermined the stated purpose of the second transport officer. Colonel Durnford, I had heard, was unstable, a reckless and habitual gambler at the gaming tables and in the field. He was the kind of officer likely to invent his own orders and follow them in the most irresponsible manner. Some years before he had been involved in a very minor affair against a very minor clan, the Hlubi, which turned out badly. Durnford had lost the use of his left arm in the fighting and been widely blamed for the debacle.

His column consisted of some fairly decent natives on ponies – mostly Basutos – and a lot of deeply questionable Natal levies. The only British element was a rocket battery (damned fireworks) packed on mules with an officer of gunners and some borrowed privates detached from the 24th. Only a day or so ago Durnford had had his knuckles rapped severely by the general for some indiscreet suggestion of crossing the river into Zululand; he wanted a pop at the savages, but Chelmsford wasn't having it.

I stood outside the bell tent, my mind was fully occupied by matters military – specifically my unappealing set of duties. Joseph was nowhere to be seen. I suppose I must have gazed around in a vacant fashion. An orderly appeared leading my charger, carefully groomed and saddled, and evidently much refreshed. How nice! At least somebody in the camp was showing consideration to a tired and disappointed subaltern of hussars! I took the bridle, put my foot in the stirrup and swung my leg up and over. "Thank you, my good man."

The orderly gaped. Clearly not accustomed to common courtesy from an officer. Politeness costs nothing, I always say.

"Sir, this is the lieutenant's 'oss."

"Well, of course it is. I am a lieutenant. 10th Royal Hussars. From Afghanistan.

Ali Masjid and all that." Probably a bit dim, but it's hard to find a good servant amongst the general run of riff-raff you find in the infantry. Cavalry troopers are considerably better material, you'll find.

"Nawssir, this be Lieutenant Fitzclarence's 'oss sir."

It is embarrassing for a cavalryman to discover he has failed to recognize his own mount. One is supposed to know these things. The appropriate thing to do, of course, would have been to say nothing, dismount, and walk away. That's what Podger Pilkington of the 12th Lancers did when he was caught with the Belgian consul's wife, and nothing ever came of it. Humiliation in front of Other Ranks is a bad thing, of course, but if they aren't *your* other ranks it's nothing to put a revolver in your mouth over.

I, however, did not follow my own advice. Too surprised, I suppose. I had to wait long enough for ---

"Get orf my horse you damned wapscallion!" Fitzclarence was fuming. A better man would have seen the humour in the moment. A worse man too, for that matter. But the puffed-up little popinjay was not laughing. He was hot. He was red. He was about, I think, to have me clapped in irons for attempted horse theft. I was at the little twerp's mercy, a commodity I suspected to be entirely out of stock. He would call the guard, place me under arrest, and speak to Major Crealock about having me flogged in front of the whole army as an example to all. Oh yes. I was definitely for it now.

Fitzclarence advanced cheeks like a washed pink toad, fists balled up. He was livid.

Then he fell over the guy line, which is what comes of not looking where you are going.

Canvas ripped. Fitzclarence shrieked. The horse bucked. The orderly, unsure of which to attend to, staggered across the horse's path as his hands fumbled for the terrified beast's headstall. Horses are not generally soothed by a twelve-stone man swinging wildly by the straps around their nose; the animal dealt with the obstacle by stepping on the groom's leg while biting his fingers.

Fitzclarence came up as the soldier went down and caught a hoof to the back of the head. Not a vital organ, at least. He went down again. There was a good deal of blood flowing by this point. None of it was mine. I was still on the chestnut's back, staying in the saddle by instinctive balance, sheer stupidity and the Music Hall humour of the Almighty. Certainly, my brain had no part in the proceedings; I sat stupidly on the plunging horse, keeping my seat by sheer luck.

The orderly had inadvertently wrapped the reins around his upper body as he fell, showing a good sense of duty but hardly to be recommended. Still, probably wasn't thinking right, what with having three fingers mangled by horse-teeth. There was a crash, which might have been the nice piece of Chippendale, a shredding of canvas, and the tent came down on the four of us. That's counting the horse, which was the key player.

It was about this time I had the sense to fall off. I've spent a good part of my life trying to avoid falling off things – mostly horses, some camels, an elephant once. My friend Evelyn Wood fell off a giraffe once, but he didn't really have the knack. The trick is to roll away from the hooves. Horses are generally good at avoiding a fallen man – they are dainty things to be such big animals – but this one wasn't doing too well. I pitched to the left, pulling my knees up, and landed *sur la derriere* in the spongy grass. Then I was up, and out through an enormous rent in what remained of the fallen tent. Interestingly enough, there was a second gaping hole in the canvas a yard from me, from which protruded a skinny – but eminently kickable – bottom in whipcord breeches and expensive boots. Well, as it says in Ecclesiastes, "Whatsoever thy hand findeth to do, do it with thy might," and that applyeth to thy foot too, so I planted my boot hard against his seat. He yelped like a cur. I was up and running – which ain't so easy with a cavalry sabre and a sun helmet dipped over your nose I can tell you. Must've looked a bloody fool. Felt one. But Fitzclarence felt it worse.

"Shouldn't worry if I were you, old man."

The voice was calm yet authoritative. "Care for a brandy and soda? Just came by some ice." The voice's owner gave a slow smile. "These things happen all the time."

Teignmouth Melvill was the adjutant for the 1/24th. If he was long in the tooth for a lieutenant, it wasn't for lack of ability. Or tact. He clapped me by the shoulder and guided me into the duty tent. There was still a tremendous racket behind us, the infuriated chestnut charger ripping the shredded tent into final indecency. Fitzclarence squealed away like a spoiled child, and the orderly moaned out some enthusiastic curses in a dialect I couldn't identify.

"Fitzclarence is a pillock."

It wasn't me that said that. It wasn't Melvill either. Another officer was addressing me from behind the tent I was entering. "Yes, a complete and utter pillock. I don't know who you are, my hussar friend, but I think you'll be the guest of the battalion tonight."

He was a light-haired man with a small beard and staff tabs on his patrol jacket. "Coghill, old chap. Attached to the staff but loafing around my own regiment, as usual. Company's much more to my taste. Is this your boy, by the way? He's done a splendid job on your horse."

It was and he had.

CHAPTER ELEVEN

Hove 1928

On Tuesday morning, George had to do the boots all over again. Young Mr. Quint had complained to Bottomley the porter that he couldn't go to work in his 'executive position' with shoes so dull and dingy. Everyone knew he was only a clerk at the bank. But he was also joint owner of the Empire Lodge, and what he wanted, went. George had overheard the conversation between the porter and Cook.

"Tell 'im to do 'em all, Fred. Not just the one pair, but all of 'em. 'Ee's got to learn the right way of doing things."

"Oh, come on Doris, he's only a lad."

"Yes, and 'ee'll turn out as idle as you if 'ee don't learn 'ow to do things proper."

"That's not fair."

"'Oo said life's fair? Are you going to tell 'im or shall I?"

Bottomley said he would. So, George obeyed. It was all part of life in domestic service. It was late when he was able to sneak up to the Colonel's rooms, to hear about another young man in service.

* * *

Joseph was turning out to be a very decent servant, orderly, what-have-you. Good with my gear, excellent with the horses, not prone to idle gossip or listening in to his betters' conversations. I liked to hear him talk, that clumsy mission English with odd Zulu expressions translated into very quaint sayings like 'Even when there is no cock, the day dawns,' and 'One does not follow a snake into its hole'. A bit strange, but sensible enough when you think of it. My own particular favourite was this:

53

'Darkness conceals the hippopotamus'.

That sounded like something my Aunt Harriet would have said, except there are no hippopotami in Oxfordshire. Perhaps down about Henley-on-Thames, by the river.

Yes, he was a nice young chap, and well worth his wages. Which, at this point, were none. I didn't know how much you paid a Kaffir boy, and he didn't seem to care. Dashed odd, when I came to think about it.

I sat next to Coghill at dinner. The officers' mess was a white marquee, done out a fair treat, with carpet on the floor and polished silver on a long table. The 1/24th took eating seriously, I was glad to see: a good regiment should. Most regiments forbid all talk of shop in the mess (politics, religion and women too – mustn't get anyone upset) but tonight was an exception. The talk was all of the morrow, and the prospects for the campaign.

I listened rather than talked, though Coghill and a severely moustachioed subaltern, Atkinson, joshed me about my circumstances. "The scout for the 10th Hussars is here. I think he's got a bit ahead of the rest of the regiment!" announced Atkinson. Everyone knew the Tenth were in Afghanistan.

"Aha! The China Tenth! The Shiny Tenth! Slumming a bit aren't we?" cried one wag – a youngster called Daly, I think. When you come from one of the really smart regiments you have to expect this kind of thing. Jealousy. None of 'em could afford the Tenth. Actually, I had serious reservations as to whether I could, but that was as maybe. We had the best hats in the army.

But they weren't really in the mood to tease the guest. There weren't any of the ribald comments about Valentine Baker[26] that officers of the 10th had to put up with from chaps in other units. Baker, you will recall, had been C.O. of The Regiment when he was quite unfairly accused of indecently assaulting a young lady in a railway carriage. It ruined his career; he was forced to spend a year in a common prison and become a major-general in the Turkish army. Anyway, nobody even mentioned him, which I thought remarkably good form.

"Coghill, how's your leg?" asked Degacher. He was senior captain, fortyish, droopy moustache. I assumed he was talking about cricket, but Anstey – who was to my right, Mostyn's sub – told me about it in a stage whisper:

"Coghill was honourably wounded charging a chicken last week. Evidently a most dangerous fowl!"

---

26. Colonel Valentine Baker was convicted of assaulting a young woman in a railway carriage in 1875, after a sensational trial. Upon his release from prison, he served with great distinction in the Turkish army, and commanded an Egyptian expedition against the Mahdi in 1883 (with much less success).

Laughter was general. Coghill wryly admitted the truth of the tale. He'd been injured in an incident with a passing hen. I like a man who can stand a joke against himself. Coghill had evidently taken a bad fall; he could barely walk without a cane, and hardly mount his horse. He was taking it all as a terrific jape, but I knew he must be concerned about it. A staff officer with a gammy leg is a man who can't do his job.

The 1/24th were a well-knit regiment, not flashy, but confident and experienced. Two years chasing the Gaikas and Galekas – the East Cape Xhosa clans – through the rough bush of the Kei country had made them tough and realistic. There was none of the wild blood and thunder you hear over the cigars at Aldershot or the Curragh[27]. Nobody had to regale us with ancient tales of the Crimea, and no drunken old fool felt constrained to draw a sword to show how they'd lopped off a Pandy's[28] head twenty years before. Usually they do themselves an embarrassment, chop up the candelabra or some-such. Sometimes dinner with a British regiment is more dangerous than actually facing the enemy.

"Will the Kaffirs stand up for an open fight?" asked a young chap, a fresh second lieutenant, Dyson.

"That's the question, indeed. We can certainly hope so." This was Wardell, a company commander. He'd held a post under siege by the Galekas for four months until he was relieved. His views were worth listening to.

"We must hope they don't play cat and mouse and exhaust the column that way. Our strength, frankly, lies in the eight companies of our battalion and those of our comrades in the 2nd. We are the ones that shoot and march and win the victory. Our weakness lies in rented transport and damn fools who work their oxen to death so as to get into camp in time for tea. Or who push their ox-teams into a swollen ford without checking the depth and drown the lot." That seemed like a terrible blunder, but one I could certainly believe.

"Which means we can successfully bring on our own defeat without Jack Zulu getting his hands dirty."

This came from Younghusband, a burly whiskery cove. He had 'C' Company.

The 1/24th had done themselves a treat. There was iced champagne, quail in aspic from Fortnums, and a couple of bottles of a Burgundy considerably older than the fresh faced young sub who'd opened the discussion on the Zulu's intentions. The joint, alas, was trek-ox; I much prefer foundered camel, myself, as long as it's not been out in the sun too long.

---

27. Aldershot was (and is) the site of the British army's most important station and training ground in Britain. The Curragh, outside Dublin, served the same function in Ireland.
28. The term 'Pandy' was coined after Manghal Pandy, a mutineer executed for his role in the outset of the 1857 rising in Bengal. All Indian mutineers were 'Pandies' as far as the British soldiery was concerned.

The mess grew lugubrious as the evening wore on, with remembrances of the regimental past. Anstey talked of old misfortunes. "Yerss, not too lucky, the 24th. Half of us died of fever at Cartagena in 1740-odd, fighting the Spanish, and who remembers that? War of Jenkins Ear!" He told of the regiment's being taken prisoner by the French at Minorca in 1756, and then by the Americans, and losing half its strength in battle under Wellington.

"Luck!" – this was Degacher – "Who but the 24th would have a party shipwrecked onto an island inhabited by cannibals? That was just a few years ago, in the Andaman Islands."

"The colours," said Anstey. "We have to watch out for the colours."

This seemed like a fairly self-evident thing for a British regiment. British infantry battalions have two flags, you know. The Queen's Colour is the Union flag, with regimental battle honours stitched onto it. The Regimental Colour is made of cloth in the shade of the regimental cuffs and collar – green in the case of the 24th – with a small Union flag in the upper corner, and a lot of fancy insignia. There's more to it than that, of course. It goes without saying that the colours are almost sacred objects. It isn't as if we regularly leave the damned things on a tram or lose them playing gin-rummy.

Melvill leaned over the table to explain to me. "We aren't the luckiest, y'know. We had to throw one set of colours into the Indian Ocean in 1810 when French frigates caught our convoy; they captured the colonel and four companies. Worse still, in the Sikh War of '49 we advanced against twenty heavy guns at Chilianwallah, and charged 'em, all on our own, through a belt of jungle. Afterwards nobody could remember who ordered the attack! Broke the Sikh line, not a shot fired, point o' the bayonet! "Hurrah, Hurrah!" as we went in! Colonel Pennycuik was knocked down as they cleared the battery; his boy comes up to bid farewell to his father and gets shot dead himself – and him just eighteen and new-commissioned! Old Gough, the general, said it was "An act of madness", and he was one to know all about that. He had the tactical finesse of a dray horse."

I nodded in agreement, as if I knew anything about it.

"We lost half the battalion, thirteen officers killed, nine wounded, nine unscathed; A young officer called Williams took twenty-three wounds, sword and lance, fractured his skull and cut off his left hand. He recovered completely. We have him come to dine at the mess quite often."

I said I'd be honoured to meet him some time. I was full of good cheer by this time myself. "And the colours?" I asked. "What happened?"

"Oh yes. Ensign Phillips bore the Queen's Colour. He fell dead in a patch of swampy jungle. Private Connolly saw it, wet and filthy, so he pulls it off the broken staff, and – God knows why – wraps it round his waist under his coat. I 'spect he thought he was keeping it safe, he never told anyone. Some fellows saw him with it. He ran back into the fray and gets himself killed. Nobody knows anything about it until Connolly's rear rank man tells his corporal, who tells a sergeant, who tells his officer, by which time old Connolly and the flag had been buried with two hundred of his comrades in big pits. Never did get it back."

I shuddered at the thought of disinterring two hundred mangled bodies from a patch of swamp in the Punjab.

"Still, the Regimental Colours were alright. Private Perry brought them back safe They made him a corporal and gave him a Good Conduct Medal."

Perry's good luck, Connolly's ill.

I remember that dinner well, with Melvill and Cavaye maudlin and tipsy, Coghill joking about his leg, bloodhound-faced Degacher and urbane Billy Mostyn, the Australian-born Anstey, Porteous, Atkinson, Dyson and the others, Colonel Pulleine at the top of the table, presiding like a squire over a hunt club dinner. Sometimes I remember a meal because the food was marvelous, the wine superb, or the company sparkling. I remember that dinner of the 19th of January 1879, with special feeling. I was the only one present who would be alive seventy-two hours later.

CHAPTER TWELVE

Hove 1928

"Koi-Hai!" boomed the Colonel. George knew this to be some kind of Hindustani instruction to enter. The boy pushed open the door. He was carrying a copy of the Morning Post, considerably late, owing to some ghastly mix-up at the newsagents in which a copy of the Daily Herald had been sent to the hotel in its stead. Old Mr. Quint had almost had a heart attack over his kippers when George brought in the papers. No Morning Post was bad enough, but to receive, in plain view of the neighbours, a copy of the Herald, was utter scandal. The Daily Herald was a revolutionary rag, a tool of the Bolshevist plan for the overthrow of all that was decent. If Mrs. Beebleborough at number 27, who had the investigative talents of a Sherlock Holmes and talent for broadcasting news that challenged the BBC, should find out that such a thing had been delivered to the hotel ---- well, it didn't bear thinking about. George had been sent immediately – clambering over the back-garden wall with his cap pulled low, and with the offending item wrapped tightly in brown paper – back to the newsagent on Western Road.

George was back, puffed, in minutes. Breakfast was over, and the Colonel had not been happy to be deprived of his daily dose of right-thinking over the bacon and eggs. He'd idled through the Telegraph; respectable, but essentially a tradesman's read, and the Times, too bloodless by half. He'd barked at Beryl (who came in to help with breakfast) and gave Young Mr. Quint a catalogue of complaints. The pipes weren't working as they ought and the England selectors couldn't pick a team to beat a collection of one legged Chinamen, and the whole damned place was going to the dogs. The porridge wasn't right, either

George had been cautioned to say nothing of the Daily Herald incident (as it would come to be known within the Quint family) in case the Colonel felt constrained to pack and move out rather than continue to abide in a house of shame.

"Sorry it's late, Colonel Bagshot, sir. Newsagent's fault."

The Colonel snorted.

"Look at this. Bloody Gandhi stirring up trouble again. Absurd little man. He seemed a decent sort when I helped him with the stretcher coming down Spion Kop[29], and now look at him! Used to wear a proper suit, quite dapper, and now he wants to meet the Viceroy of India in a dhoti – which is less than a bath-towel and not half as clean, I daresay --"

The Post provided daily exercise for the Colonel's spleen, rooting out, as it did, signs of Bolshevik subversion, the Zionist conspiracy, and the immorality of Americans; each of these cancers was eating away at *All That Was Good*, as Bagshot and other readers (including King George himself!) knew all too well. George could see that the Colonel's mood had improved; the utter collapse of civilization cheered him up enormously.

"George, my boy," rumbled the Colonel, furroughing his brow so that his eyebrows met like two caterpillars kissing. "Don't you have this afternoon off?"

George affirmed this. Every Wednesday afternoon he was a free man for a period of several hours. Liberty was a precious thing, and came only on Wednesday and Saturday afternoons, not always then. Sundays, hardly ever. The residents were very demanding on a Sunday, especially if it was raining.

"Excellent! Meet me on the seafront opposite Brunswick Lawns where that old fellow has the donkey rides. Two O' clock sharp. Oh, and bring a bucket and spade. I am going to show you the battlefield of Isandlwana. But first – did I tell you how I met John Chard, V.C.?"

* * *

Hussars are expected to ride on ahead of an army, scouting and screening and what-not; the 'eyes and ears of the army' as they say. What hussars are not expected to do is sit on their rumps and watch the army pack up and march on ahead of them. I could hardly stand to watch the tents come down and carts load up, so I took myself off to see what was going on down at the mission and the drift. The poor beggars there weren't going anywhere either.

Lieutenant John Chard of the Royal Engineers was making his own tea. He had sent his few sappers and a junior officer off with the column, leaving himself as Officer Commanding, R.E., Rorke's Drift, and sole staff. It didn't seem to bother him. He had a tent, a wagon, and a handful of borrowed soldiers from the 24th to operate the pont.

29. Mohandas K. Ghandi had served as a volunteer stretcher-bearer during the Boer War.

"Hello," he said. "Fancy a cup of tea?"

"Wouldn't say no."

"Got no milk. Sugar though?"

"Er, two."

"Lumps or spoonfuls? Got both."

"Well, four if it's lumps."

Talking to Chard was like holding a conversation with a particularly slow-witted piece of furniture. I recalled what the two sapper officers I had met on the road up, Jones and Commeline, had said about Lt Chard. What was it that fascinated him? Some sort of engineer's mumbo jumbo, though I couldn't remember what. I didn't want to get him started. A man who can bore you silly discussing a cup of tea shouldn't be set loose on a favourite topic. It occurred to me that, if only he spoke Zulu, we could get him a megaphone and bore the enemy into surrender with tales of elevations, ravelins and cotangents. Excruciating.

But what he really wanted to tell me about concerned a solar eclipse due to appear in a day or two, which was a source of considerable interest to him, apparently. I'd managed four years of polite social banter in the mess of the 10th Hussars without ever mentioning the merest possibility of a solar eclipse, which shows how highly I rated the prospect. I got my tea down my neck in about forty-five seconds and made my excuses. Here's a man who'll never make any kind of mark on history, I thought.

I was wrong on that one.

CHAPTER THIRTEEN

Brighton 1928

The colonel's idea of what a gentleman ought to wear to the beach surprised George. The lad had seen the Colonel dress for his morning and evening 'constitutionals' – long walks along the Esplanade or to St Anne's Well Gardens – but the idea that the old man would actually get among the sand and pebbles was a novelty. Indeed, it was a novelty for Colonel Bagshot too. Many persons, both male and female, had been witnessed in shockingly immodest costumes during that warm summer of 1928, but the Colonel was not among them. Remembering the last time, he had been on a beach, and what he had worn, Colonel Bagshot appeared from the direction of the West Pier wearing a large solar *topee*[30], khaki tunic, boots and a pair of shorts so tremendous in their scope it seemed likely that a fresh gust of channel breeze would propel him ignominiously inland. The last time he had been on a beach had apparently been at Third Gaza in November, 1917[31]. He hadn't brought his own bucket and spade then, either.

What he had brought was a huge Gladstone bag of primeval origin, the kind of bag you can climb into for a night's easy sleep. You can't get them anymore.

They made an odd pair, the military gent and the pale adolescent in shirtsleeves, walking along the seafront seeking a single patch of sand among the notoriously pebbly shore.

"Let me tell you how I got my first look at Isandlwana," said the Colonel. "There was bugger all to do at Rorke's Drift, so I went to see if there was anything going on there."

* * *

I couldn't find Joseph. He was a wonderful servant in most ways, and terrific with the horses, but he couldn't quite grasp the idea that an orderly's job is largely to

---

30. Pith helmet
31. The Third Battle of Gaza (Oct-Nov 1917) saw the collapse of the Turkish Gaza-Beersheba defensive line with the capture of 12,000 Ottoman prisoners. It led to the fall of Jerusalem on December 9th.

stand about waiting to see if the master – this being me – thought of anything for him to do. He kept going off and doing it himself, which meant it got done before I thought about it, but that he wasn't about if I wanted anything else. Very disconcerting when you're accustomed to British private soldiers who'd forget to breathe if somebody hadn't ordered them to. Initiative is a double-edged sword. I'm generally against it in natives and the working class.

Anyway, I couldn't find my kit or my horses, and I needed a clean shirt as the current one was beginning to pong a bit. A corporal of Bromhead's company thought that someone might have stowed my gear in the storehouse, so I went looking for it. Evidently some half-witted Welsh recruit had put up the kit, because my bag was wedged under Joseph's saddle and blanket roll. I pulled the saddle aside and scraped the grimy woolen roll onto the floor. It appeared to be full of feathers, big ones. Probably some native superstition. There was a weird little contraption that looked like a gas pipe with odd metal attachments. I was about to examine it – clearly a fetish item of some sort – when two books fell out. I picked one up, reading the title as "Emily Zulu" by Theresa Racquet – perhaps a missionary's story about a happy African convert. I opened it. It was in French. Most strange. They don't learn French in native schoolhouses in Natal, do they? Ah! It's Emile Zola's "Therese Racquin". Smut, no doubt: these Froggie novels always are. Joseph probably just looked at the pictures.

Oddly enough there weren't any. The other book was "Crime and Punishment" by Theodore Somebody. Sounded like more smut to me. Foreign depravities. There were footsteps coming into the storehouse, so I shoved the books back into the blanket roll and tugged out my own bag. It was Joseph coming in.

"Master, me clean big knife and make sharp. Nice for meet big baas Colonel Durnford."

The sabre shone magnificently as he held it into a narrow shaft of sunlight. He was a good servant even if he was a perverted little beggar.

I prodded about the mission yard to kill some time. The missionary, Witt had been thrown out of his house and seen his little stone church turned into the store where my kit, along with a barnful of military supplies, had been stowed. He'd sent the wife and three kiddies off to Pietermaritzburg and pitched himself a tent to monitor the damage a company of Welsh boyos would inflict. I'd have left it in the hands of the Almighty and abandoned all hope of the cabbages coming up if I'd have been him. He was talking to an army chaplain when I passed his new domicile. I wandered into the house, Jim Rorke's house, now serving as a field hospital. It was a very odd sort of building, singled storied with a thatched hip roof and a covered verandah at the front. The side walls were of stone, substantial things, but front and back were very basic mud brick. What was strange was that Rorke didn't seem to understand the essential idea of being able to walk from one room into another. The rooms didn't connect in the ordinary fashion, and frequently not at all. Perhaps he'd never had a house before and didn't want to waste effort on idle fripperies like hallways.

I stepped onto the verandah, pushing open a door to the right. There was a small, plastered room with a window to the front. Two men sat on cots playing cards, walking patients I assumed, as they stood wincing to salute this fool of an officer barging in on them. "Er, sorry, ah, carry on!" Moving along I pushed open the front door – surely this was a front door – into a large, open room. There wasn't much in there; perhaps it was the surgeon's operating theatre. Army surgeons don't generally have the luxury of actual medical equipment, and the room was certainly big enough for the central features of military surgery, these being a good sawing table and somewhere to throw the excess limbs. I moved through a gap in the wall to my right – no door, brickwork in a shocking state – into another large, empty room. Actually, there was one piece of furniture. A piano was hiding against a side wall, lurking under a blanket. Embarrassed to be seen here, I assumed. Must belong to the missionary. I kicked at a flimsy wooden door and stuck my head into a back room. A black orderly sprang out of the way of the swinging door, dropping a bedpan onto a recumbent figure. The patient grunted, and – recognizing what had occurred – sat up bolt upright, and yelled some particularly imaginative abuse, as he slung the bedpan back across the room. It hit the door frame, spraying its contents in spectacular fashion across the length of the tiny room, although away from me. There were sick men stacked hither and thither on wooden cots, a half dozen or more. I knew that if the wounded, disabled and generally unhealthy men of No 3 Column could find a way to slither out of bed to fight one another, they would. Pandemonium is the natural state of soldiers with time on their hands. I wasn't going in there; I had my new blue patrol jacket on, by Huntsman of Savile Row, very select. Didn't want some dysenterious corporal's bodily fluids down my front, did I?

A voice barked. "Oi! You lot! Poip down afore the sarn't comes! Orderly! Get a mop you daft Kaffir – get yur mate to 'elp ee. Bloody hell!"

It was the hospital cook I'd met when I arrived at the station. He had a natural presence; the patients slid back under their blankets, all save the one who'd had the honour of first receiving the order of the flying bedpan. The native orderly did what he was told, too, which was impressive since he clearly spoke no English whatsoever.

I decided I'd give up on my hospital visiting. There were more rooms, rooms with no doors from the inside, though you could hear men inside them though the flaking walls. I couldn't imagine being brought here to get better. But that's the British army for you. If Florence Nightingale isn't making evening rounds, they think they have carte blanche to bunk fourteen men to a pigsty with a slop bucket and a bag of damp straw. And take money out of their pay for it. Never be a private soldier, boy. I never would.

What the hell. Durnford wasn't due to arrive until evening. I could kick my heels around all day if I wanted, but frankly I didn't. I could ride up to the new camp and see how things were going, reconnoitre the area, take the air a little and still be back in time to report to my new O.C. in a clean uniform and shaved chin. Couldn't hurt to present him with some fresh intelligence reporting of mine own observing, could it? Joseph had the horses ready, with full canteens and – God knows how he managed this – a grease-paper packet of cheese sandwiches.

The new road wasn't up to much, I thought. The old one must have been horrible. I passed through the Bashee Valley, where the set-to with Sihayo took place last week. It was a sodden patch of moorland to my way of thinking, though I'm sure Sihayo was fond of the place; your average ancestral estate in Scotland looks about the same, and you can imagine how well a hieland laird would feel about a column of redcoats stopping by for tea, crumpets and a bit of barn-burning. I couldn't see the rock formations where the fight had been, but I made a mental note to cut across and do some sight-seeing there when I had a spare moment. You know, it never occurred to me there might be Zulus about! I hadn't even brought my revolver, the Colt double-action thing my late chum John Tunstall[32] had given me on young Billy Bonney's suggestion the year before. "Old Bagshot, stabbed to death while sketching a pastoral view of Sihayo's kraals, January '79". The mess would have loved that. Then again, I wasn't the only one who didn't take the Zulus as seriously as they should.

The column had been gone from the camp site since early morning, and I assumed that the entire force would be pitching tents and brewing tea by now; my watch said it was gone two in the afternoon. As the sun swung to a position peeking over my left shoulder, I came upon the rearguard of Chelmsford's army groaning its way up the path. It was like a bus accident in Piccadilly Circus, with tremendous amounts of activity but no visible progress. As I had come to expect, there were wagons failing to cooperate, much heavery and shovery, and the kind of concerted swearing that makes the British fighting man such a joy to know. Local light horsemen in shabby corduroy uniforms of controversial colour – think of sacking dyed with schoolroom ink and left out in the rain – were sent to cover the back of the convoy. Most wore a serious 'scouting for the enemy' expression under their white spiked helmets, but several had the look

---

32. John Henry Tunstall (1853-78) was a British gent whose adventure in ranching in New Mexico ended in his murder, and started what would become known as the Lincoln County range war. His employee, William Bonney, showed admirable loyalty to his memory. Today he is remembered as 'Billy the Kid'.

of clever slackers who realise that sitting aboard a pony with a carbine across your lap is better than unloading two tons of camping equipment from a stalled wagon in a treacly bog. We hussars know that look well. I moved around them, Joseph passing greetings with a young native idling beside his ox team.

Passing the column of frustrated men manhandling mountainous pieces of unwilling luggage on wheels, I spotted the great rock jutting from the earth. If the sphinx had an older brother, it was that rock. Grey, massive, mellowed with grass, it drew my attention. The column was passing close to the right of it, over a little saddle of ground, with a rise further to the right of the track.

Joseph came up beside me, deferentially keeping his pony a step or so behind Benevente. His eyes followed mine across the sweep of country, coming to rest on the imposing rock massif.

"Isandlwana," he said. "Which is Zulu word for, ah, part of cow stomach. Cow stomach most important to Zulu man."

Well, I suppose so, if they have a word for each and every segment of the bovine digestive tract; the Zulu language doesn't have a single verb, noun or adjective for 'Anti-disestablishmentarianism' or 'plum jam', so I expect language reflects matters of local interest. Still, you won't get the Sunday trippers out on a penny excursion to see a big stone cow intestine. Some enterprising local will call it after some minor member of the Royal Family, lay on tea-rooms and lavatories for visiting charabancs and make a few bob for themselves. Very nice, it was, with a plateau behind it to the north. Scenic.

CHAPTER FOURTEEN

Brighton 1928

The Colonel stood up stiffly. "Young George," he announced, "We are going to have some of those disgusting pickled shellfish you like so much. And then you are going to make a sand-table relief map of the field of Isandlwana. You do have that bucket and spade with you, don't you?"

Paying a passing urchin, a penny to guard their patch of sand, 'Until we get back or I'll pull your ear off', as George fiercely expressed it, the pair mounted the steps to the Promenade. George had to carry the Colonel's bag.

"Blinkin' heavy," he said, mainly to himself.

There was a whelk stall close to the West Pier, run by a sardonic Cockney evidently bent on making a fortune from guileless trippers in order to retire to a prosperous old age. Since the Colonel had commandeered his afternoon off, and was paying, George was happy to serve as the vendor's accomplice in swapping a wholly unreasonable amount of the Bagshot pocket change for myriad paper bags of mussels, winkles, whelks and cockles. The Colonel refused to countenance anything involving eels. Besides, he said, he had brought some cheese sandwiches for himself, "A nice bit of Double Gloucester with a dab of mango chutney". The two walked back towards the King Edward Monument, George shoveling mussels into his mouth while discarding shells with dexterity. The Colonel observed that everything tasted like small bits of India-rubber encrusted in sandstone before dousing in vinegar. George believed that this comment formed some kind of criticism but made no response. After all, he had to eat if he was going to dig out a battlefield. Who could tell how big the Colonel would want it to be? He nursed a cockle from its shell and walked on to the patch of sand. All this complaining from a man who spoke of eating insects and leaves in the forests of the Congo, and liking them, and cooking strange Indian dishes over a funny little stove in his rooms! Cockles were good. Englishmen ate cockles.

The urchin was paid off, George cuffing him briefly for his air of cheekiness, while the Colonel assembled an impressive canvas and bamboo chair. At length satisfied with the contraption, Colonel Bagshot enthroned himself. George thought of King Canute.

The morning's ebb tide had left soft furrows across the beach. The sand was warm to the touch. George knelt on a towel.

The colonel reached a bony hand down beyond his feet. "George, build the mountain there."

George dug a heap of sand into his bucket, patted it down, and upended it close to the Colonel's glistening toecaps. With additional scoops of sand on the right and a judicious amount of scraping and patting, the clumsy likeness of a sandcastle sphinx appeared. Colonel Bagshot gave artistic direction.

"Don't put eyes and whiskers on it. It's not really a sphinx. It's a cow stomach thingy. Dammit, it's Isandlwana! That will do, at any rate. Now dig out a valley in front, fairly broad, and put the extra sand over on that side. That will be the nQutu plateau. Move your towel, you simpleton. That's where the Zulus are ---"

* * *

I reached the saddle at a brisk trot, edging to my right to skip around the convoy. Joseph came almost alongside as I halted astride the north flank of the stony kopje – that's Cape Dutch for one of their rugged hills – and pulled out my binoculars. Zeiss of Jena, morocco leather, seven times actual size magnification. A present from my aunt. Damned expensive. Carefully I scanned the valley. It was perhaps eight or ten miles deep, pasture all the way. At the far horizon was a line of heights, with one peak rising behind the front range, green patched with stonework.

"The Nkandhla Hills," said Joseph. "Silutshana there, Magogo next to it. Big one, name Isiphezi."

Joseph was turning out to be a useful fellow. He had told me all about the Zulus as he understood them, with their big thrusting spears called 'iklwa' or some such, and their 'impi', which is an army, though sometimes it was just a regiment, and how they used an encircling formation based on the shape of a bulls head. Of course, he told me this in broken servant's English, with a certain amount of drawing in the mud with a stick.

To our right the Buffalo River was meandering southwards, cutting to the east behind another range of hills. You couldn't see it from where we stood, but

Joseph pointed out its line between the closest hills – the Malakathas, he called 'em, with Hlazakazi further east – and the distant green ridges of Natal.

It was disconcerting to have a fellow equipped only with what the Almighty had issued him pointing out topographic details that I could barely make out with the aid of the finest Teutonic optical design. Still, I thought, that's the nature of the savage; primitive hunting skills, animal instincts, rudimentary reasoning, that sort of thing.

The camp was being laid out below. Advance parties of the 24th had got rows of white tents laid out, pinned smartly against the grass in comforting geometry. Beyond them were the tents of the Native Contingent, sagging on slack lines while white ants pursued black ants around the canvas cones. A party of officers was gathered on horseback. Even at several hundred yards you could see – feel – the glossy coats of expensive horseflesh, the gold and the hair oil and the Old Bond Street accessories. One of them, skittering about on a chestnut that seemed likely to toss him aside, wore the deep green of a rifle regiment. He had that excitable, useless air that I had seen about him yesterday. I hate a frilly soldier. He'd probably wear corsets when he got old and fat.

Across the valley, beyond the new tents and scurrying figures, was the Nqutu plateau. It rose up against the plain like two tables pushed together and not quite fitting. Deep crevasses were gouged into the scarp wall, opening out in jumbled rocks on the valley floor. Only between the northern end of Isandlwana and the plateau was there any show of gentleness, where a broad spur sloped onto the Nqutu. About a mile in front of the camp, brimming down from the plateau, was a watercourse – a nullah, as I'd have called it in Afghanistan – washing clear across the plain. Even with the incessant rain of these last weeks, the stream that ran through it was thin and feeble. Joseph told me that he didn't know the name of the stream, but that in South Africa such a feature was known as a donga. A smaller donga joined it, looping in desultory fashion from the direction of the camp. A little further on from the camp was a conical hill, a little thing like a lone pimple. There may have been another donga beyond that.

"Binky!"

I turned in my saddle. It was Melvill. He reined in, grinning broadly. "Couldn't wait to be up here, eh? Don't try to tell me it's official. You couldn't stand to be on your tod at the drift with the deaf lieutenant and the dull engineer, so you thought you'd wander along to see if infantrymen could pitch tents and brew tea properly".

We rode together, watching the activity as wagons were pulled swearing into the park set aside for them under the lee of Isandlwana's southeast flank. The NNC seemed to have been directed towards this piece of manual labour – British infantry are utterly hopeless as lifters and carriers, which is why they can't get decently honest jobs at home and have to take the Shilling rather than starve. I was entertained by the way that, left on their own, the blacks came up with a rhythm for the work, singing and swaying in their almost serpentine manner as the wagons came in and the loads came out. Naturally this did not suit their officers and NCOs, who persisted in breaking the flow of effort with a great deal of noisy scolding, pointing and – I regret to say this – pushing and shoving. Melvill was shaking his head.

"Look at that. The quality of leadership shown by our brother officers in the Native Contingent is something shocking. And the non-coms! I've seen better men awaiting trial at the county assizes."

"Is there to be a laager?" I asked. "I'd heard we were to pull the wagons and carts into a laager whenever we halted. With a shelter trench outside for the infantry, broken bottles, prickly hedges of thorn bush and all that?"

"You mean like His Lordship mentioned in his *Regulations for Field Forces in South Africa*? Did you read that on the way up? I think the answer would have to be no. Chelmsford was very impressed with what the Boers had to say about fighting the Zulus, but when we got here, suddenly the regulations are gone by the board. I asked Colonel Glyn about it, and he just shilly-shallied about. The ground is too hard to dig, they say, and we need to keep the wagon park open so as to move freight up to the front, send the empties back to Rorke's Drift and generally shuttle things about."

"Does that make any sense?" I asked. Melvill clearly kept his eyes and ears open.

"I think that depends. If you look on this camp as a stores depot, it does. The Quartermaster's chaps would scream blue murder if half their supplies were serving as ballast for some kind of wagon fort instead of being checked and issued and properly accounted for. They would see it in the same way as if the station master at Clapham Junction were to go mad and try to form up all his rolling stock in a defensive circle around the sidings."

"I see that. But this ain't Clapham Junction, is it?"

We pondered that metaphysical truth for a moment. I considered the prospect of several thousand Zulus marauding though south London in full regalia, pausing only to purchase platform tickets to entitle them access onto the railway station.

"Bagshot!"

I knew the voice immediately. Dammit, I should have seen him coming. He was obvious enough. I'd put him out of mind when I began contemplating military matters.

"What on earth are you doing here? You are supposed to be with Durnford's motley collection, awen't you?" I said nothing. Fitzclarence's eyebrows came together in a knot. I think his brain might have been working. I hadn't seen that look before.

"I say! He's sent you on as vanguard, hasn't he? Dwat that Durnford! He's bweaking orders again! He's wefusing to stay in the wear like His Lordship has instwucted! He has, hasn't he? Out with it, man ---"

Oh Lord. I've gone and got my new C.O. in hot water and I haven't even met him yet. So much for making a good impression.

"Don't be silly, Fitzclarence." Melvill was all smooth assurance. "The fellow just came up to have a look around. Keen, you see. Enthusiastic. Interested in what's going on."

Fitzclarence was not mollified. "Oh," he said, "What do you mean by that?" An insult in everything, you see. You can't ask some people the time without getting into a bitter personal argument. Fitzclarence pulled out what he evidently considered to be the Big Gun. "We shall have to go and see Colonel Cwealock about this."

I looked around for a stray guy line or a picket rope. Anything for the little twerp to trip himself up on. It was a lot to ask, but he'd done it once already. Maybe the horse would go berserk again. I looked. One white stocking.

"Yes, the General must know," repeated Fitzclarence.

A rider came up at the gallop, a small chap in the white helmet and smelly corduroy outfit I'd seen earlier – the Natal Mounted Police. "Message for Lieutenant. Fizzclarence, sir"

The recipient of the message withered the trooper with a scornful glare, snatching the paper from his fingers. He scanned the page. "Oh piffle!" he muttered. "They can't mean this. They can't mean to leave a Fitzclawence out of the action."

So they had a job for him too.

73

When I stopped laughing he was capering over towards the group of staff officers, bouncing along on his horse like a cheap clockwork toy. I heard him shrieking about places of honour and not knowing anything about what he termed 'twansport'. I don't think anyone was taking any notice. "For whatever a man soweth, that shall he also reap," as the Apostle Paul told the Galatians. Fine lot, the Galatians; Celts you know, much like Scotch highlanders I should think.

"I think we could find you a drink," said Melvill, "If it isn't too early for you."

It wasn't.

CHAPTER FIFTEEN

Hove 1928

The Colonel was glaring at George. "You aren't putting the topographic details in properly. Fill the bucket for the hills on the right and I'll carve out the dongas with my stick. Don't build the Malakathas on my cheese sandwiches either ---"

George wasn't about to. The Colonel's cheese sandwiches were in the Buffalo River. The boy wasn't about to mention it, though.

* * *

"The Fitzclarences", opined Coghill, "Are a collection of bastards".

This seemed harsh, and I would have said so, but for the fact that he was in the process of handing me a large tin mug of iced claret. I feel a good deal of generosity to those who pass iced claret my way.

"No," he said, "It's perfectly true. I speak of the family of the Earl of Munster. My people are from County Dublin, and we old Irish families know one another's business far too well. The House of Munster has a lineage that extends back, err, fifty years at the outside. You see, the Duke of Clarence, as became William IV, lived happily with an actress who used the stage name of Mrs. Jordan, though that weren't her family name."

Coghill went on to explain the complicated history of King Billy's illegitimate son, George Augustus Fitzclarence, whose scandalous conduct led him to ruin and suicide. As the Earl of Munster he'd married a Miss Mary Wyndham, who was, as they used to say, the natural[33] daughter of the Earl of Egremont. There was a lot to it, including details of the family crest. I didn't follow all of it.

"So, what are you saying?" asked Melvill; "That our Fitz is the grandson of William IV and resents being born on the wrong side of the blanket? That would account for the snotty outlook and unbearable self-importance."

---

33. A now disused term for an illegitimate child.

"Probably not the grandson, since that would make him almost forty at the very least, and he's still a scrawny little toad. The first earl had five legitimate sons and a fair parcel of daughters. He might not even be of that lineage whatsoever. The way the Fitzclarences have carried on, he might be the progeny of a passing chimney sweep."

"That's as maybe," said Melvill, "But a man whose great grandfather was an honest greengrocer may hush that fact up, while a man whose great grandfather might have been a randy royal begetting his way through the palace laundry maids will advertise that possibility in as flaunting a fashion as you can imagine. Perhaps our young Algernon thinks he is about two hundredth in line to the throne."

"Short of an outbreak of the plague over Christmas at Balmoral, he's still a long way shy of the crown." This was the first thing I'd said in this discussion of pedigree.

"True," said Coghill, adjusting his camp stool and pouring us all another drink. "Still, if he's two hundredth, he's ahead of anyone else here."

"So why is he so beastly to me?" I asked.

"Oh, he's beastly to everyone. It's not personal."

But on the way back, I remembered something Great-Uncle Henry had told me, about the 10th Hussars when he was a young officer. It was 1814, just after Bonaparte was exiled to Elba. The regiment had a fellow called Quentin in command, a notoriously incompetent soldier, but a close chum of the Prince Regent, the Colonel-in-Chief. He was so unfit to command that the officers of the 10th wrote a letter to His Majesty, more or less requesting that Quentin be given the boot. Most of the officers put their pens to it, anyway. My uncle Henry Bagshot, the reason being that he was off getting a nasty boil lanced, and never got round to signing it before the letter was posted. Quentin demanded a court-martial to clear his reputation, and, though the evidence indicated that he was a coward, a brute and an imbecile, the Prince Regent made sure the chap was acquitted. The accusers were then on the ropes themselves, and were forced out of the regiment, leaving only my great-uncle and two others who hadn't signed the letter. The expelled officers were influential men – one was the Marquis of Worcester, another a French emigre duke, even – but the Regent wasn't having it. I think a few may have found their way back into the 10th after a few years, but not all of them. And two of those who didn't return were Fitzclarences.

So perhaps it was personal.

CHAPTER SIXTEEN

Hove 1928

"What are these, d'ye think?"

George examined a box the Colonel had pulled from the bag. It was unfamiliar to him, a red patterned lid with a fancy buff label and a banner and badge that proclaimed "Fabrique Francaise" and "C.B.G. Paris". He prised off the top. It contained a set of horsemen, in broad-brimmed hats, bandoliers and rifles. They were models of black men, the dark brown paint slopping onto collars and sometimes rubbed off to show pink underneath. Each had a bundle of pins glued behind the saddle, painted brown except for the tips.

"Don't know sir".

"Not surprised, laddie. Natal Native Horse. The figures were Boers, originally, by the Mignot Company; my chum Lyautey[34] got 'em on leave in Paris by way of an apology for getting me mixed up in the mutiny at Fez in 1912. My Gurkha orderly painted 'em as blacks for me – paint wasn't much good, was it? We were under siege by the Mohmands at the time, couldn't get the proper stuff sent up beyond Peshawar. I think he made it from the spleen of a mountain goat. He said the red was actual blood from some fanatical mullah he'd taken his knife to, that's as maybe. Still, he didn't give 'em slanty eyes. He did that once with a company of Welsh Fusiliers ---"

George rolled his own eyes, but the Colonel didn't notice. That was probably a good thing.

* * *

Joseph had pressed my best patrol jacket and shined up the spike on my snowy white helmet. I looked damned smart. I could stand up straight in those days

---

34. Louis Hubert Gonzalve Lyautey (1854 – 1934) was a French officer who served in Algeria and Madagascar before leading the operations that brought Morocco under French domination from 1907 onwards. His published memoirs make no specific mention of Colonel Bagshot.

too; I was young and hadn't fallen off any elephants yet. I sat on my charger, ready to present myself as No 2 Column splashed through the River below Rorke's station.

I knew Colonel Durnford the moment the column came into sight. He didn't look like a Royal Engineer. He looked like a bandit in a western romance, 'Wild Bill Hickok here tonight, sixpence admission'. I think his hair was a good deal shorter than Hickok's, but otherwise it was the same look, all whiskers, pistols and wide-awake hat.

I presented myself and my written orders.

"Transport officer," he said, eyeing me quizzically. "You're a cavalryman."

Evidently no fool.

"Seems a damn silly posting, but, what-the-hey, our wagons may need someone who can make 'em gallop."

No 2 Column looked as if it knew its business. No chocolate soldiers here, excuse the pun. Unlike the ragged, disheartened blacks of the foot Contingent, the men were cocky as you like on nimble ponies, bare big toes in stirrups. Slouch hats with red *puggaree*[35] wrapped around, drab clothing of European cut, bandoliers, carbines, sheaves of spears in a saddle boot. I don't think these were the men the passengers on the Pinetown stagecoach were talking about, but they looked a sight more workmanlike than the characters I'd seen escorting the wagons up to Isandlwana. There were five troops, each speaking its own dialect. Three of the troops made up Sikali's Horse, Ngwane clansmen from the hills, who hated the Zulus. Another troop was comprised of Tlokwa Basutos, under their chief Hlubi. The last troop were different, Zulu refugees from the Edendale mission station under one Simeon Kambula; unlike the usual haggard refugee types, these men appeared convinced they could take on Cetshwayo's laddies and beat them. Unlike their comrades, they wore proper boots, and sang hymns over the campfires.

Behind the horsemen came a band of scruffy native infantry, all bare legs and blankets. The rocket battery was next, mules laden with weird ironmongery, sticks and triangles, with wheezing privates in the muddied red and green of the 24th and a bloodhound-faced mounted officer cursing to himself in a low rumble.

Then there were the wagons. These were to be my adopted children. They were light things, mule drawn, painted in the colonial style of green bodies and red wheels or the reverse rather than army grey. I was relieved to see they were not the

---

35. A 'pugaree' or 'pagri' is an Indian military word for a turban. In this case, it refers to a twisted piece of fabric serving as a broad hatband.

massive Boer ox-wagons that were everywhere about; I'd never be able to keep pace with Durnford's light horse with a squadron of those wheeled warehouses. As it was the wagons – hardly more than carts really – were labouring through ploughed mud and massed horse dung. Skittering along the line of vehicles was a man on horseback in blue patrols and forage cap. What surprised me was that he had a banjo, slung over his shoulder rather than on his knee. I don't think he'd come from Alabama, at least not today.

I was introduced to him within the hour. He was my immediate superior, being No 1 Transport Officer.

He announced himself. "Cochrane, 32nd Foot. You look like a tenor. D' ye sing?"

The column pitched camp quickly in the brief twilight, beyond the fouled grounds left by Chelmsford's army. There's nothing quite as disgusting as taking over yesterday's bivouac in the rain; it's like an open sewer. Most forces will do it anyway, out of sheer lack of initiative.

The white officers were mostly colonials, as you'd expect, but not a bad lot for all that. We messed around a great fire, using wood they'd brought themselves to keep dry; this I found encouraging. There were Roberts, Vause and Raw, all lieutenants, who each had a troop of Sikali's riders. Harry Davis commanded the Edendale Christians, and Alfred Henderson led the Basutos. Captain Nourse joined us, swearing loudly about looking after one's feet, or not, in this case; he had the bad luck to command the Kaffir foot – "Company 'D', 1st Battalion, 1st Regiment Natal Native Contingent", he informed us, as if that made it a real unit – and everyone felt sorry for him. Roberts passed him a tin mug of the disgusting local gin. Not really gentlemen, of course.

The regular officers seemed happy to muck in, looking as disreputable as possible in damp tweeds and big hats; Cochrane introduced his comrades to me as a Captain Barton of the 7th foot, and Major Russell of the Rocket Battery, who had the air of a man tolerating a bad joke long after it had ceased to amuse.

Raw – everyone called him 'Charlie – was telling a story. A few years previously he had served under Durnford in the short and unlucky campaign against a chief called Langalibalele. Raw hadn't been an officer then.

"No, I was a trooper in the Natal Carbineers, and Georgie Shepstone was a corporal. Oh, we thought we were a fine body of men. The orders from above were strange, as we understood them. We were supposed to ride up onto the Drakensberg and prevent Langalibalele and his people from getting out of the province by way of the mountain passes into Basutoland. Easier said than done!

Durnford came up with a plan to get us up onto the Berg by this one pass while another force comes around from the north end. Between the two of us we'd pull a pincer move and catch 'is Majesty between us. The odd thing was that the Lieutenant Governor had said we wasn't to shoot first, but to gently usher the Hlubi – that was the name of the tribe – back to their location in Natal. Anyways, it all went wrong. We got lost and Durnford broke his shoulder in a fall on the way up the mountain. The country was terrible, really rough climbing. When we got to the top, the Hlubi were already coming up the pass. We set out to talk 'em out of crossing and persuade 'em to go home. But the carbineers lost their nerve and wouldn't listen to Durnford. The Hlubi started to push their way forward and everything blew up. Three carbineers and some of the black levies was killed, and Langalibalele and his people got away into Basutoland. It was pitiful. Thing is, when the news got back to P.M.Burg, it was Durnford got the blame. Politics, see. Didn't have no powerful chums. No friends in 'igh places, you know. Made a few enemies, or at least ruffled a few feathers where it weren't appreciated. So, when it comes to picking a scapegoat, guess who fetches up with the blame? Durnford. And he's been getting the blame ever since."

CHAPTER SEVENTEEN

Brighton 1928

There is very little sand on Brighton Beach. Those who choose to spend their holidays in Brighton or its sedate sister Hove ought to be well aware of this fact, but nonetheless, a number of trippers seemed to take exception to an elderly man in tropical garb and a youth far too old for sandcastles monopolising the only patch of damp sand for at least a mile on either side of the piers.

"Yer should be ashimed of yerselves!" shouted a passing Londoner, encouraged perhaps by the bottle of pale ale he was pawing. "Fink of all the kids 'oo want ter play."

The Colonel stood up and glared.

"I lost a leg in the War for the Likes of You!"

That silenced him. The cockney gaped at the Colonel, looked at his beer bottle, then back at the old man, who clearly had two legs poking out from his sail-like shorts. Amazing what they could do today. He shook his head and sloped off. Bagshot winked at George.

"That'll settle him down."

* * *

In the morning I had a chance to look over my, er, command. Cochrane – "do call me Willie" – filled me in on what he thought I needed to know, which was a good deal more than he actually knew. He was a cheery chappie to be certain – overage for his rank, thinning hair, fertile moustache. He was one of the Dundonald Cochranes. His famous ancestor[36] was a lunatic sailor of

---

36. Admiral Thomas Cochrane, Lord Dundonald (1775-1860) was a British naval officer, radical politician and inventor. A brilliant frigate captain, he was hounded from the navy in 1814 by political enemies and went to serve in the revolutionary navies of Greece, Brazil and Chile. He is the model for more than one fictional naval hero.

Nelson's time, became a radical M.P. and went on to fight for the Greeks and Chileans. Avoiding his creditors, more like. Our man here was a second cousin to the titled Cochranes.

His accounting of the fixtures and fittings of the column transport was off-hand in the extreme. He had no idea how many mules he had, or what was in each wagon; he had no plans for the secure deployment in case of contact with the enemy. What he did have were two things. First of all, he had a burning enthusiasm, quite odd in a foot-soldier, to be a dashing leader of irregular horse; he would clearly put the wagons under the immediate command of the nearest corporal if a chance arose to be haring off on a spotted pony, with two dozen Basutos galloping behind him, watching his rump bob up and down in the saddle.

"Wonderful laddies, Binky." he declared in his Scots burr.

I'd known him twelve hours and he was calling me Binky already. He made friends quickly. I'm always suspicious of that type.

"Lots o' spirit, good riders, fine baritone voices."

The second thing was, he had a choir. He'd said something about this the night before, with the firelight and the colonial gin giving him the eyes of a lover or a lunatic. He'd kept telling me that the Edendale men "shing well". They sang mission-taught hymns while he accompanied them with slow rolls on the banjo. He'd offered to bring them out for a moonlit recital, but Nourse had smacked him with an empty bottle and they'd all piled on top of him in a drunken scrum.

* * *

I spent all the next day checking swingle-bars and dissel-booms and such like, crawling under the carts and generally showing the men I knew what I was about. I didn't, of course, but people are always impressed by a show of activity; at least they know they won't get away with slacking while you are at your business. We had ten wagons. The column had started out with thirty wagons but had left most of them with the NNC infantry at different posts along the way. Durnford had made noises about getting more from the local farms, since the remaining wagons were much overburdened. Most of what was carried in the wagons was forage, to enable the mules to actually pull the wagons. Unlike oxen, which can be left out to nibble on the local verdure for a few hours, mules needed a special diet – five pounds of grain and ten pounds of hay each and every day – meaning that a wagon with a team of eight would need, er, a lot of fodder every day. Since the wagon would only be carrying a total load of two thousand pounds, you can imagine that a jaunt of several days between grain supplies would involve carrying vast amounts of forage. If you had to go far enough, say two weeks journey, you could carry bugger all but grub for the mules, transporting nothing and starving yourself in the process. I won't bother you with the arithmetic – I'd have to take my shoes and socks off to do it – but it's fair to say we had tons and tons of the stuff. Being wet, as everything was and had been for days, it smelt like a geriatric badger. What space was not allotted to malodorous vegetable matter was given over to human concerns: provisions – a great deal of the cheap gin, I noticed, amongst the officers' personal stores, though the black troopers were a sober lot – some camping gear, and enough ammunition to keep shooting for a good while.

There was supposed to be two hundred rounds for each man beyond what they already had, in boxes of six hundred ball cartridges apiece. I expect we had a hundred or so of them, divided amongst the various wagons. These were wooden things, weighing, I believe, seventy-nine pounds and some-odd ounces apiece – that's five and a half stone each. Your average ten-year-old boy weighs about that. I mention these boxes because they were to cause a good deal of argument later on; they were lined with tin-plate and had double copper strapping with a lot of screws. Actually, you only needed to open one screw to slide out the lid, and everyone who'd ever dealt with a box of ammunition knew that. But I'm getting ahead of myself. Cochrane had buggered off for what he termed 'choir rehearsal' around ten and hadn't come back for hours. Now I heard his voice.

"Binky! Get a wagon down to the mission station! I've found a piano!"

"Yes," I answered, banging my head on the bottom of the wagon I was under. "It belongs to the mission. That's why it's at the mission." Wit's wasted on some characters.

"Not if ye get the wagon down here smartish, Binky old man. I've often thought that the banjo isnae quite right on the slower pieces --"

"Stealing? Willie, we're officers and gentlemen, you remember!"

"Well, naturally. But there's nae kirk meetings at the mission, the missionary's cleared off, and our friends in the 24th will only burn it for firewood. We'll only borrow it. For God's sake, Binky, we'll be safeguarding it!"

I decided to go and look for the missionary, the Reverend Witt, who had not "cleared off" as far as I knew. He had a tent not far from the buildings. If he thought we'd be safeguarding his piano, so be it.

I couldn't find him there. Cochrane had got a wagon down to the hospital with a speed that amazed me considering his ignorance of transport duties; probably the thought of larceny had sharpened his athletic skills something considerable. While the black *voorloopers* managed the vehicle into place, Cochrane led me by the elbow into the hospital.

"Bloody heavy, Binky Need your help."

We couldn't shift it. We made a certain amount of noise not shifting it. The fellow I'd met previously, the hospital cook, looked in. Cochrane sized him up as a man of natural authority, though not so much as to quarrel with an officer. Muscles too, lots of them.

"What's your name, private?"

"1373 'ook, zurr!" He clattered in salute, a large pot in his hands.

"I'd be most obliged, Private Hook, is it, if you'd help us get this piano into the wagon. No need to get any other men, we'll be fine if you'd just take that end ---"

It's understood. Officers don't explain, other ranks don't ask. Hook's huge West Country shoulders had the piano into the back of the cart in a moment. He picked up his iron pot and went back to his job. Cochrane managed to look unconcerned yet furtive in a way I find incredible yet; if he'd been on that street corner in Sarajevo in '14 the Archduke's car could have gone right by while Cochrane was borrowing ten quid from Gavrilo Princip.

Talking of money, I had a suggestion to make.

"I say, Cochrane, oughtn't we to leave the Reverend some cash as a deposit, a surety, on his piano?"

"Good idea. I'll write a note to old What's-his-name saying what we've done, and leave him, what do you think, a couple of guineas?"

"I've only got a fiver to hand," I said. Money spoils the line of a man's uniform. I always carry a single crisp banknote to cover any necessities, and usually a ten-shilling note was the order of the day. I've no idea why I was carrying what amounted to a month's pay in a field on the Zulu border; p'raps I was expecting to treat the entire column to a steak and kidney pie and a trip to a music hall.

"Gi' it here, then, Binky boy, and I'll find some paper."

It wasn't much of a letter, really. Cochrane was no literary stylist – he was barely literate, really – but I'm not sure Alfred Lord Tennyson would have done much better in explaining how come he'd wandered off with some foreign cleric's piano:

Dear Revd. Witt;

This is to let you know we have temperarily purloined yr. Piano as to protect it from the ravidges of undisciplaned Enlisted Men who are Wont to make matchwood of all that they come across. We undertake to return said piano at the Close of Operations if not prior. We enclose a suretty of £5 as a Mark of Good faith.

We both signed the document and folded the banknote inside it. Cochrane folded both again and went off to give them to Hook to pass along to the missionary. I ordered the wagon back up to our camp. It could hardly move, the mules straining and the black driver yipping unsuccessfully in encouragement.

"What's in the wagon, Cochrane?"

"I dinnae know. Ah, part of the ammunition reserve I think."

"Should we do some redistributing of loads, to even them up?"

"Good idea, Binky. It's getting dark, mind ye. Do that in the morning. Let's get back and have the choir sing us through dinner. We won't use the piano yet, though. I've worked out a bonny banjo accompaniment for some of the local cattle herding songs the lads like to sing. Nice tunes about how many heifers a certain girl might be worth, that kind of thing. I might do it as a medley with 'Camptown Races'."

When he did try out the piano, Cochrane found out why it weighed so much. There were a hundred hymnals, in Swedish, stowed inside. He just left them there and opened a bottle of Glenlivet. A varied supply of what he termed 'the Creature' was the staple item of his personal stores, and served to endear him to me, at least a little. As he drank he became more and more Scottish, waxed eloquent and maudlin over the pure waters of the Spey and the rich peat flavour of the Islay malts. After a while, he offered to conduct a scientific experiment involving myself, a blindfold, and three tin cups filled with Talisker, Glenmorangie and something from a small distillery on Kintyre, which had burned down in 1865, taking four days to do so, the fire being visible from Ireland. I had Cochrane's word on it.

CHAPTER EIGHTEEN

Brighton 1928

By this time the sand-scooped landscape was dotted with toy soldiers, formations of stiff two-inch figures drawn up in front of a line of folded notepaper tents. As the Colonel pursued his story, he pulled boxes – long brick red boxes – from the Gladstone bag. There were the red-coated infantry of the 24th, gunners in blue, mounted men, black men. George was beginning to learn the lore of the Bagshot collection, of the intricate obscurata of the collector's mind. The foot and guns were, he saw, the work of the Britains factory, while the black soldiers were Zulus from "Johillco"[37], whose identity had been changed by a thin streak of red paint about the brows. There was an officer amongst them, an acrobatic cowboy of uncertain origin, six-gun in hand but holster filed off, painted with the same red blotch snaking around the crown of his five-gallon. All the work, perhaps, of the Gurkha orderly, painting with his strange improvised colours as wild hillmen cracked off shots from rock-strewn hillsides. The cavalry pieces were the same, thin washes of black over factory red tunics, matchsticks carved into carbines, and scratches of new trim in pipeclay white or an oily brown. George examined the toys carefully. He decided that he could do as well. It was then that he realised that, the Gurkha having chosen Nepal over Hove, he would probably have to.

* * *

January is high summer in South Africa. The sun was up and about its business around five, as I washed my face, dragged a comb across my head and wriggled my toes into a still-damp pair of boots. I felt as if the Royal Ordnance Factory was conducting artillery tests inside my skull. Joseph had my kit in tolerable order. I grunted miserably, and he grinned broadly, forgetting to go through the most superficial form of groveling; getting a bit big for his britches. It seemed like a lot of trouble to kick him, and anyway I was having some difficulty with walking upright.

---

37. "Johillco" – John Hill and Company – was a rival to Britains, started by a former employee of that company.

George Shepstone was in the guard tent, in a disreputable fisherman's woolie[38] and a squashed Boer hat, a kind of garb that usually indicates its wearer is either a tramp or a member of the aristocracy. Shepstone was neither. He was a captain of the Natal Carbineers, which would make him a nobody in the eyes of most of us regular Johnnies. Although actually he was a considerable somebody. He was Durnford's political agent and right-hand man. Shepstone knew the Zulus on terms of deep intimacy; he not only spoke their language – a lot of odd clicking amidst bass moans – but knew how they look at the world. He could get inside the Zulu and walk a mile in his, well, his bare feet. Moreover, George's pater was Sir Theophilous Shepstone, a grand poohbah in the Natal Government, and someone who was up to his skinny neck in the devious political trafficking that had given us the Zulu War. Not that I was complaining. A war was a war, in those days.

A soldier brought me a mug of warm brown water. Shepstone already had one. It was disgusting, but it did wonders for my head. Whoever made it knew nothing about coffee or tea – which was it? – but had discovered a veritable balm for the alcoholically disadvantaged.

"Anxious to be at 'em?" Shepstone had the laconic tone of one who expects very little of interest from his companion. Young officers in smart uniforms are expected to be keen as mustard and thick as treacle.

"I am, sir!" The 'sir' would do no harm. Most regular officers think a colonial commission rates about on a par with the poor bugger who cleans out the thunder-boxes. I am myself, as you know, no enthusiast for local settler militias, and especially their officers. Most are the kind of shiftless wastrels who left England one step ahead of the bobbies or the bailiffs. Their military service consists largely of stealing the natives' livestock, drinking themselves stupid, and recommending one another for the Victoria Cross. Shepstone seemed like the exception to the rule.

"Soon enough, I expect. Cetshwayo is showing remarkable restraint. He doesn't want war and would avoid it if there was a way to get out of it with a certain degree of honour. A mere shred of honour. I regret that we don't seem able to give him that. We haven't, so he has to fight. His regiments are as brave as any in the world. They'll fight us toe to toe in an open field, and we'll smash 'em up good. Then my papa and his friends will draw up what they will be pleased to call a political solution, and the Zulus will be pulling ploughs and singing hymns. I hate it. It's a plain fact, but I still hate it."

All this rambling didn't make a lot of sense to me, and why on earth was he criticizing his father's efforts to a total stranger? Perhaps Shepstone had done

---

38. Sweater

himself rather too well the night before. I was about to look for an egg and a bottle of Worcester sauce when he smiled at me.

"Don't worry, I'm not with the Aborigines Protection League or whatever they call themselves. It just seems a damned shame, that's all."

I could understand a Damned Shame. I changed the subject.

"The Basuto horsemen look marvellous. Practical. No chocolate box soldiers."

I was laying it on far too thick. His cheeks creased in amusement.

"Ah, you'd never say that over the mess silver with the picture of Lord Cardigan over the fireplace. Still, go out with them over some rough country a time or two, and you'll see."

I was about to say that it was the 11th Hussars that had the portrait of Cardigan, not my own regiment, when the tent flaps parted. A figure in muddy waterproofs stooped through the opening, straightened up, and banged his helmet on the canvas ceiling. Gasping an apology, he stumbled over a camp stool and thrust a paper at me. "Captain Shepstone," he blurted, "I'm Smith-Dorrien. From the general. For the colonel. Sorry. Important. Sorry."

Shepstone reached for the document. It doubtless pained him that rank and seniority were always associated with clean pressed uniforms. Then again, he did look like someone who habitually slept under hedges. He read the note carefully, his eyes narrowing. This was no birthday telegram.

"The colonel will need to see this right away."

Smith-Dorrien stepped forward. He'd made a fool of himself coming in and wanted a chance to redeem himself in Shepstone's eyes, and probably his own. Horace Smith-Dorrien[39], as I was to find out, was no fool. Gangly and awkward, doubtless, but no fool at all. Saved the BEF in 1914, I believe, but that's another story.

"I shall ride to find Colonel Durnford, sir!"

Trying too hard, of course, no sin in that, but Shepstone shook his head. No need to keep this enthusiastic young idiot dangling on the hook. "Get some coffee, man. Get your horse looked after. Get a bit of kip."

He handed me the dispatch. "Durnford's halfway to Helpmakaar. Get this to him. I'll fall the men in."

---

39. Horace Smith-Dorrien (1858-1930) went on to command a brigade at Omdurman and served with distinction in the Boer War. As commander of the British II Corps in Flanders in 1914-15, he fell afoul of the commander-in-chief, Sir John French, and was sacked.

I was aboard my pony – the little roan -and splashing though the drift. This was done in a fit of excitement that I regretted in a sharp moment of fearful cold as the water surged over and around me. The ponts were tied up, and there was no sign of John Chard or his detachment. The air was crisp, and I was quite agog at the whole thing. Despite my headache, I was able to have a bit of a sing. Bishop Heber, as died of a fever in India fifty years ago, had a way with words:

"The Son of God goes forth to war, a kingly crown to gain

His blood red banners stream a-far, who follows in his train

Who best can drink his cup of woe, triumphant over pain

Who patient bears his cross below, he follows in his train."

I suppose 'the train' means the regimental transport, which did seem to involve woe and pain and bearing of crosses. Perhaps the Almighty wanted me to be in charge of mules and ammunition boxes.

I'm a curious sort of cove, I suppose, and the dispatch was calling out for me to read it. After all, what if I should lose the paper in a freak gust of wind, or if a sudden thorn bush were to rip my saddle bag, or ----

I opened it:

22nd, Wednesday, 2 AM

You are to march to this camp at once with all the force you have with you of No. 2 Column.Major Bengough's Battalion is to move to Rorke's Drift as ordered yesterday. 2-24th Artillery and mounted men with the General and Colonel Glynn move off at once to attack a Zulu force about ten miles distant.

J.N.C.

Our friend Crealock, no doubt.

I caught up with Durnford's party in a half hour at a brisk canter. Cochrane and Barton were with him at the head of the procession. He turned in his saddle without halting and waved me on towards him with his good hand.

"Orders from Lord Chelmsford, sir." I was about to tell him what the note contained, but etiquette grabbed excitement by the shoulder. Subalterns are expected to know their place, keep their tongues still, and, oh yes, not to read confidential correspondence between superior officers.

Durnford eyed me quizzically, his impressive whiskers twitching with interest.

He ripped the sheet from my fingers and held it up to read. As his face cracked into glee, I held mine impassive. I didn't know a ruddy thing: I was just the messenger.

"Have you any idea what this says, man?"

"Nossir!" I replied, like a flipping corporal of horse.

"Bloody liar! You've read it yourself."

"Nossir!"

"Well you ought to have! I certainly would have done. Initiative, man! What if you'd lost it crossing the river? What if you'd drowned? Then I'd have to wait until I saw Georgie Shepstone, because he'd certainly have read it! This isn't Aldershot you know, we don't stand on stupid ceremonies ---"

Colonel Durnford was dressing me down for following correct military procedure. Well, I was hardly going to tell him that actually I'd lied about doing what I said I hadn't done but really I had, which is what he would have done even though we both knew neither one of us should. Could I now? My ears were ablaze. I'd gone red in the face. I really liked this fellow.

I liked him even more when he gave me an order. "Stay close by me. Lieutenant Cochrane can tend the wagons. I shall need you for staff purposes if we're busy today."

I noticed Cochrane was frowning. He didn't like the sound of that last bit and nosed forward to plead his case. Durnford spoke with him briefly, then made an announcement.

"Just what I thought. We are to proceed at once to Isandlwana camp. There is an impi about eight miles from the camp which the general moves out to attack at daybreak."

Within moments the column of riders had reversed direction. The immediate concern of harassing a few more wagons from the farmer-folk of Helpmakaar had evaporated: we were going to fight the Zulus. Not a man among the party doubted it. We were sick of 'acting in support of the main column' or 'serving the lines of communication.' The jubilation running through each of us told that battle was ahead and above us, hanging in the air. I wasn't a transport-wallah anymore. I was a bold cavalier, an officer of the Natal Native Horse. I felt like Prince Rupert driving on against the Roundheads at Edgehill. The mules could go to hell. Cochrane could have them and put on a concert party too if he liked.

Shepstone had the rest of No. 2 Column formed and ready to march. He was all got up in his Natal Carbineer rig – white helmet, blue tunic and breeches with white trim and gilt brightwork – and had the pink glow of the freshly shaved. It was about 8 o'clock by now. The Sotho horsemen were serious, holding their ponies tense in the reins. He hadn't told them anything. A good man.

Durnford said nothing, but knee'd his horse into a trot. With a flourish of that one good arm he pointed far into Zululand as the column swung in behind him. The Sotho don't cheer as white men do; a kind of exultant warbling went up, and there was an outbreak of singing. Good voices. We moved fast along the road, newly made by the sweat of the Centre Column, ten miles in two hours. The men on foot and the rocket battery were jogging to keep up the pace, but falling further behind at each turn in the track. God alone knew where the wagon train was. Ten carts full of cartridges and groceries. Far behind, no doubt. I thought of the wagon we'd hoisted missionary Witt's massive piano aboard; we'd planned on shifting the loads about to even it up, but never had. It was already three-parts full of heavy stuff, carbine ammunition. Perhaps Cochrane had done that first thing this morning. Perhaps he'd stayed in bed late. No, because he'd been out with Durnford at first light while I was still abed. In fact, I could see him bobbing along in the saddle five lengths in front of me, behind Durnford and Shepstone. Durnford must have relented and let him serve as what? Aide-de-camp? Officer of Light Horse? He did ride well for a beetle-crusher[40]. So who was minding the wagons? I remembered a fat, apologetic conductor called McCarthy or McCartney; I wouldn't myself have trusted him with delivering a Christmas goose before Epiphany. I stopped thinking about it. We were, after all, racing for the seat of war. The sound of the guns and all that. Almost.

John Chard was coming down from Isandlwana camp. I suppose we were a quarter of a mile from the rock. Durnford called out to him. I don't know that they'd met, but he recognized the R.E. insignia; sappers are like a Masonic order, so I was half expecting them to do a funny handshake. Durnford kept it simple: "You, sir! What news from the camp?"

Chard had to think about this. "Ah, well, I saw the enemy moving on the distant hills, apparently in great force. Large numbers of them moving to the left. The idea struck me that they might be moving in the direction of Rorke's Drift. I think they might be going to make a dash at the ponts. Have you seen a wagon coming this way, by any chance?"

Durnford rubbed his chin. We had, in fact, passed a wagon of sappers some while before. "You'll be Chard, then? If they wreck the ponts, you can always roll up your sleeves and make more. You're an engineer like myself. I'll help if

---

40. 'Beetle-crusher' is one of the many insulting terms coined by cavalrymen for their counterparts in the infantry.

I get the chance." I got the impression that Durnford had sized Chard up as a nervous nellie.

"Why, thank you sir!" replied Chard. Irony's lost on some people.

"Oh, Chard, pray, one favour," said Durnford. "The foot natives are behind us some way. As you meet them, ask Captain Stafford and E Company to jolly along the wagons. Tell Captain Nourse to hurry up to the camp with D Company. There's a good fellow."

As he rode past me, Lt. Chard recognised who I was. Almost.

"Morning Baggett. Looks like a nice day."

CHAPTER NINETEEN

Brighton 1928

As the afternoon wore on, George began to feel more and more like unpaid labour, much like the Natal natives the Colonel had spoken of. If he was going to dig a landscape, the lad felt he deserved a reward.

"Er, it would be a good day for ice cream, sir!" George tried to keep his tone as deferential as possible. He was good at that.

"Didn't we have those disgusting fishy things about ten minutes ago?"

"About an hour and a half, sir. And it's hot, working out here!"

The Colonel snorted. It wasn't hot, and how difficult was it to dig sandcastles? Even if they were topographically accurate sandcastles. Still, he allowed that he might consider the provision of tea and cakes, when four o'clock came along. Or, perhaps, three-thirty.

* * *

The 24th never finished their breakfast. The fall-in was sounded just as the battalion cooks were dolloping it out. I can't imagine it was all that good, mind you, but a soldier does his very best murdering on a full stomach. My tutor at Sandhurst, Old Griffith wrote a monograph on the subject. He knew never to miss a meal. Anyhow, the poor beggars were starving for something hot and starchy when someone ups and spots the Zulus, lurking about up on the plateau. They had been standing around in their belts and helmets for a couple of hours when our column came up over the saddle.

I followed Durnford, Shepstone and the others past the wagon park into camp. There were forty-odd vehicles, teams in-spanned for movement, all ready to go on down to Rorke's Drift. I remembered that Horace Smith-Dorrien was the transport officer for this stretch of the communications; the train couldn't move without his order, and the last I'd seen of Horace, he was off to cadge a stray sausage from Gonville Bromhead at the mission. I believe they shared a mess together with Chard. Either way, the wagons were in no shape to use as a defensive position. That whole section of instructions regarding the protection of a camp through trenches and wagon-forts had entirely gone by the board.

As the troop leaders brought No. 2 Column to a halt with the order 'Face Front', Durnford dismounted. He walked over to some chappie in the usual frontier garb who had a number of dejected-looking Zulus in tow. I asked Shepstone who they were.

"Couldn't tell you precisely, but by the look of them I'd say they were here to negotiate for themselves. Probably brought in a dozen rusty muskets in return for a pledge that we won't confiscate their herds. Or perhaps we already have, and they are begging to get them back."

I really hadn't seen actual live specimens of Homo Zulu-us in the natural state before this, so I was interested. Not very impressive, really, old black men in blankets and frowns. I told Shepstone so.

"Oh, these are just clan elders in cooperative mood. They aren't warriors. This is like comparing toothless old codgers on a bowling green to the Grenadier Guards."

"Surely not?" asked Barton. "After all, they're just Kaffirs."

"I'll let you decide about the Zulus," replied Shepstone, "When you see them in action. Which might well be today."

* * *

The general had gone. Before first light, Lord Chelmsford had taken his staff and most of No. 3 Column out to the east, where there had been sightings of a Zulu force. "The Main Impi", it was whispered. Nobody knew much. The tents and stores were all left behind, under the watchful eye of my recent dinner companions, the 1/24th foot.

Lt. Colonel Pulleine was seated at a table in the mess tent. Present were Melvill, as adjutant, Degacher as senior captain, and Coghill, because he was a good fellow and had nowhere else to be; evidently his job as staff officer to Colonel Glynn had rather fallen through, since Glynn had ridden ahead with the general, and Coghill wasn't riding. Pulleine addressed Durnford as he came in; "Good to see you this morning. It seems we have some little disturbance out on the left flank. We have had patrols of colonial horse up on the plateau since first light.

Reports are vague, I'm afraid, at this point. I suppose it would help if I gave you the position as it stands."

"If you would be so good as to appraise me."

"Naturally. Our force stands at two guns, seven pounder pieces, under Major Smith. Five companies, 1st Battalion, 24th Regiment – my own men – and a company of the 2nd battalion under Lieutenant Pope. About a hundred horsemen, mostly colonial volunteer with a few regular mounted infantry. Four hundred of the Natal Native Contingent. A few black pioneers, with a handful of Lieutenant Chard's sappers en route, so he reports. Something over a thousand all told, not counting your own column, of course."

"Of course. Pray tell, what orders did the general leave?"

"Only the verbal order 'to defend the camp'. To keep the infantry close in and put *vedettes*[41] out to scout. I have placed mounted patrols out on the plateau, on the conical koppie, and on the plain to the east."

"So, nothing for No. 2 Column specifically? I received orders to come up to this camp, marked 2 AM. I had rather assumed that there would be more detailed instructions awaiting me. Surely the general would not bring up two hundred and fifty light horsemen 'to defend the camp'. Not in a purely static manner, at least."

"Obviously I couldn't comment on Lord Chelmsford's intentions. He left at four this morning and did not speak to me personally before his departure. He left no correspondence for me to give to you, nor did he say anything. As to orders, all I am aware of is the single command regarding the defense of this place."

I noticed a formality about this discussion, a degree of punctilio beyond the common ceremony that the army expects of two senior officers meeting on official business. The two had the air of awkward dancers waltzing around an issue that they preferred to avoid. What was going on? Who was in charge? Was Durnford taking over command – I thought he was probably the senior man – or simply inquiring what Pulleine was about? For a plain-spoken engineer, phrases like 'pray tell' seemed odd; it was as if he had decided to quote a bit of Jane Austen for our general edification. I decided to ask George Shepstone about it later.

"Pulleine, what intelligence do we have of the Zulu movements?" asked Durnford, most solicitous.

---

41. A *vedette* is a group of mounted scouts, often more or less stationary. The term piquet is similar, although more often used for sentries on foot.

"The first report was from a mounted vedette on the escarpment. The man said that a large Zulu force was advancing towards us over the plateau from a north-easterly direction. That was around eight, or a shade before."

"Seven fifty, sir," interjected Melvill smoothly.

"Yes. Then at nine a few Zulus popped up on a rise at the edge of the Nqutu, beyond that conical hill. They had a peek at us and we at them, before they cleared off. I had a look through my field glasses, couldn't see anything, must've been three miles. We got another rider in from the vedette up beyond the spur. He said the Zulus were moving in three bodies, dense columns. Two of them had gone back the way they came, but the third took off to the north-west. The ground is fairly broken up on the plateau they say – I haven't been there myself – and the scouts could see no more. Being colonial types – I hope you'll excuse me saying this, as I know you command colonials – they tend to be very imprecise in their reporting. No idea of numbers or formations. 'Lots of Kaffirs' is what they say. Still, I expect they have better eyesight than our chaps."

Durnford appeared concerned. "You might wish your men to finish breakfast if it seems that the Zulus are withdrawing. Keep their kit on, of course. That would be my suggestion, no more than that. I don't like the sound of a Zulu sweep to the north-west at all. Let me have a word with my officers, then we'll have breakfast ourselves."

Colonel Durnford's voice was low as he spoke to Cochrane and myself; "Bagshot, will you please tell Mr. Vause to take his troop back to escort the wagons in. I expect the train is still some distance back along the trail. I hope you gentlemen had everything in good order this morning."

We left the two commanders together while Melvill conjured up something superb for breakfast; I hoped he'd keep some aside for us. Anyone who thinks you should force yourself to eat filth just because you are under canvas is an idiot; I fancied kedgeree and devilled kidneys. Cochrane broke my mood:

"I say, Binky, you did shift the piano into another wagon this morning, didn't you?"

"Eh?" I replied. "I thought you were going to do it."

Senior Transport Officer Cochrane's eyes bulged. "Oh, my sainted aunt!" was all he could say.

"Steady on, old man," I replied, "The conductor ought to know when to move loads around. He'll get it sorted out."

"You don't know McCarthy. He has the initiative of a cowpat. Last night I told him to put all the ammunition together into two wagons. I didn't want it divided up between umpteen vehicles. I didn't mention the piano to him because, ah, I didn't trust him to pack it up safely; he's not fond of the choir you know, and, well, I didn't have any confidence in him. I thought you'd put it in a wagon with some nice hay for padding. Bloody hell, if he's got them all in together we'll have eight mules pulling the better part of two tons! They could barely move up the hill from the hospital when we pinch – picked it up."

CHAPTER TWENTY

Brighton 1928

Colonel Bagshot couldn't wait for tea-time, as it happened. When a man pushing an ice-cream cart came along, the Colonel almost leapt to his feet to find some coins in the deeper capacities of his voluminous shorts. "Go and buy yourself one," he told George. "And one for me. Your choice."

As the two of them attended their ices, the Colonel was pensive. "You know," he said, between licks, "This is all a long time ago. Almost fifty years, in fact. I am amazed I remember it so well."

George was amazed as well. Some of the story might even be true.

* * *

My errand run, I returned to the mess tent with hopes of vast breakfasting awash in coffee. Moving through the lines, I saw my old enemy Fitzclarence with another officer. This fellow was obviously the senior and was giving dear Algernon a proper dressing down.

"I don't care who your father is or how much he's got in the bank, if you can't keep track of a few ox-carts you ought to go home to him and your mother. You don't have a valet to fetch and carry everything for you. You have to use your brain. You do have a brain, don't you?"

"Oh, that's so unfair, Essex. All these wagons look exactly alike. And the dwivers are so uncouth."

"Couth ain't the most valuable commodity out here, sonny Jim. And that's Captain Essex if you don't mind."

I enjoyed this considerably.

A rider was approaching from the spur at a canter, the usual grubby colonial on a light bay pony. He needed a shave and a haircut.

Durnford and Pulleine were finished eating and coming out from under canvas. The horseman reined in, announcing himself as a Lieutenant Adendorf of the NNC. He was the type who regarded a good scratch of his beard as an adequate greeting for superior officers; I can't imagine why the army sticks with saluting.

"The Kaffirs iss scuttling back'ds over ve 'igh grarnd," he announced in a strange accent that suggested a keen German making the most of a long weekend in Dartford prison.

"Yes?" said Pulleine, all expectant.

"That's it," answered Adendorff, puzzled-like.

"Give us details, man!" interjected Durnford. It was galling to him that Pulleine's low opinion of colonials was being amply proven right there and then.

"I din't zee 'em mizzelf, zir," – he almost called him 'mate' – "But that's vot the lads up on the plateau zays. A big lut of vem, scurrying abaht ve rocks and grannies. Back'ds, moustly, I reckon. Cattle, too."

Cattle. Irregular colonial horsemen like cattle. Stealing's an art to them. Show a settler a couple of cows and he'd forget any orders he'd been given. If the Lord Almighty appeared to him in a burning bush, your colonial volunteer would only use the light to look for any cattle concealed by the shadows.

Pulleine decided to send an officer, another NNC man, up onto the Nqutu to have a proper reconnaissance. I took my chance to see what I could find to eat. "Got anything good to chew on, Melvill? I'm famished!"

The adjutant laughed. "I see you wasting away before my eyes. We can probably muster some toast or porridge – nothing too spectacular, but you weren't hoping for much, were you?"

Actually, I was, but you can't have dinner at Claridges with the Prince of Wales every day, can you? I stuffed a crust down my gullet and helped myself to a tin plate of what looked like mashed cardboard soaked in oil. Actually, this was probably what the Prince got when he visited mama at Balmoral ---

One of the colonial chaps rode over with a message for me. Durnford wanted me. Immediately. The moment I reported, he gave me his instructions.

"Bagshot, attach yourself to Captain Shepstone for staff duties. Be ready to move in five minutes!"

I'd been riding Benevente, the strawberry roan. She'd done a dozen miles or more this morning. Joseph did me proud once again as he led the chestnut charger out for me to mount. It was sleek and glossy, and I wondered if he'd found a way to wrap a horse in oilskins and stick it in his saddlebags rather than get it muddy trotting along behind him. 'The horse is prepared against the day of battle; but safety is of the Lord.' I think that's from one of the Psalms. My kit was left at the mission, but Joseph had thoughtfully made ready everything a young officer might need to spend a vigorous day of sporting fun looking for Zulus. My field equipment was as follows:

Waterproof cape, one.
Expensive German glasses, on which I have remarked.
Sword, light cavalry pattern.
Small flask of Glenlivet, courtesy of Willie Cochrane, who was coming up in my estimation. Small container of comestibles, horridly inadequate.
Matches, paper, pencil.

You may consider that I think a great deal of my stomach, and I do; I echo the Frenchman who stated that life is too short to drink cheap wine. Still, you can't shove a wheel of Double Gloucester in a saddlebag, or a gallon of good mulligatawny soup. I was carrying the minimum, tea, sugar, salt, a jar of 'Bovril', four ration biscuits and a tin of oysters from Fortnums which I'd won off Coghill in a quick hand of whist. I know you wonder why I tell you this, but it comes in important later.

I strapped on my sword and carefully loaded my revolver. You may wonder why I hadn't done this previous-like; I had a good reason not to run about the veldt with dangerous gunpowder devices. I can ride an ostrich and slice a tossed grapefruit into quarters with a blunt cavalry sabre, but I can't shoot. Anyone or anything that falls to a bullet of mine has drawn the shortest of straws; you'd stand a better chance of dying from the sudden collapse of a Roman aqueduct or being bitten by a black mamba crossing Oxford Circus. Last year, at the home of my chum Tunstall (also deceased, but that had nothing to do with me) in New Mexico I had successfully shown my inability to hit any one of a prodigious number of tin cans laid out for target practice. One lad, Billy Bonney, who seemed like a nice young man and most proficient with firearms, suggested I might try what he termed a double-action revolver. What this meant was that simply pulling on the trigger served to cock and fire the weapon, without any need to pull back the hammer first; that part had always confused me. Billy said that my shooting at clouds served no real purpose, though, of course, in more picturesque American terminology. I was given the choice of a model known extravagantly as 'The Thunderer', which took a rather odd sized cartridge – .41" I think – or a smaller piece entitled 'The Lightning'. Young Bonney thought that the Colt Thunderer would blow a bigger hole in whatever I wasn't intending to shoot at, but the other one was less likely to frighten the life out of me, and consequently bring less danger to my friends. I took the Lightning; you can get .38 cartridges anywhere. Well, not at the corner grocer's shop, though you can probably get 'em there if you're in America. Yankees are mostly bloodthirsty savages, I've told you that.

I didn't take a carbine, though most of Durnford's officers carried them. There didn't seem any point. If I needed to shoot anyone, I'd get one of those obliging African troopers to do it for me. Never be afraid to ask a favour, I always say.

My loins thus girded for war, I took off at a fair clip in pursuit of the open column of horsemen streaming out of the camp. Cochrane called out to me as I passed him – "See if you can't get the wagons up smartish, Binky!" – but it wasn't wagon-ward we were going. No, as I made out George Shepstone up at the front with Charlie Raw, I knew we were headed for the plateau. We cleared the edge of the camp and took off in loose order up the spur, outriders peeling away to the flanks as the ground broadened. Ahead of us was Roberts' troop of native horse, with Captain Barton in the lead; they wheeled left and moved out towards the north-west. Our job was in the other direction, up and over the broken upland to the nor'east.

Cavaye's 'A' company was stretched out along the foot of the spur, facing up onto the plateau. The men were spread in the newfangled skirmishing order, two ranks deep and six feet between files. This meant that the company covered a fair piece of ground and was much less vulnerable to artillery fire or breech-loading rifles than the old shoulder-to-shoulder formation of Wellington's day. The Prussians swore by extended deployment of infantry, and everyone knew they were the scientists of modern war. They'd beaten the French by an innings at least in 1870. Still, it looked damned thing if it ever came to a rush; not just because a close-order line can hold its ground when it comes to the bayonet – neighbour supporting neighbour like the redcoats beating the highland charge at Culloden – but because you can mass a huge mob of fierce men with spears in the space covered by the firing line. It's all to do with the effect of a vast hail of warm lead coming down on the enemy's heads. The arc of a Martini-Henry rifle at a distance is like a rainbow; the bullets fall out of the sky in a quite discouraging manner. The more that come down on a given spot, the more likely it is that the poor bastards underneath will decide to go home. It ain't really a question of killing 'em. It's far better to pot one or two and have the others refuse to come on into the storm of shot than it is to murder half of them and have their mates come and do the same for you. Don't believe anyone who tells you that professional soldiers aim at individual targets; let 'em do that and it'd be bloody chaos. We leave that kind of nonsense to the Boers. I wasn't certain such a slender firing line would be able to put out that kind of volume of nasty little flying things. Still, who was I to know? Charlie Cavaye was waving as I passed. He seemed happy enough.

Lt. Higginson was on his way down from the forward mounted posts. He had a despatch to deliver; actually, I think it was a piece of torn notepaper from inside the band of somebody's hat. "The Zulus are gone, chum," he said. "You'll be lucky to see a-one of them. They've gone off eastwards damn smartish." All these colonial officers talked so common.

 Ahead I could make out the vedettes of Durnford's colonials, a vague rash of single riders in front of a supporting party. Not the proper cavalry scouting system with 'Cossack posts' and linking patrols, but they were only settlers out lifting livestock, when all was said and done.

I caught up with Shepstone. He was silent, scanning the rock-strewn horizon with a small naval glass, intent while Raw bawled out orders in a cheerful mixture of pidgin Nguni – I think that's the name of the language – and taproom English. I was uncertain whether to approach him.

"Er, Captain Shepstone. George. What are we up to?" It seemed a good question, if a touch obvious. "I mean, the colonel and the other colonel and all that?" If you aren't sure how to couch a question, try the route of the babbling imbecile.

He took my meaning. "You mean at the camp. Yes. The extreme diplomacy of it all. What it means is that Durnford is the senior officer, and everyone knows it, but Durnford doesn't want to take the senior man's job, which is the command of the camp. The last thing he desires is to sit down and nursemaid a stores depot. He has the most mobile force in Zululand – and by that I include the Zulus themselves – and wants to use that ability to manoeuvre against the enemy. If he takes Pulleine's post, he takes Pulleine's orders, which are to sit tight. Pulleine, of course, doesn't want to give up his command, even if it's rather a boring set of instructions. No soldier wants to be superceded, you know that."

Of course I did.

We moved across the plateau, the troopers fanning out into little knots like fingers of an outstretched hand. These were Sikali's men, members of a clan known as the Ngwane, related to the Zulu; their grandfathers had been driven up into the hills by the depredations of the Zulu impis, and they were out for blood. Unlike the Christians from the Edendale Mission, the Ngwane wore no boots but rode with their big toes through a small leather stirrup; looked damned painful to me. Each man carried a bunch of assegais and a carbine – an elderly lever-action weapon called the Westley-Richards which our cavalry had tried out in the sixties before the Snider came in; the Edendale men had the Martini-Henry carbine sometimes known as the Swinburne-Henry model, which I was used to with the 10th Hussars. They did not take the same .45 cartridge; the Westley-Richards was a percussion weapon, and you couldn't get the two confused or there would be trouble. Which was really all that mattered to me as the fellow who was responsible for transporting the bloody things. That again ---

There was excitement ahead. A party of riders began moving fast, towards a distant fold in the ground which I couldn't see into. The terrain was like a rumpled bedspread, stitched with all kinds of nips and tucks. I spotted Raw gesturing extravagantly as he called "Tally Ho!", and there was a general surge onward. Firing broke out in a sporadic, enthusiastic sort of fashion. Shepstone had his binoculars up.

"Bagshot! Take a look. This is interesting. We've drawn the fox, or something very like it." He was very calm.

I looked. There were cattle. And men. Zulus!

"Why are they herding cows? I mean, if they are an army out for our hides, why graze their animals?"

"Good question. Maybe that's all anyone has seen, a few herders and a lot of cattle. People get excited, you know, and see whatever they want to. Maybe we've caught the tail end of the impi going away from us. Still, we'll go and have a look at what's going on. In fact, I can't imagine we'd be able to stop the men if we wanted!"

The Zulus had seen us. They were driving their herds away from us as fast as possible. I'd guess they might have been a mile or so ahead, splitting up into smaller groups and pushing on so as to ensure that at least some got away. They were good at this game. The Native Horse were after them, though, and it didn't take a genius to work out that a keen cattle-thief on a pony will catch up with a tricky herdsman on foot, even with broken country in the herder's favour. Cows just don't shift that quickly. They don't see the point. Loyalty isn't a bovine virtue. They don't give a tinker's cuss who owns them. I expect that's one of the few real differences between cattle and British private soldiers.

The chase was on! I have to say the black troopers could show the Southdown Hunt a few tricks in the saddle, taking long strides on the flat and nimbly finding little paths through the rough; still, they'd never be allowed in, being coloureds and all. Also, the Southdown Hunt takes a very dim view of any kind of mounted gunfire. At least, that was what the Master of Hounds told me when they asked me never to return.

Higginson was coming back at a gallop, trying to catch Shepstone. He had another message. They ought to have given him a postman's cap and a nice big bag. He was puffing, I can't imagine why; the horse did all the work. Shepstone reined in and took the note.

"Good news, Binky. Durnford wants us to ride along and push the Zulus out to the east along the plateau. We may catch them on the flat and give 'em a trouncing. Should they elude us, Durnford is advancing the main body of our column out across the plain from the camp towards Chelmsford's position. He wants to prevent the Zulus sneaking up on the General's flank and rear. We'll be in a position to catch the Zulus between two fires. Sound enough idea, I'd say."

We both wheeled our horses, I back towards the chase and Shepstone to confer with Barton and Roberts. The leading troopers were well ahead of us, Charlie Raw close to the fore. The Zulus were driving the herd up an incline, apparently losing the race as the Native Horse hit an open stretch at a gallop. The cattle bunched and stood as their guards dropped behind the crestline. One trooper, cocky as you like at the head of the field, clipped up to take possession of the livestock. He stopped dead at the ridge.

 I was moving up fast – the charger had a good stride on the hard-upland turf – and saw the Ngwane's muscles tense as he stood in his toe-stirrup. You wouldn't do that for fun. He was staring out ahead in disbelief, craning his neck in case his eyes deceived him. His face paled to grey. Raw pulled up beside him, jocular vulgarity dying on his lips. My horse's gait slackened as I came alongside. I looked out on a deep ravine, chiseled into the plateau floor. Twenty thousand Zulu warriors looked back at me. They seemed to be quite upset at our intrusion. Words came out of me without thinking, as if I'd wandered into the wrong bedroom by mistake.

"Oops, sorry!"

CHAPTER TWENTY ONE

Brighton 1928

George had burrowed into the sand with his pathetic childhood spade, and the ravine was ready. Colonel Bagshot handed him boxes upon red boxes of soldiers. All were Zulus. There were Zulus with assegais and Zulus with knobkerries (this being a very nasty-looking club, as he explained it), Zulus running and Zulus throwing and Zulus thrusting. There was a Zulu chief, an induna, on horseback; George noted that he was actually the top half of a Zulu soldered roughly onto the legs of some unfortunate cavalryman whose tall jack boots had been filed into submission. The telltale streaks of greasy colour identified the questionable brushwork of the besieged Gurkha orderly.

"Well, don't sit gawking. Put 'em in the ravine."

* * *

The Zulus were stirred up, right enough. Imagine putting your foot in the biggest, angriest ant-hill in history. Imagine the ants have asked all their relatives over for tea and the whole lot decide to come out and remonstrate loudly with you about it. Imagine the ants are at least as big as you and armed with unpleasant sharp items. There was absolutely no chance of giving 'em a shilling and telling 'em to forget they'd ever seen us.

Joseph had joined me, silently. He'd acquired a straw hat with a red rag around it, and a couple of spears; I'd not noticed him at all amongst the Ngwane horsemen. He scanned the impi impassively; I'd no doubt it was the main impi. God alone knew who Chelmsford was chasing miles out towards the east. We'd followed Durnford's plan to run down a fox and found ourselves shoving our head into a lion's mouth. Or, as Joseph put it in equally veterinary terms:

"Darkness conceals the hippopotamus."

"Shut up," I replied, without any great wit. I wasn't in the mood for the wisdom of Zulu proverbs. The Natal Native Horse was behaving admirably for a small group of men who had just tapped twenty thousand of their worst enemies on the shoulder. Some fired their carbines from horseback, working the levers as they controlled the ponies with their knees. Others dropped from the saddle and let off shots from a kneeling position, reins looped around their biceps. Raw was drawing up a firing line, booming out orders. I gave them credit for the effort. Still, it was like throwing clods of dirt at an oncoming locomotive.

"Those are the umCijo," said Joseph, "Sometimes known as uKhandempemvu. Twenty-eight years old, bachelors, convinced they can overrun the whole of creation. Silly bastards. You'll know them by their black shields. Off over there, with the white shields, are the uKhulutshane. The uDududu are the fellows with the white spot on a black shield. The Nokhenke and isAngquboth have white shields, but when they get closer I shall point out the relevent differences in insignia."

I once heard an Oxford don explain the different effects of snake poisons after he'd been bitten by a black mamba, cool as you like as it killed him within minutes. But academics are supposed to be like that, and he knew he was already done for once the fangs had gone in. Joseph was a Natal herdboy. He wasn't meant to look his own death in the teeth and analyse the details. He was expected to brown his breeches and scarper. And – I realised – he'd suddenly begun speaking in the most fluent English. Very odd.

The Zulus were firing as they came boiling up to the brow, wild shots from ancient muskets. Still, one horse was down, and a rider was flopped out at the rim, carbine flung aside. Raw had the NNH dropping back in pairs, one firing to cover his partner's retreat. He was doing well, I thought, but it was a vain effort if he expected to hold the enraged hubble-bubble of warriors from coming on. Taut volleys crashed out. Zulus died and were trampled by their comrades' advance. The umCijo were making a weird drone, a kind of hissing between the teeth while beating the backs of their shields. I sang a few bars of something from HMS Pinafore, but my heart wasn't in it, and began the last verse of "Nearer my God to thee", which seemed more appropriate. A burly Zulu in full ceremonial fig was shouting rhythmically against the beat of his soldiers' drumming. He fell, and another took up the chant. One man called out to us. It was a taunt, I knew, from the tone of it. Sarcastic sod. Joseph grinned.

"He says 'come AmaMangwane' – that's what they call the mounted black men – 'come AmaMangwane and eat with the umCijo. Come match our appetites.' He is a funny fellow."

Carbines cracked together near me; a small man in a battered grey hat was making great sport with his Westley-Richards, smacking over Zulus with a great yell of joy, and berating himself in dialect each time he missed. He seemed to be hitting his targets more often than not. It was useless, of course, and the leapfrogging backwards kept on. Charlie Raw was everywhere, congratulating his troopers on their shooting, slapping nervous men on the back, playing the country squire at a summer fete. Retreat is the hardest of manoeuvres to pull off; too slow and the enemy chews your backside, too fast and pretty soon you have a general run for the rear.

Shepstone was up with us. He had several men with him, Natal Carbineers from the vedette. Long faced and lugubrious, George Shepstone hadn't cracked a smile since I'd met him, and was not about to break out a toothy grin at this sudden swing of fortune. The muscles in his throat were like cables. "Not good at all", was all he could say as to our situation; "Not at all." Hard to disagree, really. A musket ball slapped into a carbineer saddlebag, spent and harmless, but still discouraging. George Shepstone was giving instructions to his colonials to find Durnford, then turned to shout.

"Captain Raw. We've got our hands full here. Please keep our guests occupied as best you can. Mr. Bagshot and I will go to the camp and request assistance. No unnecessary heroics. Delay the Zulus as best you can."

There was a confidence in his words that his expression belied. Shepstone knew bad luck when it sat down in his parlour. We galloped back across the plateau, with Joseph and a civilian named Jim Hamer who was a chum of George's; he'd evidently come along for the sight-seeing, which shows how lightly we'd all taken the affair. All except Shepstone.

We rode like bloody lunatics. There's really no good time to be chased by the whole Zulu army.

It was four miles back to the head of the spur, which we seemed to cover in about eight minutes. Damn quick, anyway. As we reached the rim of the upland, I saw how things stood. Cavaye had stretched a little thinner, pitching a platoon out to the left. The rest of the camp was restful as before. Evidently Pulleine had no inkling that anything was amiss. I couldn't see Durnford's mounted command anywhere among the tents and wagons.

We plunged down the slope, legs-a-gallop through the interval between Cavaye's A Company and the detached platoon. Young Dyson waved; we didn't stop. Then we were amongst the tents, breathless, snorting, tails swishing. That was just me. Shepstone, especially, looked done up, and the horses were exhausted. Someone called Pulleine from the H.Q. tent; as we waited for him to emerge, an officer appeared from the other direction, travel-stained astride the proverbial lathered horse. He had a hussar's patrol jacket on.

"Gardner, 4th Hussars," he announced. "Message from his Lordship for Colonel Pulleine."

Firing broke out behind us, from the direction of the spur; controlled volleys, infantry volleys.

Pulleine stepped out of the tent. He looked at both sets of visitors expectantly. Shepstone was breathless, choking. He pointed towards the spur in agitated fashion. The words wouldn't come. He kept waving off towards the distance.

Gardner handed over his dispatch. Martini fire cracked again and again to our north. Pulleine read.

"His lordship wants us to send on the camping kit and supplies to his force immediately. He's out in the Mangeni valley. We are told to remain here ourselves and entrench the position." His brow furroughed. The message was rather like getting a new collar and leash for a dog that had died the previous day – quite sensible, except for certain key details. Pulleine wasn't the kind of man to simply disregard orders, but he wasn't so pig-headed as to completely ignore reality. Gardner took the initiative. "You sir," – he evidently didn't know Shepstone – "I think you have something important to say to us." Well, of course he did. He hadn't come down that hill as if the Devil was after him just because he wanted a jam scone and a pot of tea.

Still, I knew what Gardner meant.

George Shepstone had his breath back, almost. He was still a bit glassy-eyed and kept jabbing his finger in the direction of the spur. He swallowed hard and spoke with quite deliberate control.

"I am not an alarmist, sir, but the Zulus are in advancing in masses over there. They are driving our men this way. It is a matter of the gravest urgency."

Pulleine's face tightened, jaws draining of colour. He made a little strangled noise between his teeth. I recall this as being the last I ever saw of him: I don't think he was at his best.

"Ah, Colonel Pulleine," said Gardner, "I'm not absolutely certain you need follow his Lordship's instructions at this time." Damn smooth, almost like Teignmouth Melvill. Well put, I thought.

"No," agreed Pulleine. "Quite. Let me send a note to Lord Chelmsford." A note was written, which I recall, since I was leaning over Pulleine's shoulder as he scribbled.

Staff Officer. Heavy firing to the left of our camp. Cannot move camp at present.

For a moment I was afraid he'd want me to run the message and miss out on all the fun. Fortunately, as I thought at the time, he had an available rider close at hand. Then he ordered the alarm to be sounded, the second time today. Everyone came out of their tents as Pulleine went back into his. Officers ran about.

The companies were drawn up on the parade ground, such as it was, in front of the camp. Billy Mostyn was beginning to move his lads, 'F' company, up in support of Charlie Cavaye on the spur. Colonel's order, I presume, though I don't know what the plans were. I was still with Shepstone and friends. George was still in poor condition; I suppose he'd been twice the distance across the plateau that I had, and I'd taken a fresh horse under me an hour previously, where he hadn't. You'd be surprised at the difference that makes.

"Binky," George Shepstone wheezed, "Go and get word to Durnford. Follow his tracks out across the valley. He can't be too far away. Let him know what a hornet's nest we've bumped into. Check on the rocket battery too – it's always lagging behind. If it's dragging about somewhere on the plain distant from the rest of the force you might suggest to Major What's-his-name that he bring his rocket crews back to camp if it looks like he's getting too far from support; I shouldn't want him to get caught in the open. Use my authority if you need. I expect there'll be blame enough to go round later, so tell 'em Captain Shepstone's responsible. Now, go!" He was gasping.

The companies of infantry were still drawn up under arms with belts and stained helmets. I cantered past them, racing across the parade ground wreathed in a cloud of my own dust – in South Africa you have either mud or dust, depending on whether it has rained today – and headed onto the plain. I was stern-jawed, determined, stupidly exhilarated. I wasn't looking where I was going.

"Mind who you run over you silly sod!" yelled a voice I recognized.

I didn't mean to trample Teignmouth Melvill. I liked him. If I actually caught him with a hoof-clip he took it well. "Sorry Melvill. Urgent message for Durnford." I didn't stop.

"Alright, Binky. Glad to see somebody has a sense of urgency, anyway. By the way - - -"

I was galloping past, even before he finished speaking. I think it was something about owing him a drink later on. Or about being slaughtered to the last man. Surely not, though. I put my spurs to the charger and leaned onto its neck.

CHAPTER TWENTY-TWO

Brighton 1928

George was concentrating on placing the model horsemen into the channel he had scraped in the sand. The mounted figures had no bases but relied on the balance of each piece on its little lead feet. He had to push them into the wet sand to get them to stand. This was really no great task, but somehow it was easier to make a grand effort over the job than to look directly at the Colonel. The old man was singing a nonsensical chant while slapping a sporadic beat on his scrawny thigh.

"Um – bap -a, Um -bap -a ----"

George furrowed his brow and moved a handful of the glossy, red-coated infantry – the 24th, of course – out from the space in front of the paper tents. There were a group of small children gathered behind Colonel Bagshot, sniggering softly. A surly ten-year old was mimicking the Colonel, while another was presenting his version of an African war-dance to the world at large. Bagshot was completely oblivious.

George shook his head.

* * *

Sometimes it takes a lot for me to remember that war's not all beer and skittles. Seeing the rocket battery cut to pieces under a wave of Zulu warriors was like a glass of cold water full in the face.

I'd bounded across the valley toward the Conical Hill, as history has come to call it, a mile due east of the camp. There was a vedette of Natal Carbineers on the summit, I knew. A trooper came scrabbling down on foot, pointing fiercely around the base of the koppie towards the north-east. Panic was etched into his face. "Thousands of the bleedin' Zulus! I seen 'em. We're done for! Doomed!" I swear he fairly gurgled at the end of this diatribe. Melodramatic cretin! "Doomed I tells yer!" What hogwash. The man was in a blue funk. Battle hardly begun and he's demoralised already. "His hands were feeble," as it says in second Samuel. Typical bloody colonials. Good men would have paid hard cash for the view from the Conical Hill that day, I was certain, and this windy bastard can only whine. No moral fibre. Damned discreditable I called it.

"I'm looking for Colonel Durnford," I told him, snappish. I wanted no more of his blether. He kept pointing in his useless way. I rode on. A few moments later I saw what the Carbineer had viewed, that terrified him so.

I don't quite know how or why Major Francis Russell of the Royal Artillery had taken a path to the north of the Conical Hill. I expect that he was trying to avoid the broken ground where the little ravines – 'dongas' wasn't it? – cut into the plain. Probably it seemed like a short cut to catch up with Durnford's horsemen who were racing off ahead. I saw the battery in the distance, moving laboriously up towards the hill that I remembered Joseph had called iTusi, and the broad notch where the plateau knelt down onto the valley floor. The notch – the whole rim – was awash with Zulus, pouring down. It was like someone slowly upending a chest of tea onto the carpet. They had a chant, "Usutu! Usutu!" and made a pounding rhythm by beating on the backs of their shields. More were coming out of a donga between the Conical Hill and iTusi, the sneaking swines. I've no idea how they got there. They were between me and Russell, swarming like ants.

I'll give the man his due. The rocket gear was off the mules in a trice; one tube flashed deep into the mass of warriors. Whoosh! It didn't do a damned thing. Bloody ridiculous things, rockets. The Zulus were the same chaps I'd seen up with Charlie Raw on the plateau, the regiment young Joe called the umCijo; bachelors, blades, hotheads. They fired a rough salvo from no more than the length of a cricket pitch. Russell fell, clearly dead. Some of the men, the soldiers, with him were shot down too. The battery mules took off, stampeded, right into the native company behind. The Kaffirs fired once in a hopeless kind of fashion and ran themselves, with the exception of a handful who stuck with their officer; it was Captain Nourse, as I could see now, shooting with a rifle at the Zulu flank as the umCijo surged by. The Zulus all ignored him in favour of rushing towards Russell's stricken battery, blades-a-glittering and making most undignified noises. I'd pulled up, to take in the scene of destruction for a moment.

I recall one moment above all from that horror. Two of the battery mules, panicked, had clambered up onto a rock – a solitary outcrop – and stood there baying piteously while the umCijo swamped the battery, stabbing the fallen bodies and smashing up everything as they passed. Finishing the task to their own satisfaction, the black mass of warriors surged onwards. I took a deep swig of Cochrane's Glenlivet and did the same, spurring the horse forward into a gallop.

I found Durnford easily enough. It's no great task to spot a one-armed man on a prancing pony as he conducts a fighting retreat of three troops of mounted riflemen in front of a wall of enraged Bantu spearmen. Couldn't miss him. The mounted natives were falling back by sections, each buying a few yards with volleys from the saddle while the others withdrew. Hadn't I just come from a precisely similar situation up on the plateau? I ought to be more careful about these things. Durnford was in his element, cheering on each volley and waving his stage-brigand's hat.

"Good show, Solomon! Oh, fine shooting, Ezekiel!" They all had good Old Testament names, these mission lads. It was like a fond schoolmaster encouraging his pupils at cricket or rugger. Made me proud to be British. Well, I'm always proud to be British.

"Hello Bagshot, how d'ye do?" asked Durnford. "Got a message for me?"

"Yes sir. Shepstone sent me. I'm to tell you that there's Zulus all over the plateau chasing our men back to the camp."

"You don't say? Well fancy that?" He darkened, levity falling away. Sarcasm don't get you far in life. "Zulus all over the plateau. Is the camp secure, do you think? "

"Don't know sir. Colonel Pulleine was sending another company up onto the spur as I left."

"Another company! Good God, is he sending out single companies to face this onslaught? Have you seen how many of the beggars there are?"

I'm not sure he wanted me to answer that, so I spoke low. "Word is that it's the whole impi. The entire Zulu army."

He winced. "We'd best pull back and make what kind of stand we can. We'll occupy the line of the donga, use it like a trench and get the horses under cover. We may be able to keep 'em off for a bit while Pulleine sorts out the defence of the camp. If the rocket battery would get here, it would certainly help."

"Ah, sir, I saw the Zulus overrun Major Russell's battery not ten minutes ago. Up towards the notch over there." I pointed to my left. Durnford's jaw tightened.

"I see, yes. Stick to me, Bagshot. I think we're in for a tight innings this afternoon. I'll want you close by."

The Zulus were smacking the backs of their shields and murmuring like crickets. It was as if they would not advance into the rain of bullets but would not retire either. Instead they stood, some crouching or dodging, others leaning forward into the storm. Odd, how people do that.

As I turned the chestnut to make a scurry for the donga, I saw that we had friends awaiting us. The vedettes from the Conical Hill, together with some Natal coppers, were lining the eastern bank of the watercourse. I spotted the character I'd been somewhat short with earlier. Evidently, he'd regained his composure. I shouted out "Good Man", encouraging-like, but he was playing with the mechanism of his carbine. Durnford told me to go, and I went.

Mounted fire is always less effective than shooting on foot. The horses don't like guns going off right next to their ears, so they skit about like bunnies if you're not careful. Even if you can persuade the blighters to stand still, you don't have a stable platform to take aim. That's what they tell me, anyway. Makes no odds when it's me pulling the trigger; I could be prone behind a sandbag wall or hanging by the bootlaces from one of Baron Zeppelin's contraptions and make the same miserable target score. Anyway, we were in the donga after a brisk bolt for the rear, clearing a decent gap between us and the foe. The horses were under cover of the bank, a natural entrenchment which the men used as a parapet to fire over. The donga wasn't nearly as wet as I'd expected; the water runoff had sluiced down the narrow channel towards the Buffalo River as it rained, drying out with today's sunshine. Of course, the rushing water would mean the Buffalo would be in full spate. I made a mental note to avoid crossing the river today. It'd be damn near impassible.

Once again, the Native Horsemen were shooting at the Zulu impi, scything down the savages left and right. It was having an effect too. The Zulus were humming again, the front ranks kneeling behind the massive cowskin shields and beating on the leather. The devilish call-and-response song echoed from one company to another, incessantly rhythmic and near as bad as that damned Boche Wagner. I saw an induna stand up – another big chap, well-nourished in the belly department – get up and jabber something to his men. I could hear him from four hundred yards; he must have had a dickens of a set of lungs, perfect colour- sergeant material. "And cried with a loud voice, as when a lion roareth: and when he had cried, seven thunders uttered their voices," as Revelation has it. The effect was rather ruined when a twelve-pound shell landed about a furlong from him, and he ducked down quick as anything. "The guns, thank God, the guns", to quote young Rudyard Kipling, though he hadn't written that yet. He was still at school in 1879.

The shelling was rather a positive step, I thought. I peered about behind me and saw that a section of two guns – the only section of guns – had opened up in our support. There's a tremendous moral advantage in having massive iron engines of destruction weigh in with death-dealing explosions at the other chap's expense.

"Take that you black bastards!" I shouted; the men on either side of me stared in my direction, ebony faces glowering. "Er, no, not you lads. Splendid work all round." I don't imagine that any of the Natal Native troopers spoke really fluent English, but I suspect that the phrase 'You black bastard' was one they might have been familiar with. Poor choice of words on my part, really. Nothing wrong with a well-chosen taunt, but there's absolutely no point in offending your friends, however inadvertently.

There was another piece of good news behind us. Pulleine had deployed a company of the 24th a little to our left, though naturally some hundred yards in our rear. They were stretched out in a firing line, volleys blasting out against the Zulus massed to our flank. The range was long – more than half a mile – but the effect was to force the Zulus down into the passive noisiness that I, for one, found infinitely more amenable than their athletic assaultiveness. In fact, I was beginning to get an ear for the tune.

It was all going jolly well. They, being the Zulus, made a motion to get up and advance, and in return we shot down the more enthusiastic proponents of attack. You'd be surprised at the effect of those soft-nosed .450 slugs on muscle and bone; very unpleasant for the receiver, damned exhilarating for the deliverer. Hurt your bloody shoulder though, kick like a carthorse. As it says in Psalm 64, "But God shall shoot at them with an arrow; suddenly shall they be wounded." The blighters ought to be happy that the Lord smiteth not with a Martini-Henry, but I suppose the Almighty has a pretty tight code of fair play.

The officers were rousing their men on; I could see Vause, who had brought up the last of the wagons, still on his pony at the far end of the donga, and Harry Davis with his Edendale men. But it was that least likely of bold cavaliers, Cochrane, who surprised me. He came up from behind.

"Er, Binky, old man. Could I have a word with you?" He had lowered his voice. "Let's no' let Durnford overhear." We took a couple of steps towards the rear wall of the ravine. Durnford had other things to keep him occupied besides our conversation. "What, Man?"

"I sent a dozen men under a non-com to bring ammunition up twenty minutes ago. They've no' come back. I had a word with Vause regarding the wagons he brought in, and he admits he doesn't know where they were left. He spurred on at the head of his troop to join up with us when the first wagons were coming into the park area. He says that a couple of the wagons at the back of the column were very sticky indeed, but, since he saw no Zulus about, he thought they'd be alright to get in on their own. Would ye mind going to find out what in blue blazes is going on?"

"You're thinking of the piano at a time like this?"

"Oh, hang the piano. I'm thinking the bloody piano's caused the ammo reserve to sink in a bog somewhere back along the road. Seriously, Bink: I'm from the Highlands; I've seen carts melt into the peat in a minute. That's all the spare cartridges we have."

"Steady on." I said, the voice of reason and all that. "Probably McCarthy the conductor fellow got it into the wagon park all safe and sound. Probably just won't hand it over without an officer being present, you know these types. Either that or the men are trying to carry 80lb boxes on the backs of their saddles. You know how literal they are. I'll be back in a jiffy. I'm sure it will all be fine."

As I said, the voice of reason.

CHAPTER TWENTY-THREE
Brighton 1928

The Colonel was grabbing figures by the handful, pulling companies – each actually only a half-dozen glinting pieces – back towards the paper tents and urging George to shove his Zulus onwards.

"Hurry, man, hurry! These laddies are savage, man-killing gladiators! They move at the speed of a Brighton bus! Push 'em into the gaps – those are the Mbonambi – and run those chaps, the umCijo and uNokhenke, down off the plateau. Don't sit on the plateau, you fool, you'll knock half of it down --- that's it, chase Durnford's horse with the iNgomabakhosi and swing the uVe round the left flank, which is the right flank of our boys. Aha! That's the picture!"

George wasn't sure what was going on. It was quite possible that the Colonel was getting ahead of the story. He moved the toy soldiers, knocking some over – the horses really didn't want to stay standing – according to the wild gesticulations that the old man was making. Colonel Bagshot had been telling him about wagons and a piano. Now it was all "Move those Zulus!"

"The wagons, sir?"

"Don't have any model wagons. Too expensive, and they only make 'em with horse teams, not oxen. Just use the boxes the Zulus came in."

* * *

They were a forlorn band, those Sotho troopers. I knew that something was badly wrong when I came up, the men squatting by their ponies, stirring the dirt with sticks and grumbling amongst themselves. They were clumped sadly on the near side of the wagon park, in front of the orderly ranks of wagons arranged for the trip back to Rorke's Drift. I couldn't see any of our own vehicles, not that one looks any different from another.

121

"Where's your N.C.O?" I asked, loudly, them being basically foreigners, as you'll understand. The NNH men leapt to their feet and saluted. "Gone quartermaster," said one. "Red soldier quartelmaster," added another, helpfully. Mission English is a bit lacking. "No find ours."

"No find ours!" I replied, stupidly. "What on earth do you mean?"

"It means what he says," chimed in an English voice. It was Captain Essex, the transport man for the main column. I recognized him as the man who'd been quarrelling with Fitzclarence earlier. "Apparently your wagons came in late and have been, ah, mislaid." He said this with disgust rather than apology. "Lieutenant Fitzclarence has put 'em away somewhere. Safe as houses, no doubt. If you can find Fitzclarence, I imagine it will all be dandy. He's hiding from me. I think he's sulking."

This was just what I needed. The pipsqueak Fitzclarence had gone and lost my wagons. Useless fool! Then I brightened. It wasn't my fault at all! It was his! Revenge being a sweet thing, I had it in mind to swagger manfully through the officers' tent lines. I'd hear a muffled sobbing from within a foppishly decorated marquee. Ripping aside the canvas – no, silk – flaps, I'd seize Fitzclarence as he sat at his Chippendale bureau. I believe I had already smashed up this fine piece of camping equipment earlier, during the incident with the prancing charger, but a man's allowed to imagine the details of his daydreams ain't he? He'd be all teary-eyed over a letter to his mother, asking dear mater if she could talk to Prime Minister Disraeli about the shameful way he was being treated. I'd smack his fat head a few times to stop the blubbering, pull him to his feet all-a-whimper. He'd apologize copiously, his cringing manner nauseating, but – my being a clean-bred Englishman and all – I'd have none of it. "You sniveling cur!" I'd cry (I really enjoyed that bit), "Stand up like a man and give me back my ox-carts!" I wasn't sure about that last part: perhaps "Unhand my baggage wagons!" sounded better. I'd thump him about the head and shoulders a couple more times, at any rate. Certainly I would.

A noble picture, but it would have to wait. "We'll borrow a few boxes of cartridges from the 24th," I said. "If each pair of riders carries a box slung between them, we'll have, er, quite a few bullets to be going on with." Arithmetic's never been my strong point.

The N.N.H. sergeant was trying to barter with the Quartermaster of the 1/24th. The process really wasn't going anywhere for either one of them. The Q.M., a solid, middle-aged veteran was passing packets of ammunition to a mob of bandsmen, servants, anyone sent back from the firing line for replenishment. His assistant was trying to coax them into an orderly queue, alternately cursing their manners and bribing them with an extra packet. "Quieten down, you lot!" commanded the Quartermaster, "You can mill about, squealing like pigs if yer like, don't mean yer'll get yer rations any quicker." What surprised me was that they fell silent immediately.

The Q.M. glanced at the troop sergeant, who was begging sorrowfully. "Please borrow me cartridge for Colonel Durnford. Give back tomorrow. Need now." The N.N.H. sergeant was almost crying. As it says in Lamentations, "The young children ask for bread, and no man breaketh it unto them." The Quartermaster broketh no ammunition unto the pleading Sotho.

"Sorry, mate. These cartridges are solely for the use of the 1st Battalion, 24th Foot. I 'ave to haccount for every single one against the totals in me ledgers. I can't just lend you a few boxes 'til tommorer. They'd 'ave my bleedin' guts fer garters. It's not like givin' yer a cup of sugar, understand?"

The agitated Natal fellow was evidently not going to win this argument. I knew that only the calm assurance of a British officer would soon solve the difficulty. I was wrong.

"I say Q.M., can't you help the fellow out? You have my word I'll smoothe out any difficulties," I said.

"No sir, like I was tellin' your Kaffir, these cartridges belongs to the 1/24th. Unless you can give me a properly signed chit from Colonel Glyn or Lt. Colonel Pulleine, I can't 'and over nuffink. Sorry, but there it is."

You must understand that a battalion quartermaster is not simply some kind of military bureaucrat. A quartermaster is most likely a senior N.C.O. promoted to a strange sort of commission akin to a working-class Jehovah who, having made heaven and earth, has decided to keep a precise, detailed inventory of its contents. Arguing with him was like Pharaoh telling the Red Sea to remain parted another half-hour while he got the chariots over.

"Now, see here old bean" – not an auspicious beginning, I admit – "Surely you won't miss a few boxes on a purely temporary basis. I promise I shall return them, you have my word on it. Officer and gentleman and all that."

That wasn't too bright on my part. Commissioned rankers look for criticism in anything anyone says to them. The quartermaster was a burly, commanding man with a moustache like two clothes-brushes. They twitched alarmingly.

"And 'oo might you be, sir; the Duke of Marlborough?" he demanded, not waiting for my answer. "I 'ave been a soldier in 'er Majesty's army, man and boy, since before you was even a nipper. I've been a colour-sergeant, instructor of musketry, and sarn't major, all in this battalion, since before the Crimean War. After twenty-eight years I fully understand that I am expected to safeguard every round of ammunition, piece of equipment and any sundry article issued or allotted to my battalion. Is that alright with you, sirrr?" He slung an eighty-pound box to his assistant, one handed, like a loaf of bread.

The last words were spoken with the gravity, and most of the volume, of a water buffalo plummeting off a bridge. What could I say?

"Oh, but hang it all. There's Zulus all over."

"That, my fine young gentleman, is why I am keeping my battalion's ammunition supply available in its hentirity for the sole usage therof. The lads is going to need it. As you say, there's Zulus all over."

Something across the valley caught his attention.

"Lieutenant, I believe that your native pals is coming back to collect their ammunition in person. I would suggest that diligent efforts, on your part, to locate the missing vehicles would quite possibly be much happreciated. Meanwhile, as you can hobserve, I am a busy man."

I followed his cool gaze across the valley. The Natal Native Horse was in full retreat towards the camp. This was clearly not a good sign.

CHAPTER TWENTY-FOUR
Brighton 1928

Colonel Bagshot mopped his bald head. It was hot; he absent-mindedly put his pith helmet down on top of George's carefully sculpted sand incarnation of Isandlwana Mountain. "Damn!" he cursed. He looked over the panorama on laid out before him.

"Nobody can say for certain the order of events that day. I've heard it said that Mostyn and Cavaye's companies were hit in the flank and wiped out where they stood. Others contend that most of 'em were still fighting as they fell back on the tents. I'm showing it that way. It's possible that the north of the camp was falling even before Durnford retired. Everybody agrees the Natal Natives ran away as quick as you like, but nobody remembers where it was they ran away from. Damned if I know, I was arguing with the bloody quartermaster."

George was having difficulty working out which group of Zulus belonged to which amabutho. There were about twenty toy soldiers to each, but the Colonel kept throwing lumps of wet sand to knock them over, shouting 'bang!' in a spirited but – thought George – extremely unrealistic fashion. Sometimes they'd fall over in the act of moving them, and George would stand them up swiftly before Colonel Bagshot pronounced them dead from 'artillery fire' or some such invention. At last the colonel pronounced himself satisfied with the layout. The surviving red and green 24th – for he'd knocked over a few – were hauled back close to the tents, with the exception of a single group placed out on the flat sand towards the position previously occupied by Durnford's Horse. The NNH had been the first thing George had moved before the Zulu onslaught.

The Colonel took a silver flask from one of his ballooning hip pockets, swigged deeply, and pointed at the single company alone on the damp sand by his outstretched foot.

"That's Charlie Pope's company of the 2nd Battalion. I'd say they were truly buggered, wouldn't you, Georgie? Pull back the chaps on the flank so's they can put up a last fight. Oh, right, these Natal Kaffirs would have run off by now, so bung some Mbonambi through the gap. Get a few into the tents."

He frowned and reached into the Gladstone bag.

"I'll have to use these guardsmen for the camp servants, got no more 24th. Oh" – he brightened perceptibly – "This fella is me."

It was a superb figure, a mounted hussar in full dress on a rearing steed. The white plume stood boldly forth on the furred busby[42]; the gold lace across the chest was immaculate. The face was ferociously moustachio'd, pink-cheeked, with black eyelashes. It had not been painted by a talentless Gurkha orderly with improvised brushes and a pot of goat's blood for the red details. It was magnificent, vaguely Teutonic in manner, varnished to a deep sheen. It looked like Colonel Bagshot too, younger of course, with one exception. It was noticeably bigger than any of the other figures. The Colonel was, himself, five feet seven at the most generous estimate.

"A present from the Kaiser," whispered the Colonel. "Before we had the big falling out."

George thought this probably referred to the events of August 1914 but didn't ask. It might have been a personal altercation over the billiards table. You never knew.

* * *

All was chaos. Sheer bloody chaos. As the Natal Native Horse came back, no longer leap-frogging to fire and retire, but bounding headlong for the camp, I heard one of those whispers that comes as a roar.

"The Zulus are in the camp!"

Rumour has a life of its own. Fearful tales were rampant among the mass of bandsmen pressing the Quartermaster for cartridges. I heard that Cavaye's company had been overrun, or was still holding the front, or was being forced back against the tents. The foot natives had broken. The artillery was in flight and the camp was encircled. A sense of cataclysm was quite real. The Quartermaster had taken charge of the moment, pushing packets of ammunition into hands, hats, helmets, without question or requisition. The 'casuals' – cooks, servants, all the soldiers whose place was in the camp rather than the firing line – were making their way towards the sound of battle. Sick men staggered gamely from the hospital tent, dragging themselves into combat. Officers' orderlies worked

---

42. A busby is the flat-topped fur cap worn by hussar regiments; it is smaller than the more familiar fur cap of the Brigade of Guards, and features a plume at the front and a cloth hanging bag from the top.

the unfamiliar mechanisms of rifles, anxiously reciting the drills that their privileged positions had so often excused them. As these men advanced into the fray, others moved away from it. The ragged natives of the foot companies, despised by all, abandoned all pretense at soldierliness and slipped in ones and twos through the tent lines, weaponless towards home. Panic fought with avarice in the eyes of civilian drivers, torn between immediate flight and the chance to steal something before they left. A trooper of the Basuto Horse, then a cluster more of them, clipped past from the direction of the spur. I recognized one, a slender light-skinned chap with bushman's eyes who I'd watched as he shot down an induna of the umCijo on the heights – what, half an hour ago? These were Charlie Raw's men, then. Good men. Men who hadn't looked like their nerve would break. I hailed the fellow:

"Trooper! Are you deserting your post?"

He slowed. "Mister Raw say go now. Go! All up!" He fingered his cartridge pouch and slack bandolier. Empty. Raw must have given them permission to leave. It wasn't their fight, after all. Then he was gone, with more following in his dust.

"Bagshot! Good news!" shouted Alfred Henderson. He had found the ammunition wagon. "Over behind the tent lines, completely hidden. I had to argue with some twerp in a green coat about it. Wouldn't see reason. Asked who I thought I was and said that Lord Chelmsford's secretary would hear about my attitude. That was before I kicked him. Stuck up little wazzock."

I wanted to congratulate Henderson, but his discovery was too late to do us any good as far as holding the line of the donga. Now I had boxes and boxes of ammunition ready to give away, and the recipients had already buggered off for lack of a handful of bullets.

This was not absolutely the truth, though I was disconcerted to see my own ammunition party had cleared off with Raw's men. I said a few choice words, to nobody in particular, and turned to Henderson.

"Let me go and find some more of our boys. You bring the wagon up, and we'll get the ammo reserve through to Durnford yet!" Never say die, and all that.

"How d'you expect me to do that, you sodding half-wit?" expostulated Henderson. Uncalled for, I thought. "There are no mules for it. Christ alone knows where they've gone. No conductors either – that drunken bastard McCarthy's probably pissed off to Pietermaritzburg with all our gold watches – and to top it all, some cretin's left a bloody piano on top of the ammunition boxes! What fatheaded fool put that there, can you imagine?"

127

I told him I couldn't. "Do what you can. Back in a tick," I told him. Then I was back in the saddle, spurring Waterloo towards – where? Into a swirling mob of humanity, the incessant clamour of battle banging in my ears. The volley fire, so comforting, had been overtaken by a confusion of single shots. For the first time I saw groups of redcoats falling backwards into the camp lines, pressed hard by howling warriors. Still the men kept their discipline, clumping back to back around the tents, Martinis cracking fire. Horace Smith-Dorrien was jemmying his way into ammunition boxes – he didn't know how they opened – over by the tents of the 2-24th. Essex was on the ammunition issue, too. The northern part of the camp, which comprised the Natal Native lines, was lost. There were black figures swarming everywhere. A tent went up in flames. Wardell and Porteous' companies, or what remained of them, were holding the eastern face against the onslaught of the umCijo and umHlanga. There were animals running hither and yon. One caught my eye. It was a fine chestnut horse, part thoroughbred, one white sock. Fitzclarence's cherished mount, bounding away without him. I told you never to trust a horse with one white stocking: still, if I'd been Fitzclarence's charger, I'd have buggered off for foreign parts at the first opportunity. I laughed aloud, which elicited a strange look from a wounded corporal carrying ammunition to what remained of the firing line. Meanwhile the battle itself – the actual blood and guts part of it – was probably a hundred yards from me. I was headed in the wrong direction, I saw. I needed to find Durnford's command, which must be somewhere behind me – damn, what was I thinking?

"This way, baas ---" called out Joseph. He was behind me. The man was like a shadow. "Durnford him quite near, me show." He turned his pony between the tent lines; my own Basuto mare, Benevente, trotted behind him, tethered. You couldn't find a manservant like him in England for any price.

Durnford's moustache was twitching. His bright blue eyes were luminescent. I can't imagine he'd ever enjoyed himself so much. "Ah, Bagshot! Have you seen Colonel Pulleine?" Of course, I hadn't. "Do me a favour. Go and find him and tell him I shall be up on the saddle – you know, the spot where the road goes between the two hills – and if he wants to draw in the defences towards me, I expect we can make quite a decent fight of it. Keep the road open for the civilians to get clear. I've sent Georgie Shepstone to watch the back of the mountain. I've asked Essex to help him, if he has a moment free. I'd tell Pulleine myself but can't be in two places at once. Oh, do give him my regards. Thanks, awf'ly." Cool as you like. He turned his pony – I recall it was known as 'Chieftain' – and left me. Where did he expect me to find Pulleine? "I show you, baas."

A gun team thundered through the camp, smashing canvas, the horses wild. A gunner drooped grotesquely from the limber seat, eyes glazed. An assegai pinned him to the wood. A second transfixed his chest. His comrades managed to overlook this not inconsiderable lapse on his part, one clutching his sleeve while the drivers hung low over the maddened horses' necks. The near side wheeler was bleeding from a gashed flank, blood spraying as it galloped past. The iron twelve-pounder flailed behind like a rabid plough. The Royal Artillery goes to a lot of trouble to avoid losing its guns. An officer was yelling, orders unheard, blond hair flying as he lost his helmet.

Coghill was mounting, painfully, outside the 1/24th guard tent. A soldier in a cook's apron was helping him into the saddle. "Bloody leg," he offered, conversationally. "I think it's probably all up. The colonel's told me to get along now. Melvill's gone off with the Queen's colour. Don't much like the look of his horse, though." He frowned. "Better follow on and make sure it's alright." He called out as he rode away. "I'll look out for you down the road."

The regulars were fighting furiously, some holding a semblance of a line, others formed in desperate little knots among a swarm of Zulus. It couldn't be long now. I watched in dread fascination as a soldier fell beneath the assegais, blades reddening as successive warriors plunged their spears into the body, before an exultant Zulu ripped the belly open with a vicious cut. His iklwa reminded me of Goliath of Gath, "the staff of his spear was like a weaver's beam; and his spear's head weighed six hundred shekels of iron". That's Samuel 1, 17. Bloody great thing, anyway. I'd have pulled out my Colt Lightning and plastered the blackguard, but a shot from the survivors of Wardell's command brought him low as I tugged at the flap; just as well, I'd have probably peppered one of the gallant clumps of the 24th.

The line between observer and participant is a thin one. Here I was, fifty yards from the fighting and feeling oddly safe from it all. I could have been watching cricket from the pavilion, enjoying the game while taking salmon and watercress sandwiches. All of a sudden, this enormous, muscular chappie, chocolate brown and swathed in feathers, appeared from nowhere and tried to smack me about the noggin with an ironwood knobkerrie – a nasty looking club of considerable efficiency. This caught me unawares, as you can imagine, and scared the daylights out of my chestnut gelding. The camp cook yelped, dropped his cleaver, and ran for a tent doorway. Waterloo shied before I could get my sword out of the scabbard, and I found myself in a casual upside-down position with my left foot in the stirrup and my face alternately staring up at this fiendish apparition and down at the thick wet mud. Not at all Ascot week. This was no good at all, so I heaved my foot free, slipped to the ground and leaped up. The Zulu assumed he'd got me – well, you would, wouldn't you? – and thrust his shield towards my chest as he set himself up for the old coup de grace. Being a nimble little devil, and unencumbered by weaponry (still safely tucked in holster and scabbard where they could do neither me nor him any harm), I seized the sides of the big cowskin shield, and tugged like billy-o. The Zulu's bare feet slid from under him as he overbalanced, and he buried his face in the muck at my feet. I should probably just have taken my size nines to his cranium – kicking one another in the head was a popular sport at my boarding school, we were barbarous little brutes – but, instead, I swept my sabre from its moorings and brought it down on a savage downswing. "Take that you heathen devil!" I shouted, bold-like. It would have cleft him in twain, as they used to say in the more full-blooded sort of novel, if the crafty swine hadn't flipped a half-turn sideways and grabbed my boot.

"Give that back you cheeky sod!" I told him, righteously indignant, as the hand-made glove- leather polo boot came off in his hand. He looked at it disgustedly, then twisted away as I shoved my besocked toes into his face in an attempt to poison him with lethal fumes. He didn't know who he was dealing with! The Bagshots have astonishing survival instincts and toxic feet.

But, then, he had a massive club swinging in his hand. I, however, was hopping on one foot, performing dismounted sword-drill while trying to keep my feet clean. I know it makes no sense to value clean hosiery over life and limb, but the ground still seemed awfully sticky. It must have seemed funny to the Zulu, because he laughed at me, a basso-profundo sort of chuckle. Which, I suppose is why I was too disconcerted to deliver the vigorous backhand cut that my old fencing master would have suggested as the solution to my immediate difficulties.

I suppose it was fortunate that Joseph shot him, considerably dead, with a home-made gas pipe pistol. I'd seen it in the storehouse at Rorke's Drift and thought it was some manner of ritual lamp or something; in daylight I saw it was two pieces of iron pipe strapped to a wooden handle, with ancient percussion cap mechanisms soldered to the top. The triggers were simply bent nails. I expect it had an accurate range of about four feet. Then again, the Zulu had been four feet away, so that worked out nicely. I've no idea what choice items of scrap iron he had selected for ammunition, but the blast tore the Zulu's oiled chest to dogsmeat. Joseph grinned. "Blacksmith shop at mission. Blacksmith drink, sleep, mission boy work nights."

"Why, thank you," I said, seizing the bridle of my charger. I was glad to take Waterloo's reins; I thought I'd lost the horse in the fracas. I picked up my boot – damn, the sole was half off, and I'd bought it new from Old Bond St last spring – and remounted. All safe.

Joseph's pony whinnied as somebody cut the traces behind. The cook had stolen my pony. That was the last I saw of Benevente, groaning under a sweating sausage-slinger and headed south with all my kit.

"Come back here, you thieving bastard!" I demanded.

I don't know why I waste my breath.

CHAPTER TWENTY-FIVE

Brighton 1928

"Are you sure you don't want a cheese sandwich?" asked the Colonel. "You have to keep your strength up when there's a massacre afoot. I was saved from death by a bit of dried yak flesh I'd forgotten I'd even got in my pocket, once, out where Kashmir and Afghanistan and the Chinese frontier all come together. Terrible place. Freeze yer bum off. The Karakoram range, or is it the Kun Lun? Howling wilderness, anyway."

George remembered that the cheese sandwiches had been rescued from the sea a few minutes ago and hadn't actually dried out yet. He shook his head. "Starving to death, sir?"

"No, shot by a Russian agent. Bullet hit me in the chest, but the piece of yak meat took all the force out of it. Bloody tough creatures are yaks."

* * *

The camp was infested with Zulus, stabbing and shooting as they advanced among the dwindling clusters of the 24th. The one thing that prevented a complete collapse was a formed body of regulars up on the slope of the mountain. Still under orders and blasting volleys into the flank of the impi as it surged through the tents, they held; I've since been told this was Younghusband and C Company, though I don't know. Whoever they were, their efforts bought a few minutes grace, which is how come I'm able to tell you all about it.

I went into the guard tent.

Lt Colonel Pulleine lay slumped over his desk, blood seeping from a chest wound onto a sheet of paper in from of him. A fountain pen leaked ink, blending into the red stain. The right hand clutched a revolver. I picked it up and sniffed. It had been fired. Good for Pulleine. He'd been writing a letter: *To my own dear Fanny, my son Henry and my two daughters* ---

133

The last word was badly smudged. A decent man. I was quiet for a moment.

A voice, too familiar, came from outside.

"I said give me that horse you wepulsive Kaffir! It's mine I tell you! Let go the weins."

"This horse belongs to Lieutenant Bagshot of the 10th Royal Hussars!"

"Bagshot, eh! The bounder! He twied to steal my horse once before! Well, he's not going to get away with it this time."

"Stop or I shall have to shoot you!" came the swift rejoinder, as they say in melodrama. "This gun is loaded, and I shall take some pleasure in dispatching you."

Who was that? It sounded like Joseph. But Joseph did not speak the proud English of Wordsworth or Tennyson; Joseph spoke a broken dialect of kitchen English, as befitted a mission boy with the most elementary of schooling. Except that, as I remembered, he'd begun talking like an educated man, at least once, since the battle began. Which seemed --- odd.

 I ran to the tent opening and saw a sight to gladden the cockles of my heart. There stood my faithful manservant, gas-pipe pistol in hand, defending his master's property against a sworn enemy – or, at the very least, a veritable boil on the posterior of my military career. But it ain't quite done for a native valet to shoot an officer of the Queen. Really it ain't.

"Stop that right away!" I cried. Joseph lowered the weapon. Fitzclarence seized his chance, put spurs to Waterloo's flanks, and raced off. "You wevolting cad, Bagshot! I shall certainly make sure Lord Chelmsford hears of your behaviour today!" was the last I heard. I was about to countermand my last instruction to Joseph when I happened to notice he was decked out in full Zulu regalia. You know, feathers and cowtails and a funny little furry kilt. I gulped, as one might. He grinned at me.

"You English gentlemen and your beloved code of honour! If I'd shot that ghastly little man – and I'm pretty handy with this thing, even if it is only a home-made pistol – who would know the difference? I mean to say, there are British soldiers are dying all over the place. Do you think anyone would question precisely who put Lieutenant Fitzclarence out of our misery? I'd say not!" He stuck out his chest. "Besides, as of about two minutes ago, I am a Zulu warrior. Ngobamakosi regiment. We're the boys today, no doubt about it!"

"But how? ---" I asked, dumbfounded.

"Well, I had the headdress and cowtail decorations in my bedroll all along. When I killed that fellow" – he pointed airily to the fallen warrior he'd shot a moment before – "I took his shield – black, the same as my regiment – and his knobkerrie. He's umCijo. We of the nGomamakosi hate them with a passion, so I don't feel too bad about that. Old quarrel, you understand."

"But why ----"

"Zulu boys all belong to a regiment, everyone of a certain age going together to form what we call an ibutho. Mine, as I've said, is the nGobamakosi. I've always known that I belonged with my peers, my people. My father was on the wrong side in the civil war of '56, so he and my mother fled to Natal. I was educated, quite well really, at a mission school as I told you. When war seemed inevitable, I ran away and came to join my ibutho."

"But ---"

"Yes, yes. I attached myself to that ignorant Boer hoping for a passage north, but he changed what little mind he had and took off for Durban instead. He assumed I was just another Kaffir boy to whop with his jambok when he felt like it. So, when I met you, a British officer on his way to the war, it seemed rather a good idea to come along. Who would question a camp servant, after all?"

This was insane. In the middle of battle – disaster – I was getting a lecture about the rivalries between Zulu regiments. My manservant was a Zulu warrior. My jaw hung slack. As Joshua said to the chap with the sword, "Art thou for us, or for our adversaries?"

Joseph grinned. "And he said, 'Nay: but as captain of the host of the Lord am I now come', chapter 5 verse 14. Though that doesn't really apply, does it?"

Joseph seemed to be enjoying himself a great deal at my expense.

"Anyway, Lieutenant Bagshot – I hope you don't mind me not calling you 'baas' anymore, it's so demeaning – I trust you won't hold my subterfuge against me too badly. Needs must when the devil drives, as they say. You've been a decent sort. But we can't just stand about like this, what with the battle going on a few yards from us. I'd be really embarrassed if I was forced to knock you on the head after all your help getting me here. Take my pony. He's a good 'un. Please go."

The situation was, as he suggested, ridiculous. I was having a perfectly civil conversation with an educated Zulu – "Therese Racquin", I remembered, and the Dostoevsky – while within twenty feet of us two warriors of the Nokhenke were ripping the guts out of some benighted beggar in red; one pulled off the uniform coat and slipped it on himself. The other danced about in the gore.

Both took the opportunity to look at me. Joseph shouted something which I assumed meant something of the order of "This one's mine", and pushed me roughly, using his shield to conceal us from the bloodthirsty duo. "Good luck Mister Bagshot," he whispered, capering about theatrically with the knobkerrie while I mounted Joseph's Basuto pony, and took a roundhouse swing at me as I rode off damned smartish. He took care to miss me, and I took care to dig my spurs in hard.

CHAPTER TWENTY-SIX

Brighton 1928

"So Joseph was a Zulu all the time?" asked George.

"Well, yes I suppose so. He was a cunning little blighter, and he did trick me something awful, but I can't really blame him for that. He'd devised the scheme all on his own, showed initiative and all that! And the little gas pipe gun was damned ingenious. Probably he'd have made a bloody good Royal Engineer, had circumstances been different."

"You mean if he'd been white."

"I mean if he'd been to the proper school."

* * *

The camp was a bloody shambles. Zulus were penetrating what remained of the defenses from all sides as surviving soldiers fell back to find rallying points or died angrily as they pitted bayonet against spear and war-club. They were making a dashed good stand too; for every red-coated regular that fell, a muscled black body slumped in the mud. Not that I was stopping to do the arithmetic on the relative casualty rates. A naval rating was lashing out with his cutlass, backed against a wagon wheel. He was chopping away, holding back the heathen foe like a good 'un; then some crafty bastard crawled under the back of the wagon and spitted him between the spokes. "Oh, foul!" I shouted, but there was no referee's whistle.

* * *

Brighton 1928

The Colonel was satisfied at the scene of carnage. Model Zulus – with a few Red Indians, Arabs and, most incongruously, Prussian guardsmen in dress uniform, all added to make the impression of mass numbers – had swarmed through the paper tents and finished off all but two groups of the 24th. The last clusters of them, with their white helmets and belts, were defending stoutly. One group was circled at the bottom of the camp – "They've not got long left, I'm afraid, George" – while the others were posed dramatically on the slopes of Isandlwana. The great rock itself, unfortunately, had lost a good deal of its grandeur after Colonel Bagshot dropped his solar topee onto it. Still, the handful of lead soldiers stood boldly, two kneeling, two at the ready, two standing firing. An enthusiastic officer with sword aloft led them from the front. "Younghusband's company", said the Colonel. "They held out on the mountain until they'd run out of ammunition, then charged down into the Zulus with the bayonet. Very brave. They were all killed, of course. Oh, one of them found a cave further up the hill and stayed up there firing for a long time. I expect he had found some more bullets. The Zulus got him in the end." Fishing a spoon from his bag, the Colonel took a couple of scoops from the side of the squashed mountain. "There's a damned good cave, though I say it myself."

George was feeling distinctly uncomfortable. He'd been facing the sea wall, moving toy soldiers about for what seemed like hours. His whole afternoon off was fast leaving him behind; his grandmother would be expecting him for tea at five, as she did every Wednesday. He felt wet – his feet, legs, and as he sat up, the seat of his trousers. The first few paper tents were wet too, as a thin wash of water covered them. The tide was coming in.

Colonel Bagshot was oblivious, blethering on about the positions of the Zulu regiments and where the oversized personal model of himself ought to be placed on its way to Durnford's last stand up on the saddle. This particular event was now occurring on an island surrounded by a vigorous swirl of salt water. When the old man finally became aware of this development – George was never certain that the Colonel maintained a firm differential between memory and the present circumstance – he snorted like an ox. "Bloody tide. It's early. Not due for another, ah, ten minutes." He snapped shut his pocket watch. "You'd think it'd follow a proper schedule, wouldn't you. After all, it does it everyday, twice a day. Damned inconvenient."

As the pair hurriedly put the troops away, the old man had an idea. "I say, George. Are you too old to go on a donkey ride?"

* * *

I had to find Durnford.

"Colonel, the camp's as good as fallen, and Pulleine's dead," I told him.

"I've had better news," he replied. You had to admire the man, he was cool. The position on the saddle was desperate by now. Men from every unit – 24th, Carbineers, Natal bobbies, mounted infantry – were gathered in close formation. They had released their horses, symbolically abandoning all hope of leaving this place. Each man had a rifle and whatever ammunition he had remaining; some were down to their pistols and hunting knives. They were taking their places for a last stand. My English upbringing told me to dismount and die with them. 'Dulce et decorum est pro patria mori', as Horace put it. One of those Romans, anyway. I never liked the Classics, except for the battles.

"Don't be an ass, man!" snorted Durnford. "You've got a perfectly good horse and it isn't your fight, really. Bugger off to Rorke's Drift and let that bloody fool of a sapper know what's happened. Clear off this minute. Yes, that is a direct order!"

And so they gathered to die, while I did as I was bid. I buggered off.

Which wasn't nearly as easy as it sounds. The Zulus had cut behind Isandlwana mountain, swarmed the party sent to hold them off – Shepstone must be dead by now – and were all over the track to Rorke's Drift. The rush of fugitives was southward, towards the lower valley of the Buffalo River. I didn't know a better way, so I put spurs to the pony and found myself caught among a handful of terrified men with pursuers intermixed. The Zulus seemed thrilled to stab the Natal Kaffirs, who tried desperately to look innocuous by stripping off the red rags that identified them; it must have been like being able to slaughter anyone you like and choosing a particularly noxious cousin over some completely unknown foreigner. The Zulus ignored me, which I put down to my having a horse and waving my sabre about in an enthusiastic sort of way. One warrior did look interested in skewering me, but a sharp swing of the sword took the wooly thingummy off the top of his shield and he lost his urge to tangle with me. There were plenty of victims to be had that day.

I can't say I was feeling much like a fight myself, not at this point. *Sauve qui peut* was the order of things. Dying gloriously, looking the foe in the eye is one thing. Getting yourself killed while running away is the opposite. Nobody will mention your hero's death, and some will call it cowardice, no matter what the odds were. I'm against cowardice, as you know, but try to explain that once they've found your stiff corpse with a few holes in your back. So, a gallop with head down was the order of the day. Besides, I had Durnford's order to ride for Rorke's Drift. I had a few words with the Almighty, too, as you can imagine; 'And it shall come to pass that whosoever shall call on the name of the Lord shall be delivered." That's Joel 3:32.

The ground was a wicked jigsaw of rocks, panting refugees and general slippery obstruction. I've chased a few foxes in my time, and I can take a jump at a five-barred fence with military precision, but the run from Isandlwana down to Fugitives Drift – as they came to call it later – was hellish bad. The path ran through rugged country seamed with dongas cutting across the line of descent. I remember a steep-sided spruit, water rushing white. Howling Zulus leapt from rock to rock with frightening agility. As I rode I swung my blade – a good one from Wilkinson – through the manual of sword exercises. There wasn't actually anyone within striking range, but I thought the appearance of martial enthusiasm might detract from my appeal as a potential victim. Sure enough, the Zulus took my hint and set upon some poor devil of a civilian conductor, who hadn't the advantages I'd got. Still, one sour faced old warrior discharged an ancient Prussian flintlock musket, which I didn't much appreciate. I'd have sabred him good in retaliation, but the swine stepped back a pace and pulled out his ramrod. The pony found its way down through the torrent – a wise horseman allows his mount to pick its own path through water – while I dared the blackguard to come within distance of a backhand slash of good British steel. He grinned evilly and continued to load the musket. Evidently, he was confident of another shot while I was still crossing this blasted stream. He might not be wrong either. The Basuto pony was a nimble thing, but damnably cautious, and stopped to test the flow of the current. I was a sitting target. The Zulu poured loose powder generously into the musket's open mouth. They say a man shot at eighty yards by an old-time musket would be damned unlucky if the fella who pulled the trigger was actually aiming at him. How about eight yards? The Zulu had a nasty slug of rough metal in his hand. He dropped it down the barrel and banged the butt against a stone. Then he rammed hard with the iron rod. Methodical, if not quite according to the drill. My horse still hadn't moved. My enemy – for it was personal now – smiled once again. He had good teeth, too. The musket came up to his shoulder, one eye piercing my chest along the browned barrel. He pulled the trigger and my heart stopped.

There was a thunderous crash and his grin disappeared in a welter of gore. The musket had exploded in his hands, its German craftsmanship challenged once too often by huge doses of cheap powder and incongruous bits of ironmongery. In the dice game of life, he'd thrown a double one! He fell, in silence, with the flint, lock and plate welded to his teeth like a piece of that ghastly modern sculpture. My horse jumped out of pure fright, and we reached the far side of the raging spruit. I wanted to yell out something bold like "You have your reward, savage assassin!", but all I could manage was "Yeearrgh!" as we headed off. One always thinks of the really good ripostes later. I do, anyway.

CHAPTER TWENTY-SEVEN

Brighton 1928

"How much for two on the donkeys?"

"'Ere, you're much too big for my donkeys!" replied the owner of the two placid, elderly animals. "They're for the kiddies." He eyed George; "little 'uns, not like him."

George's experience warned him that the Colonel would try and damn-your-eyes his way into overawing the donkey-man. This was always embarrassing to the boy. Instead, Colonel Bagshot took what he would term a flanking approach:

"My good man, you're an old soldier, aren't you?"

"Yes sir!"

"Let's have a look at that manly bearing. Oh yes. And cavalry, eh?"

The man puffed his thin chest out. "5th Lancers, sir. I was with them when we charged the Boers at Elandslaagte. Troop sergeant, sir. Twenty-one years' service."

"Excellent, sergeant. Elandslaagte, eh. I commanded some irregular horse under Buller, only colonials though. Then I was at Mafeking, and then ---"

So the two ancient warriors refought the Boer War for a few minutes, with the result that both George and the Colonel were adjudged to be small enough – "Wiry, sir, like a good 'orseman oughter be" – to ride the donkeys. The donkeys were not consulted on this decision. The old troop sergeant even carried the Colonel's Gladstone bag while we rode.

"Now then George, this puts me in the right spirit. Wasn't I telling you about the ride down from Isandlwana to the drift?"

* * *

A sergeant of the 24th was staggering through the rocks. He was done up, wheezing like a twenty-year-old dog; his last legs had come and gone. "Give us a lift" he begged. "Oh, for God's sake, give us a lift." The rider ahead of me answered something to the effect of "It's a case of life or death for me!" and galloped on. I did the same thing. When the sergeant called out to me, I pretended I hadn't heard. Embarrassing, rather, but one has to be realistic. You can't pick up every poor blighter with the bad luck to be caught legging it from a great British military disaster. You'd need a bus. You'd have no time to yourself.

He might still be there, trying to cadge a lift. Somehow, I doubt it.

The gun team had come a cropper. I'd seen it as it galloped out of the camp. That seemed like hours ago. The broken terrain had delayed any attempt to get clear of the stricken field. Desperately lunging across a gully, the carriage had turned over and the horses trapped in their traces. Hanging over the edge of the cutting, hooves hopelessly scraping the air, the terrified animals had been speared by Zulus. So were the poor sods on board, which was unfortunate, but after all they were getting paid for it. I always have a soft spot for beasties. It was not a pretty sight. There was no sign of the artilleryman, Stuart Smith.

Not then, anyway. I came across him a few minutes later, as I reached the bluff above the Buffalo River. He was yelling out to someone, "Get on man, the Zulus are on top of you!" Stuart Smith was horribly wounded, croaking and ashy-faced. I saw that the man he was addressing was Horace Smith-Dorien, dismounted to help a wounded trooper of Mounted Infantry. Horry was the well-mannered sort, so you'd expect him to be wrapping his hanky around some grateful fellow's paw while hordes of irate savages milled about him like Christmas shoppers at Harrods. Which they were, of course. A dozen of the chaps Joseph had identified for me as the InDluyengwe jumped on the lot of them, Stuart Smith, Horace, his patient and his horse. There was a sudden flurry of blows, and everyone fell under the Zulu crush. My own horse took a sudden start. One of the bastards had grabbed its tail. I jerked around as the Basuto pony leapt forward, both of us being startled-like. From the corner of my eye I spotted Smith-Dorrien splashing about in the water, making for t'other side. Good for him. Meanwhile I had problems of my own.

I have absolutely no idea why the Zulu decided to seize my horse by the tail. He lurched forward, lifted off his feet while he drove his spear towards my august personage. I flung up a guard with my sword, driving Wilkinson's steel against the impure product of some straw-topped veldt smithy.

I have no idea whether noble British craftsmanship would have overcome solid native ironmongery, for we both lost our respective weapons at the same time;

the pony, spirited at the best of times and palpably furious at this moment, made a leap for the water, ten feet ahead and as many deep. Probably hoped to get rid of both of us in the scrimmage. I would have. It was a damned good jump. I lost my sun helmet but kept my feet in the stirrups and had a quiet word with the Almighty. We came down with a tremendous splash. I maintained my footing and balance; so did the pony. When a horse rolls in a roaring torrent, best hope the life policy's paid up. Still, you'll save the kith and kin burial costs.

"Binky!" shouted Teignmouth Melvill. He was in the river himself, splashing about with the Queen's Colour, its cover gone, under his arm. Clinging to a rock, the heavy wet silk was draping across him and pulling with the current. Another fellow was with him in the stream. Zulu riflemen were firing from the bank, bullets flecking white in the surging water. On the far side was Nevill Coghill, still mounted, emerging from the river. He turned and yelled to Melvill. I couldn't hear the words. As he entered the Buffalo again, a Zulu bullet found its mark; Coghill's horse spasmed and slid beneath the surface. Then it was Coghill alone, the crippled orderly officer, dog paddling gamely towards his friend on the rock. You had to admire the pluck of the man. The fact that Melvill owed him a fiver doesn't account for that kind of gallantry.

Melvill looked around from the folds of the soaking flag. You have to understand that an infantry colour is a damned big thing, forty-five inches by three feet, silk with braided gold stitching and scrolling and the names of ancient battlefields. The Queen's colour was a Union flag, as opposed to the regimental colour's green cloth. It is supported by a hefty wooden staff. In the days when an ensign in his teens was expected to bear the standard into battle, the regiment thoughtfully provided a pair of burly sergeants in case a heavy wind showed signs of blowing the standard-bearer off in some spectacular Montgolfier-like fashion. That was when the flag was bigger, six feet by five foot six, but the modern thing wasn't exactly something you'd mistake for a pocket hanky. It is certainly made no lighter by immersion in an African river. Nor is it the kind of handy item you can expect to toss willy-nilly from one chap to another, with one hand clutching a lump of granite in a torrential flow.

Melvill was not a careless man, a panicky fellow, as far as I knew him. But needs must as the devil drives. He shouted "Binky!" pulled himself up as high as he could on his pillar of rock and swung the staff over his head. The soggy colour circled once and flew towards me. It was an incredible throw. Hurling the saturated flag from that position was like trying to drive a Queen Anne dresser down a fairway with a nine-iron. It ought, by all rights, have flopped ignominiously into the river within feet of the thrower. Instead it sailed majestically (though none too aerodynamically) towards me, with a languorous half-turn midway. I had my hands up to catch, the pony held between my knees as it swam against the roaring current. I'd have caught it, too, but for the Zulu.

I'd forgotten about him, or at least assumed he had been flung aside in the dramatic leap from the high crag. But no such luck. He was a believer in dogged persistence, that one. He chose that moment to haul himself up onto the pony's back and grapple me. The first I knew was that my arms were pulled down and behind me. We lurched forward, the Zulu pushing my face down into the horse's mane. I threw back an elbow and caught him in the gut. We fought dirty at my school. He grunted, giving me a chance to free my right hand. It went up for the catch. The moment was gone. The colour was in the water, the staff eddying in the torrent. I had no chance for it now, even if the Zulu were to quietly apologise to me, dismount and go about his lawful business. He didn't, of course. We thrashed on through the river. I kept my knees into the horse and hoped to keep my seat. With my free right hand, I reached back and pinched the Zulu's leg, hard. I remember doing that to Jimmy "Basher" Phipps-Harrington in the fourth form. He didn't like that at all. The Zulu felt the same way, but rather than scream for the Latin master to rescue him and cane me, the plucky inDluyengwe went for the more manly option of grabbing me powerfully round the waist. Then he bit me on the back of the neck.

"Ow!" I cried. "Unfair, you blackguard!" He might have gone to my school after all. I wished I still had my sword. If I could find room for a surgical swing, I could swipe his toes off without striking the horse in the process. The mark of the good cavalryman is never to cut bits off your mount while performing sabre drill. Still, it was a moot point since I'd lost the bloody thing. I turned my head sharply to the left, which dislodged his teeth from my skin. Downstream, Coghill and Melvill were staggering from the water, Lord knows how, one gimping up the bank and the other half drowned. I hoped Melvill didn't think badly of me. I'd done my best. So, had he. That was the last I ever saw of them. They deserved their V.C.s.

We were out of the water, the Basuto pony trying its enraged best to get rid of a wriggling load far in excess of anything it could be fairly expected to carry. The Zulu had me in an arm lock and was trying to use his strength – he was a healthy, muscular chap – to choke the wind out of me. He'd torn the back out of my blue serge tunic. I was in trouble. I've never been a big man, and always relied on nimbleness and good sabre practice, neither of which looked to do me a lot of good. If he kept breathing his disgusting vapours down my neck – never seen a toothbrush, mark my words – and kept ripping at my patrol jacket, I'd have to do something rash. Something underhand. Something dangerous. I'd have to shoot him.

I'd finally remembered my revolver. If I could persuade him to leave my right hand alone – which meant letting him use his own right hand to throttle me at will – I might reach across my stomach and unclip my pistol. His left hand was occupied with keeping my own out of play – I'd caught him one under the kidneys and he didn't want another – and holding on to his shield. I'd have dropped it if I were him. This meant that his chances of strangling me were much diminished. This said, you don't just permit a hostile Zulu warrior free access to your windpipe without some considerable risk.

I'm not a gun enthusiast. Ideally, I'd have somebody efficient on hand to do the actual trigger pulling. One thing I did know was that my weapon, the Colt Lightning presented to me by The Kid as his contribution to my surviving the Tunstall-Dolan blood feud, was a metal cartridge revolver. The ammunition was sealed tight, safe from water damage. If I'd had one of the old cap-and-ball revolvers that a lot of chaps still used, I'd have nothing to fire. As it was, there was no guarantee that the thing would shoot. I eased the pistol from the holster on my left hip, in the hope of raising it over my left shoulder and shoving the barrel against the Zulu's upper torso. Evidently, he spotted the ploy, because a powerful brown right hand clamped down on my wrist and forced the pistol down across my body. I pushed upwards, in vain. The revolver was level with my belly. "Don't pull the bloody trigger," I told myself. I didn't. The Colt was thrust down and away, until the Zulu's reach limit extended his arm, and mine, out to the right. He had me.

Ah, but I had him too. As I've told you, I went to a vicious minor public school in the Welsh marches where brutality was a planned part of the daily regimen, and, being one of the smaller boys, I learned to fight dirty. My left hand slipped from his grip – as I've said, he was far too fond of his shield – and reached under the monkey tailed flap of his loincloth. He was behind me, so I couldn't see, and the position allowed no real leverage. Still, it's a tender and vulnerable part of the anatomy – three parts if you want to be technical – and it don't take a lot of pressure in that department to distract a man from whatever else he's doing. The Zulu squirmed. No training in the world will prevent a fellow flinching in that position. I hooked my right hand downwards, breaking his grip, and swung the pistol along my right flank and behind. The muzzle jammed against solid flesh. I pulled the trigger. The gun went off with quite a decent bang.

Pain seared through me. I'd shot myself in the right buttock.

Once again, I had shown myself to be a woefully inadequate gunman. Faced with a gallant foeman in hand-to-hand combat, I'd managed to pot myself in the bum. It seemed like as good a time as any to fall off the horse. The pony appeared quite happy with the arrangement and didn't stop.

'A horse is a vain thing for safety; neither shall he deliver any by his great strength', as it says in Psalm 33.

CHAPTER TWENTY-EIGHT

Brighton 1928

"So how did you know the donkey-man was an old soldier?" asked George.

"Martial bearing, as I told him, my boy. Stand up straight. Not slouching about like your civilian Johnnies," replied Colonel Bagshot.

"Yes, sir, but how did you know it was cavalry?"

"Bandy legs. Old cavalry troopers always have bandy legs. Of course, I didn't say that to him. But it's a fact." The colonel's own legs bore testimony to this.

"But not cavalry officers, sir?"

"You're a cheeky monkey, young George!"

* * *

I opened my eyes. The Zulu was on top of me. The sky above was dark. He must have been wrestling with me for hours, unable ever to quite throttle me, but determined to do his best. Perseverance; you can't beat it. Still, it made no sense. As my mind cleared, it all seemed very odd. Was he asleep? I moved my right hand and shook it. I gingerly moved a leg. All well. The Zulu did nothing. I made an experimental push at his left shoulder. No response. I shoved. The man slumped onto his right side, then collapsed onto his back. Empty eyes gaped at me. I started. "Good grief, this fellow's dead!" I said to myself. And he was, too. Blood covered his right thigh and leg, black and sticky. There was a hole, a gash really, in his upper thigh, at the artery. I forget which artery that is. Evidently the bullet I'd used to perforate my rump had not been stopped by its passage through my personage, and had continued, fatally, into my postillion rider. Damned bad luck, really, for him. Good for me though.

I stood up gingerly. It was a painful thing to do. Aside from my wound, I was soaking wet, most of my saturated clothing lying in tatters around me from my late assailant's determined efforts to kill me barehanded. From the waist down, I was covered in blood, at least some of it mine. I had lost my sword, my horse (three of them today, though I'd only paid for two), and my sun helmet. Somehow, I'd lost a boot. I was somewhere on the Natal bank of the Buffalo River. There was every chance that Zulus were prowling, poking around for wounded Britons like myself. What I had in my favour was a revolver I'd used to shoot myself with and a satchel of small items I had, by pure happenstance, slung over my shoulder rather than attach it to the saddle of a since-disappeared pony. Oh, and a dead Zulu – not usually considered a valuable resource. A sensible man would have taken off for Helpmakaar (being directly away from the battlefield) but I had promised Durnford I'd get to Rorke's Drift. I always keep my promises, especially those I've made to dead people. When they were alive I mean – I'm not a lunatic. I'd have to wait for the moon to come up, make for the river once again and head upstream for the mission station. Have to be careful, though. There would be Zulus about. What I needed was camouflage.

I opened my haversack and went through the contents.

Waterproof, ripped.
Field glasses, expensive, German, broken.
Glenlivet, tea, sugar (spilt), salt, jar of 'Bovril', ration biscuits (also broken).
Tin of oysters from Fortnums, formerly belonging to Coghill.
Matches, notepaper, pencil (also broken).

No ammunition, maps, or tin-opener, or anything useful like that. I threw away the binoculars, cape and pencil at once, the oysters with some regret. I kept the tea and sugar, because I am a hopeful sort, and that the chance of meeting a cow grazing next to a boiling spring ought not be entirely discounted. I was about to sling the Bovril away. I've never liked it much but have been told it's good for me. Bovril, in case you don't know, is a thick, sticky brown paste with some vague relationship to dead cattle[43]; you smear it on biscuits or mix it with hot water for a beef tea. Inspiration had found me. Tonight, was a bad night for a wet and wounded Englishman with one left boot. It would help considerably if I were a Zulu. It was a good night to be a Zulu. "I will greatly rejoice in the Lord; my soul shall be joyful in my God; for he hath clothed me with the garments of salvation." That's Isaiah 61. I 'spect he had this kind of situation in mind.

Smearing oneself with a jar of viscous beef extract is not as easy as you might think. Still, I told myself, my legs were black with dried blood already, and the interesting and extravagant cowtail necklace, armlets and anklets worn by my

---

43. Bovril was a recently invented product, first sold, bizarrely, as 'Johnston's Fluid Beef'. The name Bovril was based on the Latin word bos (ox or cow) and – bizarrely – 'vril' from an imaginary electromagnetic substance in the novel The Coming Race by Edward Bulwer-Lytton, creator of the phrase "It was a Dark and Stormy Night."

late adversary would cover a multitude of sins. The Zulu had evidently been something of a dandy. Most of the warriors I'd seen in action had been in light field order, loincloth and head-ring, a few cowtail ornaments and the odd feather. Not this laddie. He was rigged out in a fancy headdress: leopard skin band, black ostrich feathers at the front with a couple of big white ones, and some funny little bunches from some other bird at the sides. Not all that practical, but damned imposing. As an officer of the 10th Hussars, owner of a fur busby with gold laced hanging bag and white- over-black plume, I had to approve. I wondered if he had the same kind of overdue tailor's bills I did. The cowtail thingies dwarfed me a bit (he was a big lad) but the kilt was very nice. Monkey skin, I expect. The shield was damn near as tall as me. Pity about losing the assegai, but I was grateful he'd not had it when we were tussling. I looked, er, different. There was no mirror about. And it was dark. The little book I'd read on the train up from Durban had said that Zulus don't like to fight in the dark. I hoped this was true. I like a good fight as much as anyone, you understand, but there are times and there are times --- I tucked my revolver, matches and whisky flask in the waistband. I had to use the writing paper to stuff the headband to keep it from falling over my eyes. I left the naked Zulu under a bush, with the remains of my waterproof saving his modesty. It seemed only fair, since I'd pinched his clothes, and he'd given me a good run for my money.

I ate the broken biscuits, crumbs and all.

The moon never came up. Instead, the sky lightened. This was a bit of a blow. I didn't mind lurking about in this bizarre rig as long as nobody could see me properly, but it seemed unlikely that the blood-and-Bovril greasepaint would convince anyone who saw me in full daylight. Had I lain out all night? I'd be very late indeed to tell Lt. Chard the bad news. There might be no point at all. It'd be in the London papers before I got to Rorke's Drift. The thought of Chard stirred a recollection. What had he said? "Two lumps. No milk. Solar eclipse --"

Solar eclipse. I wasn't really sure ow those worked, but I'd been caught out by one of the blighters. Damn. It wasn't getting light because of the natural daily cycle of dusk and dawn. It was still, probably, mid- afternoon. I was dressed in full Zulu kit and improvised cosmetic colouring at a time of day when every real warrior in Zululand was poking about the countryside looking for something to kill. I had two choices. One of them was to hide under the tangliest bush I could find and wait for night to really fall. But would that be the Bagshot way? I thought of Sir Bulstrode, an ancestral Bagshot, leading his troop against Cromwell's Ironsides. I thought of great uncle Henry, in Spain and at Waterloo. I thought of my father, ready (if he hadn't inconveniently died of dysentery) to join the assault on Delhi with Nicholson in '57. None of them had ever mentioned hiding under bushes until nightfall. None of them had ever dressed so outrageously either. The honour of the family and of the regiment spoke out to me. The other choice was to go hence, in cowtails and Bovril, unto Rorke's Drift. I went.

It's not that far from the place historians call 'Fugitive's Drift' to the mission station; perhaps five miles. It seems longer when you are dodging between boulders and bushes or crawling though long grass on the spy for Zulus. My tender feet complained bitterly. I had no idea how far the bolting pony had taken the Zulu and I after we crossed the river, nor in what direction. I lurked about a bit in a general northerly direction, until I came to a great swathe of trampled grass. In the depressions of the ground, still muddy, the stirrings of many muddy feet were impressed. It was a fresh made track, running roughly east -west, towards Helpmakaar. Clearly this was not the consequence of passing cattle herds or a holiday party of wildebeeste and gazelle. The Zulus had travelled this way in large numbers. Looking left and right, as if crossing a road, I continued my northerly advance. A mile on, I met the track again. It had bent northward, more or less. Or perhaps I'd just got lost. Two things clarified the matter for me. One was the shape of the Oskarberg, the rocky hill that loomed over the old mission station. It was directly ahead, and the track aimed straight for it. The other thing was the gunfire. Musketry. Lots of it. Which, given the evidence that a Zulu impi had recently decided to visit the place, seemed like good news. The alternative would have been much worse.

I don't know if you've ever tried to sneak into a battle. It seems like an odd thing to do. I'd sneaked into the occasional music hall and out of certain restaurants when the bill exceeded my ability to pay, but this was a new experience. The advantage I had was that it was a damned unexpected thing to do.

The rear of a marching army is a messy and confusing place where you find wagons, bandsmen, commissaries, washerwomen, skulkers, small children and a lot of dogs. It would be like a gypsy caravan if gypsies had sergeant-majors. That's the way of a European army, anyway. Luckily, the Zulus had no impedimenta; they'd even left their udibi boys behind them. I wouldn't want to tangle with a couple of hundred Zulu wives with time on their hands. I firmly believe what they say about the female of the species. You've not met my Aunt Agatha.

It struck me that, if I was going to get into Rorke's Drift, it behooved me to have a good peek at the situation there. The beaten track hooked around the foot of the Oskarberg on its way to the mission. The layout of the country was uncertain to me. The firing became clearer; independent firing of Martini-Henrys, random banging of other pieces closer to me. I left the trail and carefully made my way up the broken hill. It offered plenty of cover from jutting stone outcrops, long grass and spiky euphorbia bushes. My feet were already cut to ribbons, and the broiling rocks burned like blazes. I broke off a branch as a walking stick. Climbing hills didn't bother me generally, but the absence of stout boots and the presence of a bullet hole through my nether regions did nothing to aid my ascent. I took my time. I hadn't seen a Zulu since I left the dead 'un, and when I did I was hoping they wouldn't see me. My disguise would fool nobody.

I reached the summit.

CHAPTER TWENTY-NINE

Hove 1928

It was Thursday afternoon, a day after the beach excursion, and George had no idea why the Colonel wanted two pounds of plums. Still, he was happy to fetch them from the greengrocers in Church Road. When he took them up to the Bagshot suite – he still thought it hilarious that old Quint wanted to call three awkward rooms a 'suite' – the Colonel was waiting.

"Thought I'd lay out Rorke's Drift for you, since you liked Isandlwana so much." George wasn't certain he had, what with spending most of his afternoon off playing toy soldiers on the beach, and people giggling, and getting his trousers wet. He'd been late for his grandmother's, and when he'd come back to the hotel, Cook had found a dozen things for him to do, purely out of spite as far as he could see. She'd had him move the furniture around the downstairs parlour twice, and then decided to keep it the way it always had been.

The Colonel had cleared off his table and laid out a tableau of two cardboard shoe boxes and a square drawn in chalk on a piece of green baize taken from the hotel billiards table. The Colonel had ripped the baize while attempting a shot of considerable ambition, and Mr. Quint had given him the remnants (for the table had needed to be recovered) in return for an understanding that billiards would no longer be part of the Colonel's regimen at the Empire Lodge. Colonel Bagshot had not directly agreed to this, but simply decided that he was not presently interested in playing the game. The cloth wasn't bad, as replicas of grassland went, provided you accepted that grass was neatly cut and vividly green throughout; George did suspect, however, that the table looked more like Lords Cricket Ground than a riverbank facing Zululand. The shoe boxes and the chalk also lacked the force of conviction. All in all, it was not tremendously impressive from a visual standpoint. Even the Colonel recognised this:

"Well, no, not yet. But if you don't mind drawing some doors and windows on the boxes, it'll help. That one's the hospital, the other is the storehouse. We will use the plums for a wall of mealie bags, which are like sandbags, only with dried corn inside rather than dirt. Yes, I know they aren't the right colour; I'd have asked you to fetch apricots, but they cost too much, and they upset my tummy. Then we will use this tin of Scottish shortbread for biscuit boxes, which seems only right. The chalk mark shows where they ought to be. Then I will tell you all about the battle of Rorke's Drift.

No, you can't eat any of the mealie bag walls. We can do that afterwards."

* * *

As a view, it was a fair treat. A little way off, to my right, the Buffalo River flowed southward. Below me stood the old mission buildings, their perimeter built up with what looked like boxes and bags piled in fort-like manner. The buildings were the strongpoints around which the temporary breastworks were built; the yard was swarming with soldiers. Beyond them, a shade to the right, lay a couple of stone kraals; directly ahead I could see a garden and an orchard. It would have been a pleasant pastoral scene but for the billowing smoke and rapid rifle fire, both caused by the thin streak of red-coated soldiers lining the walls. You couldn't really blame them for spoiling the tranquility of the scene. After all, thousands of Zulus were trying to claw their way into the premises.

When I say 'thousands', what I really mean is several hundred actually forcing their way over the barricades at the left-hand side, while a lot of their chums lay in the grass cheering them on. This was a popular place to be; you had to queue up for a chance to get in. I've since been told that the Zulu impi at Rorke's Drift was the Undi corps, about four thousand strong, comprising the uThulwana (a senior regiment of men in their forties), the nDlondlo, the uDloko and my own – sorry my late adversary's – mob, the inDluyengwe. What I could see from a distance of several hundred yards was as confused a scene as you'd see anywhere this side of an England-Scotland football match. It boiled down to black men trying very hard to get in, red men trying very hard to keep them out. I believe ants do much the same thing. It looked like ants. Ants with breech-loading weapons. Below me, the Zulus were making an attack on the south wall. It didn't seem to be getting anywhere.

From below me, on the lower terrace of the Oskarberg, Zulu snipers pelted the mission with rifle fire. I could see the sharpshooters from the rear, warriors with various elderly firearms – thank God, they hadn't got the Martinis from our lads slaughtered at Isandlwana depot – taking time and turns to attempt the potting of a British soldier. Each had his ammunition laid out next to him, together with a pipe and tobacco, and there was great excitement as to who fired next and at whom. They were out for a grand afternoon of sport. I daresay there was gambling, too. They were all within a hundred yards of me, and had I been provided with a Gatling gun and crew, I've no doubt I could have spoiled their game properly. However, the Almighty had not seen fit to equip me with an Angelic Gatling with which to smite them hip and thigh. I was perfectly free to call them rude names, though. I chose not to.

The soldiers defending the north face were open to the fire of the Zulu marksmen below me; there was no cover inside the fort from elevated fire from our side. They had to rely on their comrades on the south wall facing the Oskarberg, who were shooting carefully, and lethally. A warrior in a head-ring had the poor judgment to bob up for a better aim and got the back of his head blown off for his troubles. A couple of characters who tried to make a dash from one rock to another found out that bone-smashing slugs of lead did not enhance their gymnastic abilities. One Zulu chief, ostentatiously mounted on a white pony, plummeted to the ground in a riffle of feathers and a splash of red. I felt privileged to watch such shooting. One particular soldier shot eight or nine men in succession, bowling them over like ninepins. I was impressed. I'd seen the standard of shooting displayed by my troop of hussars on the range at Muttra, in India. It had been lamentable. Cavalrymen don't like to admit that our beetle-crushing cousins can do anything well, but this was something to applaud. I thought, however, that I'd better not. Cheering was also out of the question.

The Zulus on the near side – the southern face – had fairly given up on assaulting the wall. Warriors were snuggled down in the ditch or pressed against the back of the cookhouse. They were stalled there, hunkered like dogs among their dead. The main Zulu attack had shifted to the north-west corner, where the improvised wall ran along the front of the hospital.

This wasn't going to be easy for me. If I was to get into Rorke's Drift, I'd have to think carefully about it. I might sneak towards the now-quiet barricades on the near side, crawling level with the front ranks of prone warriors, or even beyond them; then, rubbing the Bovril off my face with grass and doffing my feather headdress, I'd shout out the immortal phrase – useful in battle and in boudoir – "Don't shoot, I'm a British officer!" and bolt for the fort. The Zulus would be astounded at my bold ruse (and therefore would not react quick enough to do me a mischief), while the 24th would know from my gentlemanly bearing and commanding tone of voice not to drop me in my tracks like a rabid hound.

Alright, a certain amount of luck might be involved, but it seemed like a damned good plan. Have to be very careful though ---

Of course, at that moment I was attacked by a snake.

I believe to this day that the black mamba had been quietly waiting to get its fangs into me. They're like that. As I shifted position for a better look, my hand dislodged a pile of flat stones. The snake was underneath. Doubtless my clumsiness had filed its dastardly plot against me. It reared back from its coils, hissing; they do that, you know. I sprung up to combat the serpent. I had my stick. Just as I was about to smite at the snake – I've hated 'em with a passion since the incident in the gentleman's washroom at the Bangalore Club – I lost my footing completely. I stood momentarily on the exact summit of the hill, arms flailing as if demented. A word came to my lips. Strangely enough, it was "Eeeyaaaagh!"

A hundred heads turned my way.

A hundred Zulus saw a figure in full war regalia brandishing a weapon, dancing with warrior fury, and yelling out encouragement. They did not see an Englishman in improvised blackface and fancy dress smacking at a snake with a bit of old tree. No, they saw a brave Induna pointing the way to victory! Such is fate; we see what we wish to see, which proves that the Almighty has a sense of humour, and that he protecteth his own. Meaning myself. A hundred Zulus cheered, and, taking heart, rose up from the grass to attack. I had encouraged their ardour, spoken to their fighting spirit. They flung themselves onto the walls of Rorke's Drift at my very gesture.

My antics had another audience. The soldier who had shot all those Zulus a few minutes before now decided he didn't much like the looks of me. I'm pretty sure it was him, anyway. A bullet tore through my shield and, as I ducked low – not that I duck habitually, but this was an exceptional circumstance – a second parted the feather bouquet I had perched on the top of my head. It was lucky I was a little fellow dressed in oversize costume; if I'd filled out the uniform better, I'd have been a goner.

I flopped down behind a euphorbia bush, a big spiky thing, and risked a peek. The marksman had been distracted by closer, fiercer warriors. Perhaps he thought I was dead. Still, there wasn't a lot to be gained from sitting here. The Zulus might send a man to check if I was alright, since I was obviously an important chap. Moving gingerly from rock to rock I made my way down the mountain. This was relatively safe. All the fellows I had encouraged into charging the fort were busy getting killed ahead of me, and the fellows doing the shooting were occupied with that work. As long as I worked well to the west side of the mission I would avoid stray shots. Yipping a bit at the hot stones under my feet, I edged myself down beyond the ditch and cookhouse towards the western end of the hospital. Things looked tricky there. A lot of warriors – mixed from all four regiments, with different shields and insignia – were lying prone in the grass and bushes, facing the building. This was good, in that they weren't looking at me. I found myself in a nice patch of grass, next to some dead Zulus. They seemed less likely to query who I was and what the bloody hell I thought I was doing than the more active, still alive warriors nearby. It was a chance to catch my breath. I'd got a thorn in my foot, and my bum hurt from where I'd shot myself. Sitting down was out of the question for any number of reasons.

CHAPTER THIRTY

Hove 1928

The Colonel had a map in one of his books – he referred to it as 'The Official Narrative' – and used it as a blueprint for the building of Rorke's Drift. George had wielded coloured pencils with enthusiasm to turn the shoeboxes into mission buildings, the top sides open to permit the presence of the model soldiers. A surrounding wall of plums gave the place a perimeter, divided in half by a barricade of shortbread pieces that kept the hospital side separated from the storehouse. Three apples were placed in a line on what was termed the 'south face', to serve as parked wagons brought into the defensive wall. As usual, the Colonel directed while George did all the work.

"Put the extra plums in a stack in front of the store, George. You can eat one. Just one, mind you. They'll need them for a final defense. Get the soldiers out of the boxes. We need about a hundred of the twenty fourth, so I expect you'll have to use other regiments to make up the numbers and find something to use as hospital patients. I've got a box of broken figures I need to repair, so they'd do jolly well. I use matchsticks for wooden legs if I've lost the original ones. Do you know anything about using a soldering iron, by the way? Only I had a bit of an accident ---"

* * *

From where I lay, a hundred yards or less from the hospital, I had a capital view of the fight. I realized that I was lying on a very slight hummock, a rise in the ground, where I could see the area in front of the hospital. Of course, this meant that the defenders had a damned good view of my position, which accounted for the number of recently deceased Zulus around me. I'd better not move a muscle.

I was facing the outer wall of Rorke's house, stone-built, which I recalled as being one of the less defective parts of that ramshackle dwelling. The side wall might have been twenty feet wide, single storied, with a hipped thatch roof of no very steep pitch. There was a central door, with a rough line of loopholes carved out by the infantry inside. No windows on this face at all. As I've said, it was a very odd building indeed. From the loopholes the defenders kept up an irregular but telling fire; whenever a Zulu made to rise, the bark of a Martini was heard. Not every shot was a hit, of course – only idiots talk of 'every bullet finding its mark' – but the effect was to stifle the Zulus' enthusiasm to make a rush. Indeed, this appeared to be the quiet side, the warriors watching hopefully for their chance to move forward. One lad decided he'd get up and attack all on his own; he was quickly disabused of that notion, and fell, writhing, with a big hole right through him. One thing about Zulus is that, like Apaches, they don't complain when they are wounded. Gutshot men, in my experience, tend to gripe piteously about their situation, for a little while at least. This chap didn't. He just looked a touch pained, twitched a couple of times, and went on to visit his ancestors. A European would make more noise at the dentist. This occurred directly ahead of me. The interesting stuff was going on to the left of the hospital, on the verandah and forecourt. I'd not been able to really see this area from the top of the Oskarberg. Chard and his lads had extended the line of the fort from the west wall of the hospital forward to a ledge of rock, about four feet high, which ran along the whole front of the mission. The walls – mealie bags, as I could now see – were stacked on top of the rock rim of the ledge. Its effect was to make the crest of the defenses higher than a tall man could reach, which was all to the good as far as I was concerned. This was surely the hardest place to succeed with an attack. But that was precisely what the Zulus were up to. The reason for this was clear. The Zulus had a marvelous piece of heavily covered dead ground to mass for the assault just a few yards from the defenses. The dense bush that extended from the road had not been cut down by Chard's garrison. Between that, the sunken hollow of the roadbed, and the unfinished stone wall that either Rorke or the missionaries had begun to lay out some thirty feet from the hospital front, the Zulus had a damned fine patch of cover. They used it to gather for a frenzied attack on the barricade. Wave after wave of men threw themselves at the wall, climbing over one another to grasp a shaky handhold on the mealie-bag parapet. Again, and again a soldier blasted the climbers down with his rifle, or stabbed mercilessly into face and throat. A warrior would thrust himself up, in sacrifice, to allow a comrade to reach and seize the barrel of the gun that had killed his friend; the attempt, tried over and over, never seemed to work. Others tried to use assegais as tools for the ascent, jabbing them into the gaps between mealie bags for a climber's spike. Then, at once, the Zulus would break off their attack, the living vanishing back into the bush while those dead and dying lolled in slippery piles before the wall. Within seconds a new wave of warriors would burst from cover to repeat the assault, and the thing began again. Some managed even to leap onto the barricade, there to be shot or bayoneted as they landed. All the time the Zulus – mostly it was the uDloko and the uThulwana, the middle-aged men with tummies and families at home – were howling like banshees, slapping their shields, and making an infernal din. The short distance between the dead ground and the fort wall meant that the defense had no chance of clearing the beaten zone with Martini fire. Each time the attack eddied up like a dust storm, sweeping from cover and lashing the barricade with furious humanity.

One big, strapping warrior dropped his own spear and rifle in an effort to seize the muzzle of a soldier's weapon with his left hand and the bayonet – yes, the bayonet – with his right. Yanking down forcefully, it seemed that he would either disarm the soldier or pull him bodily over the parapet. Cool as you like, the soldier kept his left hand around the small of the butt, dropped a cartridge into the breech and, letting the Zulu haul down on the muzzle end, allowed the warrior to believe he'd got the Martini. Once the Zulu moved his body in front of the barrel, the soldier squeezed the trigger. Sneaky devil.

The men of B Company were firing fast, the shots rattling in time to the attacks like a demented symphony. Beethoven, that's the chap. At the moment of impact the rifles would crash, then cease as the soldiers stepped forward with cold steel, the old lunger, to clear their front. A small brown and white dog, a terrier I think, was yapping away at the enemy, and once jumped up onto the parapet to bite a Zulu's hand. John Chard was in the forefront, firing a rifle taken from a fallen private. The commissary, Dalton, was encouraging the men, passing out ammunition with a steadying word between rushes and using a rifle when the Zulus came on. I watched him in admiration, when suddenly he dropped with a bullet through the shoulder. A fellow in dark blue – probably the surgeon – came up all-a-rush to tend his wound. Another man was killed about this time, a big blond private who had only moments before run out from the hospital. It was the amiable dullard who'd been on sentry-go when I first reached the place, Cole by name, ages ago it seemed. This was pure bad luck for him; in one of the sudden flashes of silence that sometimes occur between war cries and musketry, someone called out "Old King Cole is dead." A merry old soul, perhaps, but not a fortunate one.

All this time I lay still, with the big cowhide shield over my back to hide as much of me as possible, and the headdress pulled down. The fascination of watching a Zulu charge from such close quarters was engrossing. I almost – almost – forgot which side I was on, and what it was I came here to do. What was it again?

I was trying to break into Rorke's Drift. The marksmen of the 24th had effectively stopped my best efforts to sneak in the back way. It was clear they would shoot me down long before I could get within easy distance of calling out "Friend! British officer! Please don't shoot!" Anyway, I'd be damned lucky to find a spot close by the wall that wasn't already infested with bona fide Zulu warriors, who'd identify me for a fake the moment I rattled my jaws. However, if I didn't go in the back way meant I was obliged to try the front door, barging in with a few hundred uninvited guests of the most undesirable kind. Since Chard and company were doing a bloody good job of keeping the door locked and barred, this option appeared closed. Perhaps things would improve when darkness came. Maybe the Zulus would have taken enough, lost their pluck for storming the barricades. It couldn't be long until dark. In the tropics, there is no lengthy fading of the day. Dusk is notional. Night falls like a drunken sentry.

An uneasy feeling in the pit of my stomach spread queasily through me. Night did not favour the men of the 24th. Night meant deep shadow, brief vision, confusion in the ranks. Night meant firing blind into the chasm. Night meant the bastards could sneak up on you. Night was friend to the Zulu.

We Bagshots are resourceful chaps, as you know. I've probably mentioned how the sainted Sir Bulstrode Bagshot escaped the benighted field of Marston Moor dressed as a laundrywoman. But staving off the greater forces of nature ain't something we learned at St Botolph's Academy for the Sons of Distressed Gentlemen. I shook my head, hoping to loosen any stray bright ideas. None fell.

CHAPTER THIRTY-ONE

Hove 1928

With the models arrayed, the scene on the Colonel's table had improved considerably. The red soldiers stood inside the wall of fruit. The Zulus were coming at them with enthusiasm, this time without the aid of the Arabs, the Red Indians, or the Prussian Guard. Inside the hospital, Bagshot's damaged toys lay in rows, defended by a staunch handful of those yet unbroken.

"A capital sight!" pronounced the Colonel.

A second opinion was given by Pickles. The large ginger form of the tabby was found dozing in the mission yard the following morning, preventing the Zulus from overrunning the position by virtue of having knocked most of them over. He'd also sent most of the garrison sprawling. Some had fallen from the table and were in need of the repairs box themselves.

"Bad cat!" scolded the Colonel. Pickles gave him a supercilious look and yawned.

* * *

Things were not going well for Chard and his lads inside the mission. Bad signs were evident. The British were abandoning the front face of the hospital and withdrawing to a second line of defense based on the storehouse and the yard in front of it. I'd seen it from up on the mountain. The Zulu pressure was more than Chard's manpower – what was it, a hundred men? – could withstand. Instantly the Zulus were up and over the ledge, onto the mealie bags and rushing the front verandah of the hospital. A scything fire from the new defense line tore bloody swathes through them – nothing like a bit of flanking fire to put a crimp in your enthusiasm – but some did reach the verandah. Some, then more. A fellow in civilian garb jumped out from the barricade to fetch his hat – I suppose it had blown away or been shot off – and in the process took the opportunity to blithely shoot one warrior and bayonet another. Hat jammed firmly on his head, he climbed back to his place. The dog was still barking bravely. The Zulus were at the front of the hospital now, the recess of the verandah sheltering them from the crossfire. They were banging at the door like rent collectors. Nobody answered the knock. I didn't think that would stop them. I've seen bailiffs at work before.

The fall of the front wall was a clarion call to action for the Zulus on my side of the building to attack the west wall. They foamed up out of the grass and surged against the door and windows. Redoubled firing from the loopholed wall felled many, but simple arithmetic was in their favor. Once a few Zulus were pressed against the wall, invisible to those inside, it was merely a question of time as to when they found a way inside. Hands reached to seize the muzzles of rifles, forcing their owners to haul them back inside the hospital instead of firing. The bravest hacked at the outside door with heavy spears, smashing the wood until it splintered. Several warriors were shot through the door, but for every one that fell, another stepped into his place. They were game blighters, those Zulus. The soldier defending his post

was a demon; he fired, lunged, stuck, withdrew, fired again. All alone he held that barricaded door shut in the faces of the uThulwana. The thin wooden planking was fragmenting about him.

Suddenly I was up myself, advancing. It might have been blind stupidity, or the heat of battle, or a glimmering of an idea. Might have been indigestion for all I know. Anyway, I was going in with the Zulus.

Death can be a terrible thing, and I've been lucky enough to avoid it so far. Some men die quietly, in their beds, or decently slumping to the ground in an orderly fashion. The soldier was not one of those. As the door finally collapsed into shards of broken timber, he leapt forward into the Zulu torrent. He fired, dropping a man. He lunged briefly, plunging his bayonet into a Zulu belly. Then, stepping into the dead man's space, he fired once more into the mass, turned his cartridge pouch upside down as if to prove that it was empty, and turned the rifle around in his hands. Swinging it by the barrel, the clubbed butt smashed into a warrior's face. I winced. There's somebody's good looks gone. It seemed like a minute he stood there, daring any man to take him on. If it had been a fair fight the Zulus would have stepped up one at a time to face him in single combat. Of course, it wasn't, and six of them rushed him at once. Then they threw him bodily in the air, spread-eagled and stabbed like a sacrifice in some dreadful Aztec ceremony. They split him like a pig, chanting and grinning all over their faces. But this was my chance. While the Zulus played with their victim, I bolted forward into the doorway. I was inside the hospital!

CHAPTER THIRTY-TWO

Hove 1928

There had been an embarrassing episode in the residents' lounge. Several guests played their final rubber of auction bridge – not the new American 'contract' version, which Mr. Quint had pronounced unacceptable under his roof – while others read or wrote letters. The Colonel sat close to the fireplace with a large glass at his elbow and the evening paper on his lap. The Colonel didn't play bridge. He couldn't remember the rules, though, of course, he'd never admit it. Three things happened that evening. None of them were unusual to those of the Empire Lodge's residents who were familiar with the ways of 'The old Indian gentleman', and most were all too familiar with those ways. It was the sequence of events that created 'The Floral Sofa Incident', as it would come to be known.

First of all, the Colonel spilled his drink. He had elbowed three fingers of the hotel brandy – a vintage he often decried as fit only for cleaning the silver but drank anyway – onto the cushions of the sofa. The flowery pattern of the upholstery concealed many such stains. Then he had fallen asleep. The newspaper fell from his grasp, open at the racing results, and was seized on by a paint salesman from Luton who had put an optimistic shilling on a runner in the 2.30 at Kempton Park. The horse had come in fifth in a field of five. The disappointed punter failed to notice that the newspaper was not the only thing that had fallen from Colonel Bagshot's sleeping hand. The ancient briar pipe, reeking of his private blend (ordered from Vafiades of Cairo, very select) was nestled among the cushions. Its aromatic stench, compared by Young Mr. Quint to perfumed cowdung, already hung heavy in the atmosphere. The last embers burned unseen.

Unseen, that is, until they made contact with the brandy-soaked cloth and burst into flame.

Exactly who first spotted the fire was never agreed upon. Miss Hesketh-Prout said she had noticed something odd a few moments before Mr. Wiggins (on holiday from East Grinstead) seized the soda siphon to douse the flames. Everyone agreed that it was lucky he had done so, because, when Colonel Bagshot leapt up yelling "Oh my God, Hook, forget the bloody Zulus!" his trousers were actually on fire.

It was a subdued Bagshot who summoned George to his rooms the following morning. Yes, he wanted breakfast in bed. No, he had nothing to say to any of the residents. That idiot Wiggins had almost drowned him.

* * *

I would like to tell you that I, Charles Edward Hezeliah Bagshot, was the first man in Zulu uniform to cross the threshold of Rorke's Drift. However, that would not be true. A couple of sneaky bastards had made it in before me. They immediately fell to the task of butchering the British patients whose ward we had so rudely trespassed our way into. I'd have done my best to prevent their spearing the sick men, but they were already well on their way to finishing off the job. All I had was a broken stick, and I had other things to do.

The room was tiny, bare and wretched. I don't swing cats, being fond of the beasties, but if I did it would have been much battered about the ears, whiskers and nose leather. I've seen bigger broom cupboards. Across from the door was a hole in the brick wall, low to the ground, with the remains of the brickwork and plaster showing where it had recently been cut. It was big enough for a man to crawl through. The man who just had was looking at me. He was a young soldier, minus his helmet, plus his rifle.

"Please don't shoot," I said as calmly as I could manage; "Lieutenant Bagshot, 10th Hussars. Is Mr. Chard available? Or Mr. Bromhead?"

His jaw dropped as he fumbled with the lever of his Martini. Confusion caused his eyes to pop. He didn't shoot me, which I rather appreciated. Instead, he disappeared through the hole in the wall. I didn't have time to hang about, so I followed him, head first. "Come back here my good man!" I called out, "I really am a British officer." I didn't expect a salute. I just preferred he didn't brain me with a clubbed rifle. Talking in a reasonable tone seemed like the best thing to do, since my appearance was rather against me. But he'd vanished. There was the sound of a door shutting a few feet to my right.

Suddenly I was all on my own. I'd entered one of Rorke's central rooms, which had a window to the front, the verandah side. I expected to see Zulus swarming through, but no. I recognized the room. I'd been here, what, two days ago. There had once been a piano in here. I could have used it to block the hole behind me.

166

But it wasn't here anymore, because I'd helped Cochrane steal it, and this fact had already contributed to my having a very difficult day. I tried to pull my shield (my shield! hear me now!) through the hole. It stuck, as you'd expect given that the shield was twice as long as the hole was wide. The thing jammed flat against the edge of the wall. Inspiration touched me, and I threaded my bit of stick through the leather thonging on the back of the shield. The stick held it fast across the hole. Not that a shield and a stick would keep out the Zulus, but perhaps, once the warriors already in the room finished hacking up the patients, they would only see a shield fallen against a wall rather than a convenient passageway into the rest of the hospital. You'd be surprised what people don't notice when they are otherwise occupied. Of course, it was entirely possible that two dozen buckos of the uThulwana had seen my rear end pass through the hole after the soldier and were helplessly choked with laughter at my antics. I remembered I was wearing proper gentleman's drawers under my monkey skin kilt. Indian cotton. It breathes, you know.

I took a swig of the Glenlivet I'd tucked inside my kilt. Inspiration hit me again. I was going to set the hospital on fire.

Now, you may ask – as some did later, in a none-too-friendly manner – why I would wish to set fire to a hospital containing British sick and wounded? Is pyromania endemic amongst junior officers? Is arson taught alongside equitation in the 10th Hussars? Did I simply feel that the Zulus weren't playing well enough, and needed my assistance?

I didn't think so. To help with the decision, I made a list. In my head, I mean. I find that often helps.

Reasons to set fire to the hospital:

I) To stop the Zulus getting in.
II) To encourage the defenders to leave while they still had chance and reach the new line of defence.
III) To illuminate the field of fire once night fell.
IV) To act as a beacon for the rest of Chelmsford's force to come and relieve us, always assuming they hadn't gone and got sliced up by the Zulus themselves.

Reasons not to set fire to the hospital:

I) Patients unable to move very quickly.
II) Destruction of government property.
III) Action not properly authorised by O.C. commanding, Rorkes Drift.
IV) Waste of good whisky.

Four to four. Wait. "Destruction of government property". It wasn't. It belonged to the missionaries. H.M. Govt probably hadn't paid a farthing in rent. Strike out number two. Four to three. That made it a good plan, then. How to do it, though?

I had matches. I had a stick. I had a pistol, a flask of whisky and most of a Zulu induna's outfit. It wasn't a lot. If necessary I had the white cotton drawers, but I rather hoped to retain the use of them.

RORKE'S DRIFT COCKTAIL; a Recipe.

Take one feather headdress, Zulu. Soak carefully in twelve-year-old Glenlivet. Place on the end of a stick of suitable length. Set the headdress alight; use paper stuffed into headband as lighter, if needed to avoid burning fingers. Lift to rafters using stick and push hard into thatching of roof. Ensure thatch is burning well. Run like the clappers.

I followed the plan, and in a few moments the inner thatch was well alight in a convincing, almost appealing manner. It reminded me of Guy Fawkes' night. Here's a tip. If you ever want to set fire to a thatched roof, do it from the underside. It's always much drier for being indoors, and the flames rise conveniently upwards into the combustible straw middle. Don't try it at your granny's cottage, though.

I was glad that it was the missionary's house I was burning rather than the chapel. "And they burnt the house of God, and brake down the walls of Jerusalem" as it says in Chronicles II. That was Nebuchadnezzar did that. Nobody in my family has set fire to a place of worship since the middle ages, and I wasn't about to start.

I was admiring my work when the front door splintered, and a couple of hefty Indluyengwe barged it down. I could just see them from where I was, through the empty doorframe into the next room. At the same time the shield I'd placed across the hole through which I'd come began to shift. Someone was pulling it out of the way. I'd best be gone. I finished off the Glenlivet; I was sorry I'd had to waste most of it on saving the garrison, but there you have it. A soldier's lot, and all that.

I knocked on the door whence I'd seen the soldier disappear. Fortunately, I was careful to lean back against the wall and rap twice, high on the door, because a bullet smashed through the central slat as an immediate reply. The defenders were shooting at me again. As if a real Zulu would knock! I hammered again, stepping aside quickly.

"Open up in there! Bagshot, 10th Hussars!" I yelled.

I heard a voice inside: "You what?"

"Bagshot, 10th Royal Hussars. Message for Lieutenant Chard." The message was admittedly a touch irrelevant at this point ("The Zulus are attacking your post") but I've found that a private soldier will always listen to someone who has a despatch for his commanding officer. "And that's 'You what, Sir!'" I had my best parade ground voice on. This was no time to play languid.

I looked around me, anxiously. Would the soldier open the door? Would the Zulus skewer me while he was still thinking about it? The shield had been wrenched away from the wall, and a brown face was peering at my knees. I'd have kicked him in the face – as I've said, St Botolph's taught me to fight dirty – but I'd got no boots on. The door opened a crack. Without the feather headdress I looked like my normal self from the neck up. That doesn't count the Bovril streaks, of course. I'm not certain that it hadn't all worn off by now. I smiled at the soldier. "I think I need to come in", I said, casually. Slipping through the doorway I took a quick peek behind me. A handful of flaming straw had just fallen on the incoming Zulu's head. Being a Zulu, he said nothing. I shut the door.

CHAPTER THIRTY-THREE
Hove 1928

The shield had been a beautiful thing, once upon a time. It was made in the shape of an almond, four feet long, white cowhide with two large reddish patches of irregular shape. A stick ran up the back, secured by a system of lacing to the main body of leather by lacing of contrasting cowhide strips. At the very top was a crest of feathers, now much faded and somewhat damaged. Deep gouges ran in rips across the front of the shield. The Colonel lifted it down from the wall for better viewing.

"What do you think, George? uDhloko. Or Ndhlondhlo. I get 'em confused. I managed to bring that back with me."

"Crikey!" exclaimed George, impressed. "Are those bayonet marks across the front?"

"Those vicious marks. Er, yes, of course."

From the corner, Pickles looked at the shield and admired his very own handiwork. Good scratches. Maybe one day he'd get another chance at the thing on top, which had looked like a bird, but disappointingly wasn't. You never knew about these things.

* * *

There were a dozen pairs of eyes looking at me. British soldiers' eyes. I was still dressed as a Zulu from the Adam's apple down. Confused men with breech-loading weapons require careful handling. "Steady lads, no shooting," I said, as you would. "Who is in charge here?"

It's a funny thing. The normal chain of command is altered when soldiers are in a hospital under attack. Officers are treated with the proper deference (except by unusually ferocious lady nurses) but otherwise the hierarchy runs as follows:

healthy men with weapons, sick men with weapons, sick men unable to bear arms, the comatose, the dead. In a good ward this last category will have been removed elsewhere. Sergeant's stripes and such don't mean a lot. "I am, zurr!"

He was a broad-shouldered man with a West Country burr to his voice. I knew him. The cook who'd helped out with the hot water when I arrived at Rorke's Drift, and then with the piano. He was now helping out by skewering a Zulu at the point of his bayonet. "1373 'Ook, zurr!" He dropped another cartridge into the open breech of his rifle and blasted into the opening where the enemy had torn the planking aside. Jim Rorke could have spent more on the doors. Hook roared at the Zulus, "Come on yerr baastards!"

I looked about. There might have been a dozen sick men on cots or crouched against the walls. The ward – cramped and narrow – looked familiar. I remembered a slung bedpan clattering against a wall. It seemed like years ago. At the end of the room the soldier I'd been following was chipping away at the brickwork with a pickaxe. The mud bricks crumbled under his short, hard blows. Rorke had been miserly in this aspect of his house too. A hole began to appear. Two of the patients helped sweep the debris aside.

"Pinned like rats in a hole!" shrieked someone. It was one of the sick men, flush faced and panicky. "All right, calm down", I said. "We need to leave quickly, in a proper and orderly manner." Easier said than done, but a nervous soldier needs to hear confidence in the voice of his officer. I was his officer now. "Form a queue by the, er, hole in the wall." And they did, at least those that could stand up.

An assegai ripped through the smashed doorway where Hook was holding back the Zulus. It struck him in the forehead. 'And Saul sought to smite David even unto the wall with his javelin' as Samuel says. But David dodged Saul's shot, and so it was with Henry Hook. Luckily – and one must see the hand of Providence, even in the design of the army sun helmet, 1878 issue – the tip caught on the brass plate on the front; the helmet was knocked backwards, taking the impetus of the throw. The spear clattered off to one side. Hook shook his head, showing a gash on the brow, and straightened the helmet. Grumbling out a string of unusually foul oaths, he fired three shots in quick succession. "Nailed that frigging Kaffir – teach 'im to chuck a sodding spear at 'Enry 'Ook."

I found a rifle myself and joined him at the cracking door. A warrior's hands reach through to grab Hook's Martini. I used the butt of mine to smash his elbow, and he yelped. That's a thing about elbows. I held the rifle underarm, like a cricket bat, while Hook fired and stabbed with the bayonet. More arms reached at Hook's rifle, one big fellow seizing the muzzle and bound into the room a pace or two. I swung and cracked him across the shins; at the same time Hook tore the gun from the Zulu's hands, slipped a cartridge in, and fired. The man's chest crimsoned and he collapsed into the doorway onto his friends. Very nasty indeed.

"Bloody hell!" observed Hook, somewhat testy at this point. "Got an 'ole made yet, Williams?" I doubt that Williams could hear him. 'And the posts of the door moved at the voice of him that cried, and the house was filled with smoke'. Isaiah 6;4

The room was, indeed, filling with smoke.

CHAPTER THIRTY-FOUR

Hove 1928

George had found an advertisement for Bovril in a magazine. It featured a large, if somewhat truculent, picture of a man that George immediately recognized as one of history's great generals, conqueror of half Europe and, apparently, drinker of the liquid meat extract. The copy read as follows: "Napoleon's Secret! The Secret of Napoleon's power was his immense vitality. The same is true of most great men – Julius Caesar, Michelangelo, Gladstone, Cecil Rhodes – they were successful because they were never tired. Don't get tired, drink Bovril!"[44] There was no mention of any benefit to be found in smearing it all over your naked body. George cut out the page. He'd give it to the Colonel.

And he did. Colonel Bagshot had just returned from an afternoon at the County Ground, watching Maurice Tate, owner of "The finest bowling action ever seen,"[45] as he took a succession of wickets for Sussex. Actually, the Colonel hadn't seen much at all, because he'd fallen asleep. Cricket did that to him. However, the consequence of a good nap on a summer's day was that the old man was refreshed. Definitely. He was positively frisky.

"Bovril, yes. Never tired, just like me. I haven't had any Bovril in ages. D'ye think there's any in the pantry?" George thought there might be. "Could you bring up some? Just a jar. Two jars. And a feather duster, or a mop, or something in that line."

A conspiratorial look crossed his face, though that same expression might equally well indicate indigestion.

"I say, George. Would you like to be a Zulu?"

* * *

---

44. This excellent piece of advertising copy appeared in several British publications in the 1920s.
45. Maurice Tate (1895-1952) played cricket for Sussex and England, and was noted for his development of a style known as seam-bowling.

"Help me with the fat bloke."

Williams had broken through the wall and taken the patients through into the next room. All except one. A very large private of the 24th would not fit through the hole. I think he had a broken leg. Williams was pulling from the far side while I pushed. Hook was still raging at the doorway, fighting mad. He was coughing from the smoke, but so were the Zulus, so it was a fair fight.

"Oww!" shrieked the fat private. "Shut up Connolly", replied Williams, in a heavy Welsh accent. "I'll break both your bloody legs if it'll get you through this bloody hole." But Connolly wasn't moving.

Then Hook was with us, face blackened and blood running from his scalp wound. He stepped over Connolly, ducking through the hole and dragging the invalid through by the shoulders. A powerful man indeed. Connolly screamed. I scrambled through, following the track of Connolly's ammunition boots. As I looked back – I always look back, don't ask why – I saw Zulus advancing through the billowing black smoke. It was like the bottomless pit in Revelation, ' and there arose a smoke out of the pit, as the smoke of a great furnace', though not as bad, of course. Still, we'd be at the back door in a moment.

The new room was no bigger than the last, the men cramped together as Williams hacked out yet another hole in the far wall. Hook and I played our same batting partnership, he shooting and stabbing while I swung a smooth rifle butt against the heads and arms of anyone fool enough to poke his nose through the gap. The patients were crammed like kippers in a tin, anxious to be out of it. The roof was crackling with fire, the flames still a couple of rooms behind us I calculated. Still, wounded men lined up in front of a hole tend to be short on patience – no pun intended – and telling 'em they had a good ten minutes before they frazzled like rashers of bacon didn't seem the best way of holding their confidence. I looked up at the rafters. Smoke was curling among the beams. I wondered if Jim Rorke had saved money in that area the way he'd cut corners everywhere else. Tight-fisted bastard.

Suddenly a Zulu came through the roof. Looking up, I saw a face peering down through a gash in the thatchwork. Evidently the enemy had climbed up onto the roof – like everything else, cheap and badly put up, probably leaked like a sieve – and were cutting their way through, the better to get at us. I spotted the beggar and would have shot at him if only I'd had any ammunition for the Martini. I'd not thought to ask if anyone had any to spare. Hook was occupied at the hole, while the healthier patients held a door that faced the Oskarberg against some warriors who were demanding to come in. The Zulu sprang. I only managed to point my finger and call him an offensive name before he landed on me, feet first on my chest.

I went sprawling, which was hard to do in a room crowded like the Black Hole of Calcutta. For the second time that day I had a fully paid up Zulu warrior on top of me. His face was squashed right up in mine. He obviously didn't believe I was a Zulu; I wished I'd kept the feather bonnet. He had a headdress of his own, a skin turban-thingy with a tail at the back like Davy Crockett; it tickled my ear, and I couldn't scratch. Oddly enough he didn't stab me, which I had to consider a Good Thing, though precisely the kind of heathen savagery you have to look for at moments like that. I saw why. One of the patients had taken a crutch and wedged the upper part of it over the Zulu's spear arm. "Oh, good show!" I squeaked – the fellow had knocked most of the wind out of me – as the patient twisted the crutch to lever the Zulu's blade away from my ribs. Then the other patients mobbed him and beat him unconscious with bed pans. Damned ignominious fate, really. Still, I wasn't going to complain. I grabbed the Davy Crockett hat and put it on. I've no idea why. Groggy, I suppose, what with the smoke and the excitement and the Glenlivet. But I shall return to this point shortly.

We were through another of Williams' patent wall demolitions and into what I hoped would be the last room. Actually, it wasn't, but an open doorway led to it. Two private soldiers, one old and one young, were holding the ward, which had a window and door facing south. They had plenty to keep themselves busy, what with the Zulus outside, but they were happy to help the patients move on through the building. One man was yowling at the top of an impressive set of lungs;

"Shirkers, the lot of you! A bit of fever! Don't want to work is what it is! And here we've got the Russians all around us!"

"Sergeant Maxfield's a bit mad," confided the elder of the privates to Hook. "Thinks we're in the bloody Crimea. He wasn't even hardly born when there was a war in the Crimea!"

"Yes, young Jones," responded Hook; "But you were there, weren't you, you old sot?"

"Oh, aye, I was a corporal then!" Both laughed. It seemed an odd place to share a joke.

"Hurry up, man!" I said; "Let's get everyone out of the back door." The old soldier looked at me, apparently unsurprised at my garb. His deep brown eyes set in a sallow complexion appeared troubled. "Don't you know there's no back door?"

177

CHAPTER THIRTY-FIVE

Hove 1928

Being a Zulu wasn't all it was cracked up to be, thought George. For a start, being sponged over with Bovril was a sticky and smelly process. Moreover, it didn't work very well as a cosmetic. George had heard that in the theatrical trade something called 'greasepaint' was used. As far as he was aware, it was not a meat by-product. This was horrible. Boot blacking would be an improvement.

"Zulus aren't really black, George. That's a common misapprehension. Sort of a pale chocolate, mostly. Then again, white people aren't white. They're pink. So, I was the pink Zulu if you want to be pedantic about it, though I never am. Pedantic, I mean."

George didn't want to be pedantic. He wanted the smell of Bovril off him. Still, dressing up as a Zulu had its attractions.

It took half an hour. The Colonel's collection of Zulu militaria ran only as far as the shield and three strings of white cowtail ornaments, somewhat ratty by almost any standard. Colonel Bagshot thought that a spear was perhaps not the best idea; he provided a nasty looking club of questionable provenance ("The Congo, somewhere, I think") instead of a Zulu knobkerrie. The rest of the ensemble was less impressive: a bath-towel, the feathers from a duster held around the head with a piece of elastic, and a pair of disreputable sandals. "Real Zulus don't wear sandals, George. The great king Shaka made 'em harden their feet by dancing on thorns, but I don't suppose you'd do that, would you?"

* * *

It was a damned nuisance that there was no back door, but at least there was a window. I used to know a chap, Podger Pilkington of the 12th Lancers, who swore a window was as good as a door any day, and he used many a sliding glassy pane to avoid an irate husband. But, of course, he wasn't an invalid in a military hospital; in fact, he went to great effort to avoid becoming one. This was a tiny opening, high up in the wall facing the yard. The two Joneses (Young Jones was the elder of the two) had widened it by smashing out the frame with an axe. They had already got half-a-dozen patients out, defending their loopholes at the same time, while the 24th still held the entire walled perimeter of the fort. But by this time the soldiers had been forced to abandon the main yard and drop back behind the transverse line of biscuit boxes that cut the fort into two. While Hook and the Joneses kept up the fight, I helped with the patients. I stooped next to the window, forming a stirrup with my hands to hoist the men up; Williams aided them with a gentle push to set them on the ledge. The drop was six feet. On the other side two soldiers, both wounded, took a terrible chance by crouching under the window to help the patients down. One invalid used me as a ladder to get up into the window, then stiffened as he stared out from the ledge:

"Holy Mother of God! Have you seen that drop?" He hesitated, more afraid of the height than the Zulus. Williams shoved him with no pretence at delicacy, and he fell with a squeal to the hard dirt below. Williams sniffed in disgust. "Wait 'til we get to the ones as is really sick. That silly sod's only got a case of the runs. I should've stuck him with me bayonet."

I stood up on a piece of plank to look through the window. It was an unnerving sight. The yard was thirty yards of open ground from the window drop to the safety of the biscuit boxes. As a race course it wasn't bad – better than Epsom Downs most Derby Days – but then Epsom doesn't feature the considerable disadvantage of hostile armed spectators all along the sidelines. The Zulus had pushed up to the mealie bag wall on both sides and were able to keep up a hot crossfire with muskets and thrown spears from the grandstand, with occasional brief rushes onto the turf. The redcoats behind the boxes kept up a brisk hail of fire on the Zulu position; without that, nary a one of us would have crossed that yard.

As it was, not everyone did. Williams and I helped a trooper of the Natal Mounted Police up into the window. He had terrible rheumatic fever and squirmed stoically as we hoisted him up; he was in appalling pain. A patient in the queue behind called out, "Good luck, Syd." We tried to lower him gently, the men below gingerly offering their hands, but he stood no chance of getting across the courtyard. If we'd thought about it, we'd not have let him try. As it was, he made a pitiable effort to drag himself over the ground by his elbows. The strain was evident, and you could almost see the Zulus slavering over an easy kill, like jackals around a sickly antelope. Bromhead was directing fire from the redoubt and trying to buy the poor beggar enough time to haul his battered carcass across the yard, but an impetuous warrior leapt over the wall to show off and did for the trooper with a spear in the back. You could hear the groans from our men, and the maddening approval from the Zulu grandstand. Naturally the killer was almost blown apart by the volley that opened up on him, but too late for the lame copper.

Williams sighed bitterly; "Poor bastard. We'd best get the real cripples over ourselves. Sons of whores!" I assume this last was directed at the Zulus. He wasn't in a charitable mood and vented by firing three fast shots from the window at the hunkered Zulu mass, cursing them with considerable obscenity but little imagination.

Private Roy was next, a patient whose enthusiasm for the fight had proved better for his health than anything the surgeon had to offer. "Me gun's broke, but I've still got me bayonet!" He made sure the two-foot blade was securely fixed, performing a vigorous display of bayonet drill towards a body of Zulus forty feet away while we lowered an old soldier, a real invalid, down beside him. Brandishing the weapon fiercely, with extemporised leaps and yells, he charged across the open ground as if assaulting the box wall itself. The invalid tottered along in his wake, reaching the barricade safely. The Zulus all seemed impressed. "Oh good" said Williams. "'E's got rotten eyesight. I thought 'e might run toward the Zulus 'stead of our lads. That is a relief, boyo."

Between us, we got out everyone who was willing to come out. Another Natal policeman almost bought it as a Zulu slug knocked him off balance, but a comrade from his unit and another man dragged him to safety. A staggering artillery bombardier was rescued by a gunner who ran out from the box wall. Regimental pride's a wonderful thing.

"Let's be out ourselves!" yelled Williams. "No time like the present!"

"We've still to get out Sergeant Maxfield" called back Old Jones (being the younger of the two Joneses). "We've got 'is trousers on but the silly sod won't shift."

Being a willing sort (and everyone else busy with clubbing, shooting, jabbing, that sort of thing) I staggered back into the smoke to the Jones's room. The fog was dense and the thatch fair crackling with flames. Maxfield was on his pallet, roaring something about the Russians. Jones was pleading with him to show some sense.

"Come on sarge. We can get you out nice and easy." I knew this would have no effect, so I shouted out something closer to the mark. "Fall back on Balaclava camp, sergeant! The cossacks have captured Florence Nightingale!" Maxfield sat bolt upright and reached for his boots. "Yessir, Lord Cardigan sir!"

It was a bloody shame that half a dozen Zulus swarmed in just then. The sergeant was their first target. Maxfield was dead in moments. He never got the chance to rescue Miss Nightingale.

Jones and I fled for the window. Williams and Young Jones had already left, covered by the two soldiers at the foot of the wall. I helped Jones up and out and pulled myself up into the window frame.

A fusillade of shots smashed into the brickwork, damned close to me. "Careful, you ignorant bastards!" I shouted, falling back into the room. As I pulled myself back up, I saw Jones and the two soldiers had made a run for the breastwork. Another rough volley blasted against the wall, one shot much too close to my head. The 24th were firing at me.

The stupid pillocks thought that I was a Zulu. You'd have thought that one of the patients would have had the sense to let on who I was, and not to shoot at me. Instead, they just hobbled off to see the surgeon. Ungrateful sods. Meanwhile I was the bulls-eye in a shooting gallery.

I wasn't going out through that window, not today.

CHAPTER THIRTY-SIX

Hove 1928

It was Cook's practice, each night, to have what she termed a 'little drop of gin' in the servant's parlour – a sitting room just across from the kitchen – before she went to bed. The Empire Lodge had known better days, and, like most large Victorian establishments, had a sizeable 'downstairs' from the time when a house would have a good number of servants 'living in'. Now it was just her, that old fool Bottomley, and young George Chapman. Too cheeky for his own good was young George, especially since that Colonel Bagshot had started up with all his silly stories, filling his head with nonsense. George was too big for his boots. What you wanted in a page was somebody who was presentable to carry luggage and clear the breakfast tables, run out for errands, and clean the boots. Very important was cleaning the boots. In a bigger hotel that's all George would get to do. Bloody lucky, he was. He ought to be grateful, 'stead of running about with that senile old geezer and never being about when she wanted something fetched from the shops. She'd tell him so again.

* * *

Somebody said something behind me. I won't attempt to repeat it. I'm generally good with languages – I can ask "Would you have a glass of fermented mare's milk, by chance?" in several Central Asian dialects – but I'd only been in the country a fortnight. But it wasn't English, and I didn't believe it was Welsh. I couldn't see any choice but to turn around.

I'd not learned the Zulu for "What the bloody hell do you think you're playing at?", but I'm pretty sure that was the gist of what he had to say. As I turned to face him, his eyes grew big. He did not think I was a pal from the inDluyengwe. I thumped him on the nose and scuttled past him.

I ran through the Jones's room in a flash. Fortunately for me (though not, alas, for him) the bunch of rabid Zulus who had descended on Sergeant Maxfield were busily engaged in the bizarre and disgusting task of ritually disemboweling the poor beggar. There was a lot of smoke about, which helped my sudden rush past. I dove for the hole – the work of Private Williams – in the opposite wall and hoped that the Zulu I'd smacked wasn't too swift on his feet. Unfortunately, he was.

He grabbed me by the back of my kilt as I scrambled through the hole. I'm not certain if this was a good thing, but the kilt fell down about my ankles, causing my assailant to slip at the same time. I think I've told you that the dead chappie I got the Zulu togs from was a deal larger than me. Anyway, I stepped clumsily out of the kilt and turned to face my pursuer. He had an *Iklwa* with a blade a yard long. I had a pair of gentleman's drawers, Indian cotton, first grade, from a little place in the Burlington Arcade. It wasn't a fair fight.

It was then I noticed the revolver. I'd shoved it down the kilt's waistband with the whiskey, matches (etc) and had forgotten it in the excitement. It lay temptingly close. I grabbed it from the ground as the Zulu rose, and did what young Bonney had shown me out at the old fence at Tunstall's ranch. I fanned the hammer like a western desperado.

Bang! Bang!! Bang!!! Bang!!!! Bang!!!!!.

I traced a line of bullet holes through the top of an old wardrobe, which stood next to the entrance hole. I'd not hit the Zulu at all. I'm not a pistols man. But I've told you that.

The Zulu glowered, evidently a bit put off his game, if nothing else. I held the Colt out almost to touch him and pulled the trigger. Click. Six-shooters, Bonney had called 'em. Click.

Bang! The Zulu spasmed in pain and fell. I didn't even touch the trigger this time. The shot had come from the wardrobe. A smoking muzzle emerged from a crack between door and jamb. The barrel was moving hither and yon in a strange manner, while a dialogue emerged between two voices inside the cupboard.

"Stop that. I need to shoot the other Kaffir."

"It ay no bleedin' Kaffir. It's that officer as dressed up like a Zulu as 'elped with the wounded. Ee's a whoit man!"

"Nah, that blork's gone owt t'winder wi' t'others. Let me do for this 'un ---"

I was not about to be the silent victim of this argument, so I turned towards the next Williams-hole. Smoke was belching through it, suffusing the room in acrid fog. I tripped over a dead Zulu on the floor and looked up at a hole in the thatched roof. This was the room I'd been fallen in on. The ceiling was ablaze. There was an open door to the outside, smashed in. Outside was full of Zulus, and dusk had not deigned to drop yet. I was in a fair pickle and wouldn't have put a shilling on my chances. I stepped back.

"In 'ere, sir!" whispered one of the voices from the wardrobe. "Mind, Beckett, take yer finger off the bloody trigger." A faced peered out at me from the crack in the door, a small, fortyish face. I don't usually climb into wardrobes (although there was an incident once, at the Viceroy's Ball at Simla) but this offer seemed tempting. I got in.

The wardrobe was, well, cramped. The missionary had left a variety of sombre clerical garments hanging from a rail, and his shoes in the bottom. I threw a pair of elastic-sided boots out as I tried to get comfortable. Nobody else had shown any respect for the preacher's possessions; it seemed foolish to start now.

"That's orroight, sir" said the old soldier. "We've got plenty of room. Me sister's 'ouse up Cradley 'eath is more crowded 'n this." I had no idea what he was on about. I'd learned some of the Pathan dialects, but this man's tongue was a mystery. Afterwards I found out it was a strange Midlands form of English known as Black Country; it is a region of wild tribes and primitive cultures[46]. I know this, for I was later to serve with a troop sergeant from West Bromwich, deep in that territory. But that was, as I say, later.

So, there we were, three of us, sweating in a cupboard with the flames crackling overhead and smoke siphoning through the cracks in the woodwork. The other man was a young northerner, an invalid. He kept demanding to use the rifle – we only had one – to poke out and shoot at passing Zulus. I'm not sure he didn't still want to shoot me; he'd taken my shots into the wardrobe (high, fortunately) somewhat personally. I'd have cursed him roundly – thus proving that I was, in fact, an officer and a gentleman – but silence seemed a better policy for the moment. Looking out, I could see Zulus moving about through the swirling smoke, most of them having the sense to go outside. There's really not much advantage in hanging about inside a burning building. I was only staying for lack of anywhere better to go.

The young soldier cracked. "Ahm no' sticking it 'ere no more!" he declared, flung open the door in a most irresponsible manner, and was gone. I didn't see where.

"Daft as a brush," sighed the old one.

---

46. I can confirm the phonetic accuracy of Colonel Bagshot's transcription of Black Country dialect, for my own family come from the borders of that region.

Still, it was becoming clear that we couldn't stay here much longer. The temperature had reached the level of a fourth-class railway carriage between Calcutta and Benares on a sultry July afternoon. I'd got a preaching gown pulled over my nose and mouth to breath. A crash in the room behind us suggested that the roof beams were falling down in flames. A peek through the crack showed a distinct orange glow replacing the darkness of smoke. I had no desire to baste gently in my own juices. It was definitely time to go.

The old private felt the same. He had an idea. "Pull the robe on sir. That's what oim a- dowin'. They won't see us in the dark."

"Ah, but I am still dressed as a Zulu!" I stated, with confidence. "I shall be alright as I am."

"Not unless yow've got some more o' that brown stuff. It's all washed off."

I'd sweated my disguise away. The preaching gown was a good idea.

Waters – his name was Waters; did I say that? – opened the wardrobe door. We reached the wrecked door to the outside. Night had finally shown up, like a boozy baronet at his own dinner party. I pulled the robe over my head, with a narrow gap open to see. All was darkness ahead. "Good Luck, sir" mumbled Waters through his woolen robe.

We ran like the clappers.

It can't have taken thirty seconds, stepping on bodies, shields and weapons. There were warriors milling about, focused, I suppose, on the fire and the raging battle. Nobody took any interest in me at all. I stumbled and fell into a ditch, no more than two feet deep. But I couldn't get out.

I'm not exactly certain what the thing they call adrenalin is, but I do know I'd run out of it. They say a man can be as strong as a gorilla, lift buses off the ground, for a little while, then slump and feel weak as a kitten. I'd ridden thirty-odd miles, walked half a dozen more, been wounded in the seat of action, half roasted alive, shot at by everyone who had a mind to, feet torn apart by thorns and stones, all on a few ration biscuits and half a pint of single malt Scotch. I'd have had more whisky if I hadn't needed it to burn a hospital. I was very tired. The ditch was a nice one as these things go, not too wet. 'The sleep of the labouring man is sweet, whether he eat little or much' as it says in Ecclesiastes. I pulled the preaching gown over my head and went to sleep.

CHAPTER THIRTY-SEVEN
Hove 1928

The scheme was all George's own idea. The Colonel would never have suggested anything that might get the lad into trouble. That being said, he was more than willing to help.

Probably, it was the bit about Waters and the wardrobe that made George think about it. That and the Zulus waiting to ambush the stores depot at Isandlwana.

George wasn't given to introspection. He didn't dwell on the many petty slights that cook had inflicted on him. Not very often, anyway. Nor did he consider the possible consequences of the action he was about to take. He was, after all, sixteen and dressed up as a Zulu warrior.

"Certainly, George. I shall cause a diversion to distract Cook's attention while you take up position."

* * *

They say – though I have no idea who they are and how they'd know – that death comes upon you like a warm bath. Or a deep sleep. Or a tremendous surprise and a pain in the guts as you wonder what to do about the half-yard of iron sticking through yesterday's steak-and-kidney pudding and out the other side. Anyhow, as the wet warmth crept up my arm and across my chest, gently dampening me, I knew I was due to report to St Peter at the orderly office outside the Pearly Gates. I was sorry to be out of uniform – considerably so – but consoled myself with the thought that he'd seen a lot of chaps worse off. Besides, although Church of England doctrine is lamentably hazy on the details, it was pretty certain you'd get any dismembered limbs, heads etc back on correctly, all wounds sewn up right, and no gangrene either. Heaven wouldn't be all it's cracked up to be if you had to put up with gangrene. The Vikings were pretty clear about this being the order of things in Valhalla, and I was sure that the Almighty, the One God on High, could offer at least as good a bargain as those vulgar Norse deities. Once I'd reported in, there'd be a grand reunion with Dear Mama (lost to typhus in '56), Papa (ditto dysentery on Delhi Ridge during the Mutiny), Great Uncle Henry (no, wait, he was still alive, though incredibly ancient), various aunts, several uncles and perhaps a cousin or two. Most of my cousins were still living, and those that weren't seemed unlikely to be plucking harps upstairs. I could ride with Prince Rupert or attend drill with Wellington and Marlborough. Our deceased soldiers would fight with dead Frenchmen and Americans and Sikhs and Maoris (but wait, these last two weren't Christians, so they couldn't be there, and how many Frenchmen could there be in Heaven?) and then we'd all go and have dinner together, even the ones who had been killed again today ---

Death licked my nose. I awoke with a start and took in a whiff of breath that would have felled a rhino. Brown eyes stared seriously into mine. A succession of barks almost deafened me. It was the dog, the little brown and white terrier I'd seen yapping at the Zulus from inside the fort. I'd awoken while he licked the last of the Bovril off my skin. He'd pulled back the black robe that had covered me.

A soldier came running, fixed bayonet at the ready. "Another live 'un, Pip?" he queried. "I'll do fer 'im, too."

"I'd really rather you didn't," I croaked.

"You again!" The man gawped down at me. "Ah, zurr!" This last, I felt, to cover his initial note of disrespectful surprise. It was Harry Hook, in filthy shirtsleeves, braces hanging loose. "Let me 'elp you up, zurr."

The sky was light. It was daytime; I must have slept for hours. The fort still held. As I staggered out of the trench, I witnessed a scene like a charnel house. Dead Zulus lay in grotesque positions, stiffened with weapons in hand, piled deep in places. The hospital was a blackened ruin, its roof caved in. Soldiers were picking through the bodies for survivors, rescuing ours and (I regret to say) disposing of theirs with a shot or a stab. Some picked up spears and shields for keepsakes.

"Oi remember you now," said Private Hook. "It was you as pinched the minister's piano; oi 'ad to 'elp you get it onto a wagon."

"It was not!" I replied, hot. "Did you never give the Reverend a deposit of £5 as the surety of an Officer of the Queen? It was with a letter that Lieutenant Cochrane gave you."

"Nozurr. That gen'lman with you gave me a letter, but there was no money with it. I did look at the note, and it said something about money being left. My corporal told me if the preacher saw it, 'ee'd think oi 'ad already took the money, and oi'd be up for a charge. So I burned it. The letter oi mean. Oi never saw any foive pounds."

Bloody Cochrane, the thieving so-and-so!

Hook led me through the shambles, past the wreckage of the fortifications to the makeshift dispensary. To my surprise, Private Waters was there, still draped in his preaching robe, having a nasty gunshot wound in his arm dressed. His face was smeared with soot.

"Took a leaf out o' yow book, sir," he told me. "Blackened me foice at the cook'ouse stove, and 'id out all noight with the Kaffirs all about. Some bastard shot me, though. Then I nearly got shot this morning troyin' ter get back in the bloody fort ---- sorry ter say, young Beckett copped a spear wound. Dow look good fer 'im."

He was interrupted by the surgeon giving me the once over. "Good God man, just look at you! Corporal, get this fellow a tot of rum forthwith! You'd be the maniac half my patients have been blabbing on about. 'A white Zulu,' they said, 'But he talks like a toff'. I had assumed they'd all lost their wits in the process of getting out of the burning hospital. Somebody shot you in the arse, I see, though it could be a lot worse. Just don't try riding a horse anytime too soon. Let me look at your tongue. Open your eyes wide. "

I was rapidly losing connection to the world around me. I could barely mumble but spat out a phrase I hadn't planned to say; "Doctor, I have cholera, but I'm feeling much better now".

When Gonny Bromhead appeared, I told him what had happened. "I burned your hospital, you owe me a large whisky!" Being deaf, he didn't take this as being tactless or rude.

All of a sudden, it seemed, the garrison fell silent. Those out picking through the bodies and debris stood transfixed, looking out towards the southwest, the shoulder of the Oskarberg. There, massed, was the impi. "Oh my God," muttered Waters. "Not again. 'Ow much can they tek? 'Ow much can we tek?"

This last seemed to me to be the more important question. Soldiers nervously checked through their buff leather pouches, counting the brass cartridges. The NCOs turned to examine the remaining ammunition boxes, far too few. The commissary, the man I'd seen fall early in the fight, was up, bandaged heavily, shouting instructions.

My mind was fading in and out. I thought of myself up on the Oskarberg, in full induna clobber, smacking at that damned black mamba with a bit of stick.

The Zulus below, hailing me as a hero dancing to spur them on. Then I was up on there again, right now, no snake this time. I stood proud, lofted my shield, and stabbed my broken stick portentously across the Buffalo River. "Go home, you ugly bastards!" I said, sort of under my breath as they were only half a mile away and I didn't want them to hear. The impi stirred in obedience to me, their commander, and moved off towards Zululand. I smiled. A shout from the storehouse roof snapped me back into reality.

"Column of men coming from across the river." Fear gripped the innards in a way I wouldn't recommend. More Zulus, a fresh force from the army that had swept over the camp at Isandlwana. What might that be, ten thousand men? More? I wished for my horse, my sword, even the miserable Colt Lightning I was so inept with. Red coats, one man said. But I'd seen Zulus ripping the red coats off slain soldiers and dress themselves in stolen garb.

Then it was over. The men on the roof went mad, waving homemade signalling flags. A peal of laughter rang out, relief not funny ha-ha. "'Orsemen" said someone; "British 'orsemen". "It's 'is lordship," said another, "Bloody Chelmsford". And they were right. The Zulus on the shoulder knew it too. Across the field of dead men and broken weapons the impi shook its head, grumbled, and slowly went home.

I'd not seen Chelmsford before, but I knew it must be him, bearded and sorrowful. The defense of the mission was no true consolation for the disaster that had overcome him and – more pointedly – his command. He was talking with John Chard while his officers stared their way across the battlefield and the men trudged in. A skinny, supercilious cove was drawing a sketch from his saddle. He surveyed the burned hospital, the tumbledown breastworks, and the exhausted soldiers. I'd met him before, in Fitzclarence's tent. It seemed like ages ago. When his eyes reached me, his jaw dropped visibly, and his pencil slipped from his grip. "Good God, sir, and who might you be?"

"Bagshot," I said. "Tenth hussars. I set fire to the hospital roof. I do hope nobody minds."

There was a stunned silence, followed by a roar of voices. But I'd fallen over by then.

My recollection of the next few days is patchy. The bits I do recall are not wonderful; riding in the wagons laughingly designated as ambulances, receiving the tender ministrations of medical staff of highly doubtful competence. At Helpmakaar I had the chance to glimpse the survivors of the Isandlwana disaster; Gardner, Essex, Horry Smith-Dorrien, Charlie Raw and Alfred Henderson. Not many, really. Cochrane had survived, but somehow wanted to avoid me. Not that

I was really up to talking. I slept most of the time, and it seemed that I was kept separate from anyone else when I was awake. My mind was anything but clear. I kept hearing words like 'turncoat' and 'renegade' associated with myself, no idea why. I do remember a voice that I had heard before and had hoped never to hear again:

"I pwomise you, that bounder wobbed me of my horse. Twice he twied it. He's a blackguard and a thief. He deserves to be shot. And thwown out of the army."

What I couldn't understand was why they insisted on treating me as a cholera patient. I know I'd said something about it to surgeon Reynolds, but medical men don't usually trust their victims (sorry, 'patients') for self-diagnosis in the face of all evidence to the contrary. Especially army doctors. There'd be nobody fit for duty if you listened to what soldiers said was wrong with themselves. I'd obviously not been quite in my right mind when I said it. And I knew the symptoms of cholera, since I'd carelessly picked it up in Afghanistan not too long before. "And thou shalt have great sickness by disease of thy bowels until thy bowels fall out by reason of the sickness day by day." That's Chronicles II. A bit of an exaggeration, though. Headache and fever to start, cramps in the calf muscles, tremendous thirst, hiccoughs and a faint, high pitched voice. This is followed by continuous and violent throwing up, and a case of the trots that defies belief. "Like rice-water" is what the medicals say; they have a morbid interest in other people's lavatory habits, I've noticed. Anyway, cholera's pretty distinctive, and if you take you six-year-old to the school nurse with a tummy ache, she's not likely to confuse the symptoms with Asiatic cholera. So why were these bastards injecting me with a saline solution when it was patently obvious that all I had was a bit of exhaustion, loss of blood, and too much whisky against too little food?

They took me to the hospital at Ladysmith, then on to Fort Napier at Pietermaritzburg, all the time keeping me out of sight of anyone I might have a chinwag with. I was given a private room in the old barracks, really just a storeroom with a camp bed. I'd been there a few hours when there came a knock at the door. "Koi-hai!" I answered, India-fashion. An orderly ushered in the skinny, pencil-necked officer I'd last talked to at Rorke's drift. Behind him, officious-like, strutted Fitzclarence.

"Lieutenant Bagshot," intoned the fellow, "My name is Crealock. We met briefly some days ago. I am Lord Chelmsford's military secretary, and I have some, ah, matters to discuss with you."

"Oh yes" I replied, eager to clear up the misunderstanding. "I'm really quite well now, thanks. No cholera at all. I think I became a little over-tired, that's all."

He ignored this. "Bagshot, I have to say that your actions during the 22nd and 23rd of this month have come under considerable scrutiny. It might, after all, appear unusual for a British officer to dress as a Zulu, join in an enemy attack on one of our positions, and actually burn a military hospital flying the Union Jack."

I was about to protest that there had been no flag flying over the hospital (or else I would have felt compelled to rescue it myself before starting the fire) but Fitzclarence had to have his two ha'pence worth. "Tweasonous!" he whelped. "Deserting to the enemy at the height of battle! Dwessing up like a damned barbawian. And stealing a fellow's horse, not once but twice!"

I started. "No, sir, it wasn't like that at all ---"

"No?" queried Crealock, in the peremptory manner that precludes further discussion. "Captain Cochrane says that you lost the baggage wagons and deserted your post during the action at Isandlwana camp. He says that you stole a piano from the mission at Rorke's Drift, and that you left the firing line to make sure the Zulus didn't get at it. D 'ye think that Johnny Zulu likes a sing-song round the parlour piano, my good man?"

I was dumbstruck. Calumny upon calumny! Fitzclarence glared hotly at me and expressed his opinion. "Court-martialed. Shot from a cannon. Badges stripped off and flung out on his ear. Hanged. Flogged in front of the whole army. Cut dead by society ----"

"Enough, Algy. Please go and fetch the officer selected to act as escort to Lt. Bagshot." Fitzclarence scuttled from the room. "He doesn't seem to like you, Bagshot."

You have to be damned observant to be Lord Chelmsford's military secretary, obviously. He continued, in a more measured tone. "There are, however, some who speak of your, ah, assistance at the Rorke's Drift affair. A number of the private soldier's report that you were of some help in defending the hospital and moving the invalids to safety. As to your garb, well, we do understand that some officers have a weakness for local colour; most restrict it to corduroy jackets and colorful hat-bands. You were the only man from Isandlwana to reach Rorke's Drift on foot, which signifies some effort on your part. Anyway, it has been decided that in view of your, ah, condition and the infectiousness thereof, you should receive treatment in the hospital known to be best equipped and experienced in cholera cases. An officer will escort you to Durban. I think he's coming now."

"The hospital, sir? Durban?"

"Ah, no."

"Cape Town?"

"Ah, no. Bombay."

Fitzclarence came in. My escorting officer walked behind, as if hiding behind the mincing figure of the Rifles officer. I looked at him and he reddened, shame faced.

"Hello, Cochrane," I said.

CHAPTER THIRTY-EIGHT
Hove 1928

"Bloody 'ell" mumbled Cook to herself. "Who's ringing the bell at this time of night?" She'd settled down for the evening. Dinner had come and gone, with some surprising words of compliment from Colonel Bagshot. He'd pronounced the spotted dick, "A tour de force of English cuisine," which was all tosh, of course. Still, the old fool seldom said anything good about her cooking, so that was, well, quite nice. The residents were mostly settled in the lounge playing bridge or reading. She'd finished for the night. But now she had to get up and see who was at the door of her parlour.

It was the Colonel. "Ah, sorry to disturb you, Cook, but, is there any chance at all of a bit of that marvellous spotted dick? Only it was so good, and I'm a bit peckish."

Well, thought Cook, he must really like it. She'd had a large glass of gin and was in a mood of what passed, in her, for bounteous generosity. This mood equated to mere surliness in others.

"Yes, Colonel, if you don't mind waiting a few minutes." She returned to her gin, calculating the time needed to show him who was in charge here.

In those minutes, sneaking through the kitchen to the pantry, a Zulu warrior took up the position for ambush.

When Cook decided that she'd kept Old Bagshot hanging about long enough, she drained her glass, stepped out of the parlour and gestured for the Colonel to follow her. He tamely followed her into the kitchen without any of the snooty attitude she always expected from him. Obviously, her excellent cooking had made him respect her abilities. She hoped he'd remember this night.

She opened the pantry door. There was no electric light in there but Cook knew where the remnants of this evening's pudding had been left. The sudden shout of "uSutu!" from the back of the closet came as a terrible shock to her. She shrieked. The sudden rush forward of a black figure, capering, chanting, and draped with outlandish accoutrements caused her to turn and flee headlong through the hotel. She tore along the corridor, taking the steps up into the lobby in ungainly bounds, and terrifying the bridge players before disappearing out of the front door without her hat and coat.

Guests later remembered her screaming about "Devils from 'ell", banging into furniture, and loudly wailing that she'd been a good woman all her sixty years. Some of them also recalled an odd whiff of beef extract in the hallway.

"No discipline," said the Colonel, later. "She could have made a last stand at the top of the stairs. She'd have held you off for hours." George smiled at that.

Colonel Bagshot had never got his leftover spotted dick, but he suspected that Pickles wouldn't have eaten it anyway, and he had no intention of touching any more of the wretched stuff. Bloody horrible, as usual. All her puddings were like bricks and mortar.

The colonel examined George, now out of the Zulu costume. "You've still got Bovril on your forehead. Best get rid of the evidence."

Pickles showed no interest in licking it off, either. He had his standards.

* * *

Willie Cochrane wasn't really a bad fellow. In fact, propelled by guilt and his own good fortune, he stood me several good feeds and a fair amount of whisky on our way to the coast. It was common knowledge that brandy is good for the cholera, but Cochrane was a whisky man, and since we'd rather given up on the cholera story anyway, he plied me with a selection of the peaty malts of the Western Isles. His Scots roots were in full blown flight. We rode, with an escort of horsemen from the Edendale troop under Sergeant Major Kambula. They gave me a pony, a tame, slow pony, with extra padding on the saddle for my, ah, honourable wound. I had hoped for a chance to steal my own horse back from Fitzclarence, but they never let me near the stables.   "You've to promise me ye'll no try to escape and cause consternation and embarrassment to the high command." I said I wouldn't dream of it. I was happy just to have my baggage back, which had survived as a small part of the defensive line at Rorke's Drift; if I'd known where it was, I could have crept up to the barricade, opened one of my trunks and slipped on a fresh new uniform under cover of darkness. Cochrane had gone to great efforts to have my gear restored to me, for which I was grateful.

"No, I'm sorry I told a few whoppers about you and the wagons and that bloody piano. I had to explain why I was up at the firing line and not knowing where the ammunition reserve was. You were dead, as far as I knew, and everybody was blaming everything on dead men anyway. Chelmsford and Crealock – especially Crealock – are determined to fault Durnford and Pulleine for the loss of the camp. Trying to cover their own miserable arses, they are. I expect London'll go along wi' it. Politics as usual. So, I did the same thing to you."

"So, you get promotion and what? A troop of irregular horse? And I get the first boat back to India?"

Cochrane was quiet for a moment. "I canna deny that, laddie. You can blame me if you like; I'm an aging sub in an unfashionable regiment of infantry wi' a wild desire to play Red Indians on horseback. But they were going to get you out of Natal anyway. Don't you see it? They need the fight at the mission as a wonderful example of British pluck and heroism. After such an appalling cock up as the Isandlwana battle, they – and by they I mean the General and the High Commissioner and very probably Mr. Disraeli and his cabinet – need a success. Ye ken, British boys standing toe tae toe wi' the bloody Zulus and whipping their behinds. There'll be a dozen Victoria Crosses, mark my words. They've probably got the citations already written. So what they don't need is anything that complicates that nice little picture. And you, my friend, are a complication. If ye'd kept your uniform on and managed to rush into the fort to join the defence, I believe ye'd be promoted major and gi'en the V.C. and asked tae visit wi' the dear old Queen. Now ye ken as well as I that ye'd have been skewered by the Kaffirs before ye got within five miles o' the fort, but that makes no difference. Ye showed up, aye, but in the Zulu outfit (which makes ye suspicious, understand), and then you tell half the bloody world that ye set fire to the roof, which they will think was neither the proper action of a British officer, or a sensible thing to for ye tae do. I ken that those things dinna necessarily have much in common. Then ye dinna even get inside the barricade so that anyone -by which I mean an officer – could actually see you heroically fighting off the hordes. So, all ye do is muddy up the story and bring up some questions they'd rather were never asked about the shambles at Isandlwana. Ye're an embarrassment my lad. So, they have a choice between court-martialling you, or pretending you were niver here in the first place."

I stared incredulously. "But I saved the garrison! If it hadn't been for the light of the hospital burning, they'd all have been overrun in the dark."

"That's as may be, Binky. Ye didn't exactly explain your actions very weel."

"I was sick!"

197

"Anyway, it disnae fit wi' the version they want the London papers tae print. They're all terrified o' Gladstone."

"Gladstone! Has he joined the Zulus?" I'd always held deep suspicions about the leader of the Liberal Party, but this was infamous behaviour.

"No, ye fool. But a politician that lets his opponent have evidence of his own failures isn't long for his job, and Disraeli likes being prime minister. Chelmsford likes being a general too, or at least he disnae want tae be publicly throon oot on his ear. It's lucky you are who ye are."

"What do you mean?"

"An officer of the Tenth Hussars. Your colonel won't stand for any embarrassment."

"My colonel?" I thought of Lord Ralph Kerr, the C.O., in Afghanistan. A good man, but unlikely to help me in this situation.

"Your colonel-in-chief, ye daft loon. The Prince o' bloody Wales. He loves your regiment like a child, better than in fact. He'd not allow any public embarrassment tae the Tenth – not after the incident wi' Valentine Baker. It'd reflect badly on himself, and he'll no' allow that."

"Do you think he knows?"

"Ye'd best hope not, laddie. But my guess is that they'll not mention it tae him. The Prince's circle likes to gossip. It'd be in the racing papers on Monday and the dailies on Tuesday. All the same, ye'd best go along wi' the idea that ye were never here at all."

"Where have I been?"

"Oh, that nice cholera hospital in Bombay. I'm sure that the records of your stay have already been written. I think you might be making a good recovery at this moment. Mind, any trouble oot o' you, and ye might relapse."

CHAPTER THIRTY-NINE

Hove 1928

Cook swore up and down that she had seen the very hounds of Hell hiding in the pantry, while winged demons pursued her through the length and breadth of the Empire Lodge Hotel. The Colonel told Mr. Quint, confidentially, that he'd been in the hallway when the distraught woman came screeching up from the kitchen. No, there was nothing following her; he'd gone downstairs himself, with his stick in case it was burglars, and found nothing. Young George had been a big help in setting the place straight again. He thought she might have smelled, just a little, of strong drink. Quite a lot of strong drink.

He said that as if he'd never touched the stuff himself.

Cook decided to go and visit her sister in Kent for a week, to calm her nerves.

* * *

Durban was as little interested to see me go as it had been to see me arrive. Arrangements had been made for me to travel on a cargo steamer bound for India. Cochrane pushed a bottle of Glenlivet into my hand as I left. I think he really did feel badly about the piano, and his behaviour towards me, and so forth. He got his wish, incidentally and commanded the Edendale troop at the battles of Hlobane Mountain and Kambula, but the choir was never the same after the Zulus stole his banjo.

He never did tell me about the five-pound note; I expect he pinched it himself.

They took me out on a lighter to the vessel moored beyond the bar. I did not get lunch at the Belgrave Hotel.

* * *

199

"I tell you Edward, Colonel Bagshot is exactly the kind of guest we need at this hotel. I know you think it's old fashioned, but where would we have been with a bunch of those 'bright young things' present when Cook had her unfortunate episode? They'd have run out screaming into the street, those flapper girls. Now, the Colonel, he's a man who can take command at a moment like that. And luckily, young George showed a good deal of British pluck, I'm told.'"

Eddie Quint grimaced at his father. So much for progress, improvement and making a profit. So much for making a statement with a flashy new car. The Vauxhall saloon was out. He'd have to borrow some cash to buy the Morris Minor. One day, though, it would be out with Colonel-flipping-Bagshot and in with the twentieth century -----

* * *

As I watched the sun go down over Africa's shore that evening, I came to a conclusion. If I was to do my part to preserve the empire, even little bits of it like Jim Rorke's broken down establishment, I should not expect to get any credit for it. Durnford and Pulleine and poor, lugubrious George Shepstone, whose father had had so much to do with starting the war, had got none. I thought of Admiral Byng, my chum Bungo's ancestor, *shot pour encourager les autres*, as some Frenchman said, because he failed to retake Minorca in seventeen fifty something. Nobody was shooting me, so that was good, but there was no credit, no medals, no brevet rank or mention in dispatches. In fact, I was being conspicuously *not* mentioned in dispatches. But I made a decision that I have stood by my entire career long; if ever the sun should threaten to set on the British Empire, Binky Bagshot would be there, with matches and whisky, ready to set fire to the roof.

* * *

The colonel was tired. Storytelling, with the theatricals that went with it, exhausted the old man. "Pour me another, George. Just four fingers, well, perhaps five. A *burra peg*, yes."

"What happened to the others, sir?"

"Let me see. Chard got a Victoria Cross, as did Gonny. Both were promoted to major, but never got on beyond that. Chard died in India in the nineties. Bromhead was a bit of a noodle, never showed up to visit the Queen at Balmoral when she invited him, said he was fishing in Ireland and didn't get the letter. Neither fellow ever really lived up to that night, ever again. Hook and Williams and both Joneses got the V.C., but Waters didn't; I don't think anyone really believed the wardrobe aspect of it. Young Beckett died, unfortunately. Some others got the V.C. – the commissary and the surgeon and the young colour-sergeant. He took a commission and has made a fine career, but of the several privates they put up to non-com rank, all got broke back. Hook worked at the British museum for years. Lord Chelmsford was allowed to stay on, more or less, and finished the war before Garnet Wolseley arrived to supersede him. There were a number of battles, some large and some less so. A young chap called Louis Napoleon, whose pater had been Napoleon III of France, managed to get himself killed while scouting for Zulus; he found 'em, of course, his horse bolted and his stirrup-strap broke – I recall it was something like that – while he tried to climb on board the galloping animal. His escort had already run away, leaving him on his own against a lot of angry fellows with spears and a quarrelsome attitude. Very brave, a bit stupid, completely dead. All a bit embarrassing to explain to his mother, and the French government didn't take it too well. All kinds of wild talk that our own queen had arranged an assassination! Anyway, Lord Chelmsford never got another field command. As I recall, he dropped dead over a billiard table. Horry Smith-Dorrien commanded the 2nd division in the retreat to Mons in 1914. Joseph the Zulu I met again, which is another story. I don't remember what happened to Crealock."

"What about Lieutenant Fitzclarence?"

"They say it's wrong to speak ill of the dead, don't they?"

"Yes, sir."

"Well, that pustulent little bastard is alive and well and living on a general's pension in Cheltenham Spa, so I can say what I like. He crawled his venomous way to the top, treading on good officers the whole way, me in particular. But as it is I do not wish to speak of that vile toad. Not today, anyway. Where did I put that drink?"

HISTORICAL NOTES

While there is no convincing reason to believe Colonel Bagshot's account of his Zulu War adventures, it is worth noting that the chronology and course of events matches closely with the most recent examinations of that campaign. Indeed, much that was not generally known in 1928 – or at least published at that time – matches the Bagshot memoir.

Bagshot appears in no known history of the Zulu War; we may or may not accept his explanation for this absence. Nor, oddly enough, does his nemesis, Lt. Algernon Fitzclarence. With that exception and the understandable omission of the Zulu refugee Joseph from period recollections – African servants are seldom mentioned by name – all the people recalled by Colonel Bagshot are attested to by historical record. Where their characters, histories and appearances are known, they tie in closely with the Bagshot account. This is not only true for senior officers like Colonel Durnford (see his biography by R.W.F. Droogleever, *The Road to Isandlwana*, London 1992), but also for relatively insignificant figures. John Waters, for instance, was a middle aged Black Countryman, who spent some time hiding in a wardrobe with the unlucky Private Beckett, while Henry Hook was a Gloucestershire man of good character, rather than the delinquent Cockney played by James Booth in *Zulu*. Both left eyewitness accounts, neither referring to a white officer dressed in Zulu regalia; however, one suspects that if Colonel Bagshot were alive today, he would tell us that they had been warned off by higher authority at the threat of losing their pensions.

In tracing the Bagshot account, with the help of George Chapman (now quite elderly, but still sound in mind and memory, especially if lubricated by a few pints of Tamplin's Bitter), I have been able to trace a number of threads. The Empire Lodge Hotel burned down in the early thirties, together with portions of the buildings on either side, while the Colonel was still in residence. George had by then moved on to a career with Southern Railways, but firmly states that the investigation made no definite allegations regarding the origins of the fire. He recalls that the Colonel, with Pickles in tow, together with the unmelted portion of his collection of model soldiers, moved to the ancestral property in Oxfordshire at that time. Some angry letters to the Morning Post in 1936 regarding the Italian invasion of Abyssinia, though credited to 'An Old Hussar', suggest by their references to the writer's being present at Adowa in 1896, that they might be the work of Colonel Bagshot. He appears to have lived on well into the thirties, though no records indicate that he was still alive when his centenarian Aunt Agatha left the estate to a charity for cats in 1944. It seems unlikely that Pickles was named as a beneficiary.

The advertisement for Bovril is attested by Robert Graves in his informal social history of Britain between the wars, *The Long Weekend* (1941). The cost of various motor vehicles considered by 'Eddy' Quint matches actual prices offered by Sussex dealers in 1928.

George confirms that 'Cook's' meals were indeed as bad as Colonel Bagshot considered them, and that, when she later opened a short-lived restaurant in Portland Road, he did not frequent it. It was bombed by the Germans in 1942, to nobody's regret. George claims that if the Colonel were still living at that time, he would have undoubtedly have sent a congratulatory telegram to Goering.

I have made no attempt to explain each and every one of Colonel Bagshot's odd proclamations in Urdu, Zulu or any other language. Those who really wish to know that an '*ayah*' is a children's nurse might consult the authoritative work on Anglo-Indian jargon known as *Hobson-Jobson*.

The classic accounts of the Zulu War are Sir Reginald Coupland's brief *Zulu Battle Piece: Isandlwana* (1948), and Donald Morris' monumental *The Washing of the Spears* (1964). More recent work, which revises the story in some details according to recent research, has been done by Ian Knight, a prolific writer whose *Brave Men's Blood* (1990) is a good survey of the whole war. His *Nothing Remains but to Fight* (1993) examines the defence of Rorke's Drift in detail, as does James Bancroft's *Rorke's Drift* (1988). Interestingly, Knight, as the most thorough researcher, is much less willing to provide categorical statements of fact than some other writers have been. The events of January 1879 cannot be precisely accounted. Frank Emery's soldier's letters, *The Red Soldier*, and Norman Holmes' detailed record of the 24th Foot, *The Silver Wreath*, are also recommended.

AUTHOR'S ACKNOWLEDGMENTS

This book has been a very long time in coming. I first started it more than twenty-five years ago, convinced that – although I had never before written any fiction – that a historical novel that followed the exact sequence of events at two separate battles, written alternately in third and first person, was somehow a good idea. Of course, it wasn't; it was over-researched and ponderous, but it had some good bits in it. After publishing a series of novels and gradually learning the craft, I returned to The White Zulu, chopping out the most obviously 'information you'll never need about ox-wagons' aspect, rewrote it once, and then again to make Bagshot's arcane slang and apparently drunken sentence structure a shade more approachable.

I'd like to thank all those who've helped and encouraged me along the way. Patrick Wilson, Dave Babb and Hal Thinglum were enthusiastic about early excerpts. My late mentor Dr. Paddy Griffith and John Curry helped me bring it back for revision. Roderick Robertson, my partner on Pulp Action Library, fixed some technical issues that would have flummoxed me completely. Vince Rospond, of course, for actually agreeing to publish the book at all. Lastly, my love and continuing admiration go to my wife, the Reverend Doctor Lori, for putting up with me and my nonsense for more than three decades.

Look for more books from Winged Hussar Publishing, LLC
E-books, paperbacks and Limited Edition hardcovers.
The best in history, science-fiction, and fantasy at:
www. wingedhussarpublishing.com

Follow us on Facebook at:
Winged Hussar Publishing LLC

Or on Twitter at:
WingHusPubLLC

For information and upcoming publications